DOWNLOAD A FREE STORY

To say thanks, I'd like to give you the award semi-finalist story about Bahar's gripping and redemptive past for **FREE**.

amyearls.com/behind-walls/

PRAISE FOR THE KING'S FEATHER

Brimming with adventure and intrigue, *The King's Feather* is an out-of-this world journey of faith, loss, and redemption. A story to savor and an author to watch!

— TARA JOHNSON, AUTHOR OF *ENGRAVED ON THE HEART* AND *ALL THROUGH THE NIGHT*

I stayed up way too late reading. This is biblical retelling at its best. I fell in love with the characters, couldn't put the book down, and now want book 2. Well done! A must read for fantasy lovers and especially for Christian fantasy lovers.

— KANDI J. WYATT, AUTHOR OF DRAGON COURAGE SERIES

Amy Earls has penned a thrilling portal fantasy. In *The King's Feather*, teen heroine Pero must navigate two very different worlds but also complicated relationships and impossible choices. Readers will love this clever biblical retelling that reveals timeless truths with a fantastical flourish.

— KAREN GRUNST, YA AUTHOR OF *SACRED FIRE*

[*The King's Feather*] combines fantasy elements with faith material in an unforced way. The Old Testament allusions add depth and interest to the story. Some of the faith material, when the Lesaries are marching around Moon City, is especially powerful.

— *WRITER'S EDGE* REVIEW

The characters were relatable and believable, the romance, oh my gosh, it was the best, and the plot was fantabulous! I know bookworms shouldn't have favorite books, but this one is the best I've ever read.

— VIOLET, TEEN BLOGGER

This book was absolutely amazing! And now I can't wait until Amy writes the next book! I want to know what happens.

— ALISON, TEEN *GOODREADS* READER

The King's Feather transported me into an ancient, other-worldly universe full of mystery, suspense, and non-stop adventure.

— JANNETTE FULLER, BLOGGER

THE KING'S FEATHER

UNDER HIS WINGS
BOOK 1

AMY EARLS

PORTAL
PUBLICATIONS

ISBN 979-8-9874017-1-2 (hardback)
ISBN 979-8-9874017-0-5 (paperback)
ISBN 979-8-9874017-2-9 (ebook)
ISBN 979-8-9874017-5-0 (audio)

Cover design by Seventhstar Art, www.SeventhStarArt.com

Find out more at www.AmyEarls.com

BOOKS BY AMY EARLS

Under His Wings

Behind Walls (Prequel)

The King's Feather (Book #1)

Forbidden Reign (Book #2)

For my sister Katie, who flew with me on many backyard adventures.

For my favorite man, Eric Earls, who gave this dreamer wings.

Shout, for Yahweh has given you the city!

— JOSHUA, SON OF NUN

The wall that shuts you in
May be hard and high and stout,
But the Lord is sun and the Lord is dew,
And His hedge is coolness and shade for you,
And no wall can shut Him out.

—ANNIE JOHNSON FLINT

TERMS

- Koach (pronounced ko'-akh)—the Hebrew word for strength, power, might
- Onwerto—a combination of the word *onward* and the Proto-Indo-European etymological word for *ward*, meaning to turn toward
- Origo—a fictional universe named after the Old English, 14c. root word for *original*, meaning "first in time, earliest"
- Lì (pronounced lee)—fictional Chinese plants made of huang qi, calabash, and a rare species
- Green Meadow—a fictional American town comparable to those found in Oregon's Willamette Valley

1

פַּחַד

I closed my eyes with Mom's pendant in my fist. My mind replayed her scream from the night Dr. Carper found her. Every morning for the last fourteen years, I awoke from the nightmare and expected her to appear and replace the scream with a whisper: *I'm home, Pero, and I'll never leave again.*

But when I awoke, she was gone, and now on the afternoon of my seventeenth birthday, the same man who took Mom away would come for me.

I opened my eyes and stretched up to peek out the car's window. Teens chilled on the lawn in front of the high school. I scanned the entire area, but no one looked out of place. No strange men dressed in dark clothes lurked nearby, ready to snatch me.

I jolted when the car door opened. Henry slid into the driver's side and slammed the door. "Hey there, birthday girl. How was your last day of school?"

I buckled my seat belt. There'd been no strangers inside the classrooms or halls. I'd watched.

"You okay, Ro?"

"Why do you keep calling me that?" I glanced back toward the lawn.

Henry shrugged. "What's wrong, Pero?"

"Nothing."

"You're twirling your hair again." Henry put the keys in the ignition and turned on the engine. "You do that when you're nervous."

"Since when did you notice my habits?"

"I picked up a few things over the last four months."

"It wasn't my idea to make you my bodyguard."

When Henry appeared at our front door one day, Dad insisted on hiring Henry and converted the garage into a room for him. Dad and I would've thought Henry was some stalker looking for a way to ask me out if he hadn't shown us the feather necklace. It wasn't all that terrible with Henry's kindness and good looks. He was cool for a Lesarie. His blonde bouncy curls, light-blue eyes, and long, slender nose caused many heads to turn toward him. But not mine.

Henry waved back to a girl getting into her car.

"Is she a senior, too?" I asked.

With the girl's naturally wavy hair and sweet smile, Henry had to find her attractive. A flash of adrenaline tingled through my body. Why did I care if he did?

Henry moved the gear to reverse. "Who?"

Henry backed up without looking. Someone laid on their horn, and he slammed on the brakes.

I lurched forward. "Wowzer."

"I haven't killed us yet, have I?"

As soon as Henry arrived, he got his driver's license and insisted he be the one to drive me to and from school. He ran red lights, jerked the car, and swerved toward on-coming traffic while looking for deer at the edge of the meadows.

I rolled my shoulder, working out neck tension from gripping the seat. "Where you live has to have cars. I think your parents didn't *let* you drive."

Henry laughed and filed into the line of cars leaving Green Meadow High. The traffic snaked along the driveway, toward a banner that read Class of 2025 in colorful letters. One more year until my turn. I'd make it, right?

"It'd be faster to run home," I said.

Out the passenger window, large trees and lush grass surrounded the school's perimeter. A sign on the lamppost ahead said, "Keep our meadow green." Green Meadow rain did a fine job on its own.

"Faster for you." Henry tucked a stray blonde curl behind his ear. "But I can't run that far."

The car lurched forward a few feet before stopping.

Henry leaned back. "Any sign of Dr. Carper today?"

I clasped the wooden feather pendant in my fist, waiting for energy to pass from the necklace through my hand. I sucked in my breath, then exhaled. Deflated. Lightning didn't flash. I didn't feel different. Nothing.

Dad said that Mom wore the same necklace with a feather pendant and a word in ancient text inscribed on the back. I didn't know the word's meaning, but I did know that Mom and I both were two of the three chosen, and if I wore the necklace on my seventeenth birthday, I would inherit a gift. Like a power. And the necklace would lead me to Mom. But it might also help Dr. Carper find me. That's what Henry was here for, to protect me from Dr. Carper and help me find Mom.

Dr. Carper caught Mom at seventeen. After Mom escaped years later, she married Dad and had me. Dr. Carper found her again, but the second time she disappeared before he reached her.

She never came back.

"No sign." I let go of the pendent. "Maybe he won't come."

"If your power comes today, he'll be here."

"I can't be one of the chosen. Nothing's happened."

"Not yet, but it will."

"I don't want anything to happen. I mean, I want to find my mom, but I don't want anyone to take me, either."

"I won't let anything bad happen to you, Pero. Doors rarely open between Earth and Origo, so if Elohim doesn't want you to be taken away, then Dr. Carper won't be able to find you. No one can get past God's plan."

"You seriously still believe there's another universe?"

Henry leaned to look out the window and pointed. "Right there. The evidence is in the sky. How can you not believe that Origo exists?"

"Just because a planet is visible doesn't mean life's there."

"How else can you explain your mom disappearing out of thin air and never returning?"

"I was three, Henry. It could've been a dream." But it wasn't.

"Your dad remembers, too."

"We've argued about this so many times. Can we talk about something else?"

The car behind us honked, and Henry moved forward. "Pants are finally a trend in Origo."

"What other option is there? Fig leaves?"

Henry chuckled. "We wear robes."

"That explains everything. You're from the Middle East, and why are we talking about this again?"

Henry stretched his arm out of the open car window as he took a left turn from the school's driveway. Peppermint wafted from a field of herbs. Henry adjusted his arm, and the movement brought a whiff of citrus and woody tones. Of course, he'd smell nice, too.

"I'll miss high school," he said.

I snickered. "You weren't here freshman year."

Henry told me once that his parents educated him all his life. When I mentioned that's called homeschooling, he said the Lesaries in the other universe differed from the 21st-century ones here on Earth. The Lesaries here wore jeans and t-shirts, drank coffee, and took their dogs for walks like average Americans. Henry said that in the older universe called Origo, the Lesaries didn't have homes but traveled wherever Elohim sent them and slept in tents. The Lesaries' next mission was a place called Moon City. Or so Henry believed.

"Why'd your parents name you Henry?"

"My parents traveled the world before they settled. I guess they chose a name they liked the best from different places they'd visited."

"But Henry's a common name in many places."

Henry shifted. "No questions, Pero. Remember?"

"You always say that."

We passed a brown building with a steeple that pointed toward the sky and a dozen people in front holding signs that read, "Pray for a king." What would a king do for them when they already had priests? Dad took me to a sanctuary a couple times a year. He said Mom used to go every Saturday. I couldn't imagine why. The prayers and songs bored me. And although a few stories about Elohim had me curious, I didn't care for Him. He hadn't brought Mom back.

Henry stopped at the light. "Let's go for a run."

"My dad said we shouldn't go anywhere today."

Henry shrugged. "We'll check in with him before we go. It'll be good for you to get out, and it's not like we've seen anything unusual today."

In the afternoons, with Henry a few paces behind, I ran the three miles from my home to Green Meadow's border. Without people around and only sheep and horses grazing, the open space felt alive.

My muscles ached to run.

When Henry's phone vibrated at my foot, I picked it up and read Matthew Moshe.

"It's a text from my dad."

Henry glanced over. "What does it say?"

"You're right. It's time to tell her," I read.

Henry swerved.

I clutched the seat. "Look where you're going!" *Ouch.* "Since when do you and my dad keep secrets?"

"We'll talk about it later." Henry reached to turn up the volume on the stereo and sang along to an upbeat song. His tenor voice stopped. "Come on, Pero." The sway of his head resembled a cobra. "Someone told me you played guitar and sang at a school assembly once and a line of guys asked for your number."

I rolled my eyes. "Was it Jamie? She exaggerates."

Henry put both hands on the wheel. "I believe her."

"No, you don't."

"Do, too. I would've been first in line."

I squirmed. Was he serious? "You have my number."

Henry raised the volume. "And you're still hard to reach."

Henry sang again to a slower song. I wanted to hum along, but his words had hit my gut and left me breathless. I rubbed the ache in my chest. Dr. Carper may not have found me yet, but I still felt trapped.

Would I ever be free?

2

לָרוּץ

My feet pounded the pavement at the side of the highway. Tiny pieces of gravel grated against the bottom of my shoes, like Dad's text grated my heart.

The sun didn't bother me. I wanted to let the rays melt me into a puddle. Then I wouldn't grieve that Mom had disappeared and Dad worked too hard. Wouldn't ache that Dr. Carper could steal me away at any moment. In reality, Dad was who I had, and I'd give anything to keep him from losing love again.

Henry muttered. I paused my music, alternating between thankfulness that Henry was near and aching from the pressure in my head when he got too close.

"What?"

"I asked if you wanted to talk."

I huffed. "About what?" When I'd started my music, the lyrics said to hold on. Hold on to what? To hope that Henry and Dad withheld good news? I doubted that. The possibilities I'd come up with: they found Mom, Henry worked for the FBI, Dad was a spy... I had a big imagination.

I pulled off the ear buds. No point in music when Henry wanted to talk. "You and my dad keep secrets."

"You're hard to keep up with," Henry panted.

The sheep in the distance bleated as if they wanted to warn me before I crashed.

Henry sped up to me, and I stopped.

Was the secret about Mom? Her disappearance was the one day I wished to forget. I'd closed my eyes every night, hoping to erase any memory of her disappearance, but Mom's screaming face rushed into my dreams.

"Pero—"

"I'm fine." I wiped sweat that had trickled down my chin.

"Are not." Henry watched me. "You're avoiding me."

I glanced away. "Fine. I'm not okay. You're keeping something from me, and I want to know the truth."

He touched the back of his neck. "You won't like it."

"Try me."

"In the older universe," Henry said, "Elohim brought the Lesaries to a place called Moon City and asked us to march around the walls to bring them down. Moon City looks similar to a village surrounded by a big steel wall with teen slaves locked inside. Their leader is a scientist and experiments on the teen warriors. He's got them eating some plant that keeps them alive forever... or something like that. The plant also makes them numb to emotions and want to fight. They're like human robots trained to kill Lesaries for fun."

"Thanks for the disturbing history lesson. What does this have to do with me?"

"Your dad told me Moon City's leader, Dr. Carper, is also the one who was after your mom. That can only mean that Elohim sent me to you because He wants you to...."

My pulse increased, and it wasn't from the run. "To what?"

"To... go."

"Go where?" I struggled to swallow the growing panic. "You're not making sense."

Henry rubbed his head. "We should wait for your dad. I wanted you to trust me first without feeling like I'd take you away."

"Why would you take me away, Henry?"

"Let's head back."

I stepped closer and looked up into his eyes. "You. Tell. Me. Now."

He brought his hand up near my hair as if he was about to touch it, then seemed to change his mind. Too close. But hadn't I been the one to step forward? I wouldn't back down. He'd give me an answer.

Henry's eyes drank mine in a way that I hadn't seen before. At my first blink, the look dissipated.

"Your mom—Bahar—is the first of the three chosen," Henry said. "We know this because Elohim used her gift of the staff to bring Bahar great power. No one had seen this kind of power, which means it must've been a fulfillment of the prophecy, especially since Bahar is a descendant of the prophet Abram. You are one of the chosen three because you are Bahar's daughter. The prophecy says that—"

"That three chosen would travel between the universes. They would bring power to save Elohim's people—the Lesaries —and provide them the king they've begged for. I know. My mom, Bahar Abram, is the first of the chosen. But I don't have a power."

"Your power is music."

"Don't you think I would've seen laser beams shooting from my guitar if that was true?"

Henry touched my arm. "You light up when you talk about music. It's beautiful to watch." He quickly let go, a blush trailing up his neck.

I smiled. "It is? I mean, that my power is music. Not the whole I'm beautiful to watch part." Now it was my turn to feel my face heat.

"Yes, to both."

I glanced the other way. He had never been so forward. But how did I feel about him? I was attracted to him; he was kind, and I'd known him for four long months. But I still wasn't sure I could trust him, not with this secret lingering between us.

"You still haven't told me the whole truth," I said.

"Right." Henry paused. "I need you to come with me to Origo."

"No."

"Listen, Pero. I found your mom."

"You what?"

Henry briefly closed his eyes, as if bracing himself for a slap. Maybe I should slap him. He found Mom. *My* mom!

"I can't bring her back myself," he said. "Bahar asked me to find and bring you to her."

My heart beat faster. "You found my mom?"

Henry's compliment about me being beautiful had to be a lie, a way to coax me into going along with his plan. "Why didn't you bring her home?"

Henry shook his head. "The only way to bring her home is through the chosen wearing the necklaces."

"You kept this a secret. My mom's alive and you didn't tell me." I brought my hands to my face, holding back a sob that lodged in my throat. "I can't take any more of your stupid secrets."

I ran into the forest, torn between fear and longing for Mom.

"Pero! Your dad doesn't want you in there!"

Bright green ferns splayed like tattered skirts. I pressed on. Harder. Faster. For once, I'd run beyond the boundary.

When trees up ahead formed a shadow, I stopped and spun.

No Henry. Great. How long had I been running? Three minutes? I peeled off pieces of hair that clung to my face. A twig snapped and the sweat on my arms turned cold. Trees trembled as branches parted and a man walked toward me. At my gasp, he moved behind a tree.

"Henry?"

The trees seemed to spin around me, then settled back into focus. I scanned the area. Absolutely nothing. My mind playing tricks on me.

Henry appeared from the clearing to my left, and I jumped.

"Pero, that was not smart. You could've..." He cupped my arm with his hand. "Was he here?"

"I saw someone. It was so fast." So was my heartbeat.

"Are you hurt?"

I shook my head. The woods weren't dangerous, only in Dad's head. They couldn't be. Running in the woods, trying to escape beyond Dad's paranoia, looking for where I belonged wasn't wrong.

Henry nudged me away. "Come on."

Something moved behind a tree. Dark eyes blinked at me.

Grabbing Henry's hand, I picked up speed. "Run!"

Henry met my stride and glanced behind. "I don't see anyone."

I let go of Henry's hand and raced ahead, jumping over fallen limbs and pushing through thick brush. Don't be real. Don't be real. Please, don't be real.

Henry panted as I approached the clearing. "Slow down!"

I'd never been as fast... so fast. I wouldn't stop until I was in my house, where no one should find me. We'd moved to a small town away from danger. Was there nowhere I could go?

I climbed up the porch steps to the house. The third step squeaked as I rushed to the door, the handle immovable. I jiggled it harder, but it refused to give.

No. Why is it locked?

Blood thundered in my ears, my fists slamming against the door. Dad locked me outside of the one safe place. I wouldn't enter before the man—

The door flew open. Dad dodged to the side before my fists met his face.

"Where's Henry?" he asked.

My breath grew steady as I leaned against the door frame. I couldn't make Dad more nervous, telling him I'd run into the very place he'd told me not to go. Henry hadn't seen eyes blinking through branches. Dad's nerves had to be getting to me.

"I'm fine, Dad. Henry's coming."

"You know I don't want you running without him." Dad nudged me inside. "Go take a shower while I wait for Henry. Dinner's in twenty minutes. Your favorite."

I sniffed the air. Smelled like Dad's special, what I called mashed-a-roni and cheese. Usually, I made dinners. I wasn't much of a cook but at least didn't mash the macaroni. Dad took care of me by working to pay the rent. While he did his own laundry and maintained the yard, I grocery shopped and cooked and cleaned.

I closed the bathroom door behind me.

"Pero?" It was Henry. I could hear their muffled voices through the wall.

"She's in the shower," Dad said. "Is everything okay?"

"She ran off again," Henry said.

But never so far.

Turning on the sink, I drank from the faucet and peeled off my socks and leggings. I checked the shower's temperature and stepped in, letting the water wash away my anxiety. Everything was okay. I'd have a nice dinner. I had a home, Dad, friends.

Yes, I had everything. Nearly.

Back in my room, I dressed in jeans and a t-shirt and threw

my hair—tangles and all—into a sloppy bun on top of my head. A blast of wind whooshed through the open window. The curtain lifted as if trying to escape. I held the curtain with one hand and placed my other against the pane. My breath stalled. A man at the edge of the driveway watched me. The same man I'd seen in the forest. Hair lifted on the nape of my neck. The sun shone red behind him. He didn't move.

I swallowed. It had to be Dr. Carper. It had to be.

I closed the pane and curtain, as if that would shut him out. Racing into the closet, I slammed the door behind me, leaned against the wall, and switched on the closet light. Hide. I needed to hide. Only my winter coats and a couple of dresses smashed to the side. Not much of a hiding spot.

I could run and tell Dad, but he'd flip out. I could text Henry.

I yanked open my backpack and emptied the front pocket. Erasers, pencils, and lip gloss scattered on the floor. I shuffled to the side of the closet and lifted pillows. No phone. Besides, what would the police do? It wasn't like they'd lock away a man like this. If that was Dr. Carper, I wouldn't forgive him. Never. He took Mom, but my purpose in hiding was to avoid another disappearance—to wait for Mom to return, not to get snatched as well.

A beep from the corner of my closet signaled a text. Lifting a shirt and socks, I found it. Henry's picture showed close-up blonde curls framing a face that held sky-blue eyes and a slight smile. I hadn't taken the picture. My gaze scanned the message.

Hi. When can we talk?

My fingers shook as I typed.

Now.

Henry's reply was immediate.

You okay? You never agree that quickly. lol

I texted the message I'd hoped to never have to send.

He's here.

3

———

לְהַסְתִּיר

A knock on my bedroom door jolted me from the floor.

"It's Henry." Through the closet, his muffled voice told me the walls were too thin to tell secrets.

With a hanger in my hand, I flung open the closet. Nobody was in my room. I bolted to the door, unlocked and opened it wide.

Henry barged in, shut the bedroom door, and charged to the window. "Where is he?"

I didn't dare look out the window as I waited for Henry to tell me to duck down or run. But he said nothing.

"Is he there?" I asked.

Henry scanned outside. From my angle, the sky looked like a gray dragon eating the light. "I don't see anyone. You're sure he was here?"

"Yes, I'm sure. Unlike some people, I don't lie."

Henry dropped the curtain. "I never lied. I just didn't tell the truth."

"Same thing." I collapsed on a pillow in the open closet.

Henry slid to the floor underneath the window. "We need to tell your dad."

"Shh. He can hear you through the wall."

"He needs to know."

I pulled my hair and twisted it. "But he's worked so hard to make my birthday special."

"This can't wait."

"At least till after dinner. Please? The man's gone now."

Henry sighed. "Fine. We'll talk to Matthew after dinner. But if we hear a single noise outside, we're hiding. Got it?"

"Agreed."

"What did he look like?"

I shivered as his image appeared in my mind. "His hair was black. Maybe about Dad's age. Same man I saw in the woods."

"Did he dress classy and look Asian?"

"Yes!"

Henry nodded. "That's Dr. Carper. You've had no sign of a power yet, right?"

I shook my head and tucked my legs close to my chest. "Will he hurt me?"

"No way, Pero. I'm here to keep you safe."

"And to take me away. You said so yourself."

"I won't force you to come with me. But if you decide to go, we should leave tonight. Let's make your dad happy with a birthday dinner and then we'll tell him."

I nodded. Get through. Hang on. Isn't that what life was about?

"Hey." Henry's expression was soft. "Have faith. Elohim will work it out."

I'd never believed in anyone, but maybe trusting in someone else was what I needed to survive. If Elohim existed, then I wouldn't have to worry about control. Was the answer just letting go?

"I remember—" I gulped the emotion in my voice. "That day you mentioned, when I sang at school assembly...."

Henry nodded, then rested his chin on inter-laced fingers as if praying would keep me talking.

"It reminded me of when Dad and I used to sing together, just for fun. Then, Dad stopped singing. Instead, we stayed home. Dad used to say, 'Never can be too careful.' He was only trying to keep me safe, but somewhere along the way, I lost my voice." I looked to Henry, then back to the floor. "I don't know why I told you that."

Henry bounced up. "You've got a voice, Ro, and I'm going to help you find it."

A smile grew on my face. I didn't want to pretend that Henry meant nothing to me. I held out my hand, and he gave it a firm squeeze.

Henry smirked. "You told me friends hug and acquaintances shake hands."

I gave one last squeeze and held on. I craved his embrace, a squeeze without a dismissal, but I was uncertain if that would make Henry more than a friend.

"Take what you can get." I let go.

"You also told me that couples hold hands."

I rolled my eyes. "That is *not* what we were doing."

Henry laughed.

"Now I have to tell my dad why you were in my room."

"Tell him we wanted alone time."

"He'll never fall for that."

"Then tell him we're together. We held hands, after all."

"*I'll* never fall for that."

"Never is a very permanent word, Pero."

Henry reached into my closet, picked up my guitar, and held it out to me. "Play."

I glanced at the guitar, dust settling on the wood's surface, then up to Henry's eager face. "You think my power is singing?"

"You have a gift."

"But will it bring my mom home?"

"Try it."

I took the guitar, my fingers aching to play. There was still beauty in this crazy world, and I needed music to remind me.

I strummed. *Ooh. Off.* I tuned two strings. Better.

If I could write Mom a song, maybe my voice could bring her back. It was a silly idea, but so was taking off with Henry to find her. Maybe she waited to hear my voice, or maybe hearing my voice would resurrect the dream of her return. I strummed a few chords and hummed. I stopped playing and focused on the melody forming in my head.

Da-da. Da-da-da.

"I'm running after you," I sang.

A memory flashed. I was three years old, and I wore the necklace. Dad came into view, and there was Mom. This was quickly becoming less like a memory, and more like a vivid dream. She was beautiful. Brown eyes, oval-shaped face, a direct and probing gaze. She seemed sure of herself, confident, and calm. Did I look like her? Could I be like her? Unafraid.

I opened my eyes, and the vision faded. I gasped. What was that?

Henry watched me. "Keep going."

I closed my eyes. No vision. I took a deep breath in and sang out a little louder. "I'm running after you."

Mom came into focus again. So did Dad. They were standing in front of a closet. I could see myself at three, like I was a ghost watching a movie clip of a memory. I took in my small wrists and fingers. My wispy hair hung at my shoulders. So tiny.

Mom's color drained as she said to Dad, "He's here."

"How?" Dad asked.

They looked at me and saw it. Mom gasped and covered her mouth. "That's not possible."

Dad rushed to me and pulled the necklace over my head. "We should've destroyed this long ago."

"But the prophecy has to be fulfilled."

Dad glanced at me. "What about Pero?"

The doorbell rang.

Mom leaned in to give Dad a kiss. "Hide."

Another ringing of the bell. A knock. Mom took the necklace and tucked it into her front pocket.

"Wait," Dad said. "Won't Pero need the necklace later?"

Mom stepped toward the closet and opened the door. "I don't know now."

"But the prophecy. She's an Abram."

Mom stepped into the closet.

My three-year-old self ran to Mom and clung to her leg. "Where you go, Mama?"

She knelt by me. Her eyes widened and darted from me to the bedroom door. Pounding fists echoed through the walls.

"Why are you scared, Mama?"

"Mama will be back soon." She kissed my cheek. "I love you."

She placed her hand against the wall of the closet. When she closed her eyes, more tears fell. She gripped the necklace and hesitated. The closet lit up in a rectangular shape. The light became brighter and brighter. The wall on the inside of the light vanished. A door-shaped hole appeared. Through the door, more light shone, dim enough to watch but so dense that nothing was visible beyond it.

Dad eyed Mom, then her necklace. "If they come for Pero, they'll look for this. It's her only way back home."

"But." Mom's eyes pleaded. "How will I get back?"

"I'll hide the necklace. When the time's right, Pero will wear it. She'll find you and bring you back."

"No," Mom said. "Trust me. The necklace shouldn't be for her."

I gripped the necklace that was over my neck as I watched the vision play.

Dad studied her face, placing his hand on her cheek. "Come back quickly."

"I will." Mom looked at me. My little arms clung to her leg.

My hand wrapped around the necklace from Mom's pocket just as Dad pulled me from her and she stepped through the doorway. I wrapped my arms around Dad's neck, and the necklace landed on the closet floor.

Oh, no.

"No!"

I walked toward the necklace.

Mom turned around. Her eyes bulged as she reached for the necklace.

"Pero!" I saw her lips move, but I couldn't hear her. Her voice was muffled by the light from the other side. An unseen barrier prevented her from stepping out.

The light blinked, then Mom vanished. I screamed. The door shut and returned to a plain wall in the back of a closet.

Dad picked up the necklace. The chain dangled from his fingers, and his tears covered the pendant. I clung to him and cried.

"Pero?" Henry's calm voice pulled me back to the real world.

I opened my eyes, pulled off the necklace, and set it on the floor. Henry had brought back Mom's necklace, the same one that had taken Mom away. All those years. But it made people disappear and never come back. What was this power?

4

לָלֶכֶת

After we'd stuffed ourselves with green beans and mashed-a-roni and cheese, Dad handed me a package wrapped in a brown paper bag. "This will make you feel better."

I sat on the couch by Henry. Inside the bag, I recognized Dad's white wool sweater that his dad had given him on his eighteenth birthday.

"I know it's a year early," he said. "But you could use some comfort."

Breathing deeply the scent of dust and musk, I jumped off the couch and hugged his neck. When I stepped away, tears had gathered in his eyes. "You alright, Dad?"

"Yeah." He dabbed at his eyes and smiled. "Your mom would be so proud."

I returned his smile, a slight ache in my heart. Dad still missed Mom.

"Does it fit?" he asked.

I pulled on the sweater and felt it land on my upper thighs. I rolled up the sleeves. "Perfect."

"Good." As his eyes lingered on my neck, Dad's complexion paled to ash. "Where'd you find that?"

I looked down. The sweater must've pulled the necklace from beneath my shirt. "What do you mean? It's mine."

"I told you not to wear it."

"No, you didn't."

"I said that you needed to wait till tomorrow. Take it off."

"Dad, why did you give—"

"Now, Pero!"

I pulled it over my head like it was fire around my neck. Dad snatched it from my hand. "You can't wear this on your birthday. He might find you."

I braced myself for the impact my words would have on Dad. "He already has."

"You didn't tell me?" Dad's gaze shot to Henry.

"She didn't want me to."

I rolled my eyes. Why was it always the woman's fault?

"Did you see him on your run?" Dad asked.

"Yes?" I twisted my hair.

Dad sat back down, which was a good idea, considering his skin now had a bluish tint.

"You want the truth? After you lied to me about Mom?"

"Pero, sit down."

"I don't want to sit down."

Henry headed toward his room in the garage. "I'll let you two work through this alone."

"You too, young man. Sit."

Henry blinked, like a burglar caught under the streetlight. After a moment's hesitation, he plopped himself on the floor.

I grunted and threw myself next to Dad. "I've decided I'm leaving with Henry for Mom, and I'll bring her back."

"I've changed my mind. I don't want you to go."

"Dad, I have to. When I saw the man in the woods...."

"You were in the woods?"

"Just this once."

"Pero also saw Dr. Carper from her window," Henry said.

Dad dropped his head in his hands and rubbed hard. I moved next to him and placed a hand on his arm.

"I'm sorry. I should've told you." Should I also tell him that the necklace seemed to bring powers? But I couldn't hold back the truth. Hadn't we kept enough secrets from each other? "There's more."

Dad looked up.

"Right before dinner, I wore the necklace and sang. I had a vision, a memory of Mom when she disappeared."

Dad clutched my hand.

"In the vision, I saw myself at three, like I observed the memory from a distance. I heard everything that you and Mom said that day. She said there was something she hadn't told you about me, but she disappeared before she could explain. What was she trying to say, Dad?"

"I don't know. I've tried to think of things she may have said when we were together, but I have no clue. Do you think singing is your power?"

"Seems like it is."

"You won't go. I'm calling your aunt. I'll check flights to Florida right now."

Was running away and hiding the answer?

"Before you do that," Henry said, "I think we should show her the other necklace."

"There's another necklace?"

Dad moved his head toward Henry. "Show her."

Henry reached inside his shirt and pulled at a chain. Attached to the chain was the same pendant as Mom's necklace, a feather.

"It's your mom's," Henry said. "She wanted me to show your dad so he'd trust me."

"How did she have another necklace when she dropped it before she disappeared?"

Henry shook his head. "She didn't tell me, but you should take it so that if you go with me, you can give it back to her." He placed it in my hand.

I put it around my neck, next to the other.

"I want your mom back." Dad's voice choked. "But going with Henry isn't the way. Not when Dr. Carper is after you. He could—I can't let him have you."

A RAP SOUNDED at the windowpane. I ducked behind my bed and covered my face, as if whoever waited on the other side would kill me with just one look. The tap sounded again, followed by a muffled voice.

"Pero. It's Henry."

"What—" I jumped up and threw the curtain aside. Color had drained from Henry's face. I shoved the window open. "You gave me a heart attack. What are you doing outside?"

"Listen, I need you out here. Trust me."

"Why?" It was too dark to see beyond Henry. "You look like a ghost."

"If you want to find your mom, we need to leave. Now. Don't tell Matthew."

I glanced behind me. "But my dad said no. I can't go without him knowing."

"Goodbye's not forever for us." Henry took a shallow breath and touched my hand. "Don't forget that, Pero."

"You're scaring me, Henry."

"Grab some things and find the necklaces. Quickly." With that, Henry disappeared.

With trembling fingers, I shut the curtain and picked up the backpack I'd just stuffed with a change of clothes for my aunt's house. My pulse spiked. Something was wrong.

I wished I was like Dad and had enough fear keeping me at home, but I was not *that* fearful.

I smoothed my sweater down, and when I looked up, my reflection was hardly recognizable. On my frame hung a sweater that was too large. Yet my jaw appeared stronger, my wide eyes alert and alive.

For a moment, the room was silent. I took in the closet that held my guitar, a note on the desk for Dad, fuzzy pillows on my bed. My room represented me. Would I ever return? If I did, would I be the same?

Heart pounding in my chest, I opened the door and slid down the hall. Dad would try to stop me if I told him where I was going. Part of me wanted him to. Every inch of me screamed to run back into my room and hide, but I couldn't. Not when Mom needed me.

I heard Dad's voice from the living room talking with my aunt on the phone. His tone was tight, anxious. I pushed my palm along the wall behind me until it met Dad's coat on the hook. The left pocket held the necklaces. I didn't move my focus from Dad's voice but found the coat pocket with my fingertips, clutched the two pendants, and lifted. I draped the chains around my neck, then opened the front door slowly. Dad stopped talking, and the screeching of the door replaced his voice. I paused.

Dad started talking again. I sighed and slipped out the door, bringing it to a firm close.

All would be okay.

I tip-toed across the graveled driveway, scanning the silhouetted trees. "Henry?" Crickets chirped like sirens. Stars blinked against a black sky.

Fingers clasped my mouth, and an arm pushed me against

a chest, hard as steel. I protested, but the fingers pressed harder and the arm that was not Henry's squeezed tighter.

"Hello, Pero." Dr. Carper crept from the shadows. "Nice of you to join us."

My captor shoved me forward.

"You promised you wouldn't hurt her," Henry's voice said from somewhere behind me.

I squirmed and grunted, trying to reach Henry, but the man's grip around my waist made it difficult to breathe. A limousine was barely visible in the shadows ahead. As I neared, a door opened from the limo and the man who held me leaned his mouth against my ear.

"I've got your back," he said, as if to reassure me he wouldn't hurt me instead.

The man pushed me into the car and gently shut the door. I wished he'd slammed it. Then Dad would've heard and rescued me. I pulled at the door's handle, but it didn't budge.

"Henry!" I banged my fists against the window, then froze when I saw a gun pointed at him.

No!

I covered my mouth with my hands.

The man who'd held me opened a door of the limo. "You will stay quiet. Carper never hesitates to kill."

Dr. Carper said something to Henry, then walked away. An open target. I waited for Henry to charge after the gun and kill our nightmare. But he didn't.

Henry's face turned dark and his eyes locked with mine. He was sorry. I could see it. Sorry that he'd given me away. Henry's last words echoed like an everlasting throb. *Goodbye's not forever for us.*

I studied Dad's face through the dining-room window. Still on the phone, he glanced out the window but didn't see me. Seventeen years with someone and you'd think you would have memorized what they looked like. The years had added creases and receding hair. Anguish is all I saw. And he was about to have more.

The car took off. Taking a deep breath, I watched my house fade from view.

Onwerto. Dad would've said that to me if he'd known I was leaving. It meant to move forward. Then why did my chest feel like it would burst with grief, as if someone had re-opened the wound Mom had left? I needed Dad's hug to tell me everything would be all right. I longed to comfort him.

Instead, I left him behind.

5

———————

לְהוֹפִיעַ

My hand shook against the cold glass. We passed through my neighborhood, quiet in the late evening. Lights were off, cars parked. It was time for Green Meadow to sleep, but not me.

"My name's Jimmy," said the man who'd taken me. If the circumstances were different, I would've swooned over one of the best-looking guys I'd ever seen. Perhaps early thirties, shaved head, sharp brown eyes, perfectly chiseled features. But I didn't care. They'd taken me from Dad. Even if they brought me to Mom, this was not the plan.

"We won't hurt you," Jimmy said.

They already had. Not physically. Yet they'd ripped me away from my home, from Dad. *Should I cry?* I couldn't. I had spent my tears on sleepless nights when I thought of Mom.

"I used to live in a field like the ones here," Jimmy said. "It was a farm, actually."

"You think she cares?" Dr. Carper asked.

In a flash, Jimmy's eyes told me of his suffering before he averted his gaze, as if he tucked the wound he'd exposed back inside. Maybe I could trust him. Was Jimmy a victim of Dr. Carper just as much as me? Or had I misread him?

Dr. Carper sat down in the seat facing me on the other side of the limo, then pulled off his leather jacket and rolled up his sleeves. With black hair gelled forward and a small gold earring looped around one earlobe, he appeared to be prepping for a photo shoot rather than abducting a seventeen-year-old girl. How much money did a scientist make? I rubbed Dad's sweater. It was a scratchy soft. I imagined the material of Dr. Carper's shirt was so expensive that I'd never know its name.

"Do you have the band?" Dr. Carper asked.

Was he talking to me? It was difficult to tell when he hadn't looked at me.

"Yes." Jimmy fumbled through his suede bag and pulled out a strip of cloth.

"Good." Dr. Carper wiped his neck with a cloth. "You searched through her things?"

"All clear."

"The thing of value?" Dr. Carper opened the window that separated us from the driver, then swore. "Would you turn down the heat, Blue? I'm dying in here."

So, he was dramatic. I'd have to watch what I said.

Jimmy's face flushed. "If I remember correctly, you said you didn't want my dirty hands on it."

The driver named Blue must've turned down the heat. Chilly air passed from the vent. I hugged Dad's sweater tighter.

Dr. Carper pulled off his shirt. To my relief, a white tank was underneath. His arms were smooth with no defined muscle. I might escape him if he were to grab me.

"I thought you took care of this." Dr. Carper moved toward us just as the driver made a turn. The doctor fell against the seat with a grunt.

"Blue! Watch where you're going!"

Dr. Carper threw himself between us, and Jimmy retreated far to the other side.

"The band, Jimmy."

As soon as Jimmy handed him the material, Dr. Carper reached toward my neck. I ducked my head and closed my eyes. His fingers grazed along my collarbone. Could he feel the thump of my pulse? He yanked the necklaces. My neck stung from the force of the snapped chains. My key back home was gone, and we hadn't even passed the "Thanks for visiting Green Meadow" sign.

"How'd you find two necklaces?" He handed them to Jimmy, who put them into his bag.

"You'll give them back," I said.

"If only it were that easy."

What a fool Henry was for turning me in. He lived without being shot, but I may not return to anything.

"Turn around," Dr. Carper said.

I faced the window and watched the end of my town fade as Dr. Carper wrapped the band around my eyes.

"You'll call me Carper." He yanked on the band.

"That hurts!"

He pulled tighter.

"You're bold, Pero, but like your mom, you could use some manners."

"Carper," Jimmy's voice said.

"Stay out of this, Jimmy." Carper's voice was suave. I imagined he picked at his nails or smoothed his hair with a silver comb.

"Are you taking me to my mom?" I asked.

"You'll see her," Carper said, "but don't expect a grand family reunion."

I sensed more than heard Carper slide to the other seat. The space between me and Jimmy felt too far. Without sight, I was disoriented and empty. Had Mom felt the same all these years without me and Dad? Without a home? Or had Moon City become a sad place to belong?

A hand pressed on mine, and I jerked back. "You need to take this," Jimmy said close to my ear. I felt something placed in my hand.

"What is it?"

"It's a drink to relax you," Jimmy said.

"I don't need to relax." I'm sure my shaking voice was very convincing.

"No questions," Carper said.

Bringing the cup to my lips, I downed the sweet liquid in two gulps.

"You'll rest when we arrive," Carper said. "Jimmy will show you the training rooms. Marcus will supervise your conditioning. You'll stay off lì for now to test your natural abilities without it."

"What is lì?" My speech slurred.

Carper chuckled. "Where've you been the last decade? Hiding in your room?"

If only he knew how true that was.

"They're plants made of huang qi, calabash, and a rare species grown underneath the forbidden—"

Colors flashed over my closed eyes, then the darkness beneath my blindfold grew darker.

"I bet you didn't know—"

My head spun.

"—turn seventeen—"

I faded out, then in.

"—find you."

Carper's voice dwindled as the darkness swallowed me whole.

I BOLTED UPRIGHT in a strange bed. My heart thumped loud and
fast, but it was there. I was alive.

The small room held a kitchenette, an enormous wardrobe,
and through an open door, a stand-up shower, all modern. I
shivered, even with the two blankets over me. One small
window framed no glass, only metals bars. Was this Moon City?

I got up, carrying the blankets around me, and walked to
the window. I strained to my left and right and could barely see
a shiny steel wall. Reaching my hand out the window and
between the bars, I tapped against the wall. It clanged like a
gong. Solid. I looked down as I brought my hand in. About
three stories below, guards patrolled around the entrance.
Ahead, a field stretched toward a forest, similar to Green
Meadow. A planet in the sky resembled Earth. Maybe Henry
told the truth and Moon City really was on another planet.
Perhaps Mom waited for me somewhere within these walls.

I walked over to the door and pulled and twisted the
handle. It didn't move. *Now what?*

I sniffed my arm and smelled sweat and a hint of Jimmy's
pine scent. A shower might be nice. I entered the bathroom and
turned on the water.

Ah, cold.

I looked for soap and shampoo and found both in small
bottles, along with a toothbrush and paste, as if I were in a
hotel. I couldn't be in a prison. No one would bother treating a
prisoner like a guest. Did it mean I was on Carper's good side?

My shower never warmed up, so maybe I was in prison. I
wrapped a towel around myself and noticed a sheet of paper on
the bathroom counter.

> *Pero, welcome to Moon City. Call me when you're up. I left*
> *a few things for you. Let me know if you need anything else.*
> *Jimmy*

He left a four-digit number at the end of the note. Call him with what? I hadn't brought my phone.

A shiver passed through me. What had I gotten myself into? No, it wasn't my fault that Carper took me away. I would've been gone, hiding again. At least here I'd find Mom.

"Onwerto."

My hair dripped on my running clothes as I pulled them from my pack. I opened the wardrobe.

"Alrighty, Moon City. What've you planned for me to wear?"

Yoga pants, mesh shorts, tanks, and jackets in black draped on hangers. White athletic shoes lined the bottom. Apparently, there was no night club in Moon City.

I touched glittery black pants, softer than mine. The sparkle moved like tiny lights. I held the familiar blue pants and gray tank and sniffed them. My laundry detergent brought an image of home. What was Dad doing right this minute? If only I could come home at the end of this day to give him a hug and tell him I'd be okay. I sighed and tucked the clothes into my pack. I'd keep them safe and smell home to remember the reason I'd come. Mom. I put on the stupid jazzy clothes to embrace my new identity: somebody's sparkle.

A knock on the door startled me. The handle turned, and Jimmy stepped in with a paper bag in his hand.

"You mean you can do that?" I pointed to his keys. "What if I was getting dressed?"

My bluntness surprised me. Either I'd become used to Jimmy or craved seeing someone familiar.

He eyed my outfit. His face was expressionless and stoic. "You look the part. But even as a guest, there's no privacy."

Jimmy closed the door behind him.

"Aren't I some prophetic fulfillment?"

"Prove yourself. Your life is no longer your own."

I crossed my arms. "Whose is it then? Dr. Carper's?"

"Do you want it to be his?"

"No." I didn't want it to be anyone's.

"Then do what he says, but don't let him control your mind. Make sense?"

I nodded. I had a choice.

I put a hand on my torso. "Want to tell me why my ribs hurt?"

Jimmy set the paper bag on the kitchenette's counter and opened the mini fridge. He pulled out two plastic bottles of pink liquid. When the fridge closed, I noticed an intercom against the wall with numbers. The phone.

"You passed out," Jimmy said.

"You mean you drugged me?"

"I carried you over my shoulder when we arrived."

"How did we travel from one universe to the other?"

"Magic?" Jimmy shrugged. "Our bodies from Earth hide until we return. We are in different bodies while here in Origo."

I shuddered at the idea of my body left behind in some mysterious place on Earth. "What does Origo mean?"

"It means 'first in time, earliest.' That's why we call it the older universe. It existed before Earth."

I'd never learned that in geography. "Okay. What's next?"

"I'm taking you to the ammo room. You'll want to look at your choices to practice your combat skills. If you have Warrior skills, Marcus will train you. Carper wants to see what power you may have that he can use in the future. It might be overwhelming at first, but pick something up and try it. You may be surprised by what you can do." He nodded toward the paper bag and moved a drink toward me. "Eat while I talk."

I picked up the pink drink with no label and frowned.

"It's like Gatorade. Gives you energy."

"How do you know about Gatorade?" Maybe Jimmy had also lived in America. I opened and took a swig. Fruity, not too sweet. I opened the paper bag and found a salad, apple, and nuts. "Where's the sugar?" I tipped the bag upside down. "And carbs?"

"Moon City likes to keep us fit and healthy." He took a drink of his own pink water.

"And starved?"

Jimmy shrugged. "Could be worse."

One wrong word and I'd be begging for crumbs from Carper's hands. I shoved a handful of cashews into my mouth to keep me quiet.

"I want to get straight to the real reason you're here." Jimmy's tone grew serious. "No one has ever defeated the Lesaries. Carper wants power and to be king of the Lesaries."

Should Jimmy tell me about Carper's agenda? This seemed personal, like he mocked Carper's authority. Couldn't he get in trouble for saying these sorts of things?

Jimmy leaned against the counter. "The problem is when the Lesaries find out that Carper's raised a teen army, they're never going to want him as their king. He thinks they'll surrender because of the impressive power he's given the Warriors through lì plants."

Henry had told me that the Lesaries would destroy Moon City's walls. "How do you know Moon City is even a target?"

Jimmy shifted. "The Lesaries have demolished more cities in the last few years. Moon City has to be next on their list. Then there's your family line. Carper thinks if he has you and your mom, it will force the Lesaries to surrender."

My chest burned. He would use me and Mom to get what he wanted.

"Your mom has a gift," Jimmy said, "and Carper knows that the Abram family are the chosen."

"Wouldn't he want us dead?"

"Not when he has plans to rule the Lesaries and make you and your mom his advocates. With the two of you together and your powers ..." He paused. "Stop him."

It was a big call, one that I couldn't possibly do on my own. "If Elohim really calls the Lesaries to destroy the city, everyone could be dead. Including us if we don't get out of here."

"Carper's made plans," Jimmy said.

Could Carper take over an undefeated people?

Jimmy didn't seem scared or threatened. He may have doubted that Moon City would collapse. Maybe he had to see it before he could believe. Or maybe that was me.

"Do you believe in Elohim?" I asked.

"I believe in what He can do, so yes, I guess I do."

A shiver passed through me. If Elohim brought power, as Henry had said, could anyone stop Him? "So, why are you not scared?"

"I'm afraid. Not of what He can do, but of who He is." Jimmy opened his mouth, closed it, then opened it again. Nothing came out.

"Yet?"

"Yet I'm not afraid because He finally brought you here."

"What does that mean?"

Jimmy tapped his fingers before he looked directly at me. "Deliverance."

6

לְחַפֵּשׂ

Destruction.

Weapons hung along all four walls of the ammo room. Swords, pistols, and knives all seemed to point at me. I shivered under the weight of what they represented.

Jimmy scanned the rifles. "Hmm. Not the greatest to start with." He placed a finger on his chin.

He was wasting his time. I didn't know how to use any firearm. Wait a second. "Are there guitars in here?"

Jimmy eyed me.

"It's the only weapon I know how to use... I mean, play."

Jimmy swiveled back to the wall.

"I'll take that as a no." If I had to choose, a bow and arrow might be the easiest to learn. I couldn't imagine being comfortable carrying a gun. "Give me the bow."

Jimmy walked over to a shelf. "I have something better." He threw a long, skinny object toward me.

I flinched before I caught it. "A stick?" I balanced it on my hands.

"It's called a staff. It's been a common weapon for centuries."

"You think I can learn how to use it?" If only I'd taken the karate class Dad signed me up for in first grade.

"You caught it."

"Beginner's luck."

Jimmy almost grinned. "Your mom is very skilled with the staff."

For some reason, when I'd dreamed of Mom, martial arts skills weren't what had come to mind. I pictured her looking similar to my Bakery Barbie doll with a tray of cookies balanced on her double-jointed fingers. But now I imagined Mom as a warrior with wavy, flying hair and fierce eyes.

I planted the stick on the floor and gave my best effort at the sidekicks I'd seen in movies, resisting the urge to say "Hiya." When I landed on my feet, I threw the stick above my head, but instead of landing in my outstretched hand, it crashed to the floor.

"So much for being like Mom." I picked it up and tapped it. "I'll take it."

Jimmy's grin spread a little more. "Come on." He nodded for me to follow him out of the ammo room and into the courtyard adjacent to a mansion that must've been Carper's.

Inside the perimeters of the steel wall, Moon City resembled a village from a Disney movie. It was beautiful but simple. The mansion towered above the rest and was surrounded by a manicured lawn, trails of colorful flowers, and a large balcony. Beyond the courtyard, walkways scattered with islands of trees and fancy trash cans in-between. Wooden food carts spread throughout. Workers set up their displays of flower bouquets and hand-crafted jewelry that, according to the sign, represented moons.

I leaned close to Jimmy's ear. "Why's this place called Moon City?" It looked like an amusement park in the middle of a grand hotel.

"Many of the people who've joined Carper believe that he

received power from the moon. It never disappears from view, even in daylight. Carper called this place a city because he likes to appear big and powerful."

I looked at the moon above us that appeared bigger in the light of day, or maybe we were closer to the moon in Origo. Another planet showed clearly in the sky. There was no doubt it was Earth. Henry was right. Origo was real, and here I stood from a different planet, home so far out of reach. A chill passed through me. Would I ever return?

Commotion came from young adults fighting each other in the courtyard. One pair was wrestling. An orange-haired girl with gritted teeth squeezed the neck of a boy who eventually passed out. I couldn't move. Should I help him? Beat up the girl? I lifted my stick, aimed it at the girl, then dropped it. What was I thinking? With my luck, it would bounce off the girl's solid muscles like a tooth pick against metal. The boy didn't budge.

"Is he—?"

"Don't get too curious." Jimmy moved forward. "It doesn't help."

The winning girl walked away but not before she turned to look at me, as if she hoped I was next on her list.

I glanced back toward the wall, my small room sounding more inviting. But Jimmy nudged me toward the middle of the courtyard where I could see all the action. Another couple jousted on horses, which wouldn't have bothered me if I were at the Renaissance fair. But these lances were real, and the moment one of the young men didn't stay alert, the tip of the other's lance plunged into his chest. The young man fell from his horse and to the ground, deep red blood darkening his shirt.

I stifled a scream with my hands. The trainees nearby stopped to watch me with no expressions on their faces.

Jimmy rushed over and put his hands on my shoulders.

"You have to be tougher than this." His whisper was harsh. "Carper's watching you."

Carper sat in a chair on the balcony in front of the mansion and sipped from a glass. A few adults sat by him with similar glasses in their hands. I searched for a woman who'd resemble the vision I'd seen of Mom. Would I recognize her? The spectators chatted and occasionally pointed out the Warriors. No. Mom wouldn't be one of these. She couldn't be.

Carper watched me as if gauging whether he should intervene or let Jimmy settle me down. But I didn't want to take another dumb deep breath. I wanted to live in the panic so that at least someone acknowledged what had happened here. A person, possibly two had died. It was murder. My stomach cramped as bile rose in my throat.

"You didn't prepare me for this."

"They're not dead forever," Jimmy said.

"You saw what happened."

"Pero, listen. The lì plants will cure them." Jimmy's gaze didn't leave my face. "*Lì* means power, force, and strength. When they eat lì, they won't die."

Nope. I was done. I'd find the necklaces and a way out. "I can't do this."

"You have to." Jimmy was close enough for me to see that he wouldn't let me go. Not because he'd hurt me if I left but almost as if he'd watched and endured many years of death and was done also.

I closed my eyes for a moment. Mom lived in my mind. I wanted her to live in front of my eyes. *For Mom.* I nodded. "Okay."

Jimmy exhaled. "I'm taking you to Marcus. He's the trainer."

Two men dragged the boy who was lanced from the arena. Jimmy was right. My life was no longer mine. What if I really did have to die a thousand deaths? What if the lì plants didn't cure? Surely, they wouldn't start my first training with someone who'd kill me. A bald man stood between two teen girls with bows in their hands and arrows in bags strapped on their backs. The man's arms crossed, and his legs splayed in an up-side-down "V." The targets were not people. A knot in my stomach relaxed a little. Maybe this pair wouldn't kill each other. Just as one girl was ready to let her arrow fly, the man kicked the back side of her leg. She groaned, but right before she fell to the ground, she corrected her aim and released the arrow toward the target. It landed three rings above the center.

"Again," the man said.

The girl quickly stood and pulled another arrow from her bag. Giant bruises, raised and purple, covered her legs where the man had kicked her.

I gasped.

Jimmy put a finger to his lips. He could've stopped me if he thought I'd try to help the girl. But he must've had me figured out. My greatest weapon was my mouth. Not a good sign for a prophesied warrior.

I anticipated another kick, but when nothing happened, I turned to the man and the girls. All three studied me.

My face flushed. I should've held it in. Instead, my reaction screamed "New Girl" louder than a name tag would've.

"Well?" the man said.

I tried to smile. Did manners accomplish anything in a place like Moon City? Should I introduce myself? Tell him I'm ready to be trained, just not yet in archery? I held out my stick, feeling as much a fool as I probably looked.

"I'm here." Wow, was I smart. I cleared my throat. "For training."

"Marcus," Jimmy said, "this is Pero."

Marcus looked me over and smirked. "You're not anything like your mother. Did Carper see this girl before he dragged her here?"

With all the female Warriors around, his insults couldn't be because I was a girl. Maybe it was because I trembled as I held out my pathetic peace offering.

"She can't even hold a staff," he said.

I didn't disagree.

Marcus snatched the stick from my weak hold and pressed it against his knee. His muscles bulged and his face shook as he snapped it in half. Nausea waved through me. What would he have done to me if I'd held out myself instead?

"Lesson one." Marcus dropped the pieces on the ground. "Don't hold out your weapon."

"Got it." With nothing to hold onto, I placed my hands on my hips.

Marcus's face distorted to disgust. "Say it."

"Say what?"

"You've wanted to the second you saw the first one die. So, say it."

Was I really that easy to read? I guess I would be, an innocent seventeen-year-old who thought losing her mom was the worst pain she'd ever have to experience. Oh, was I wrong. "What will you do to me if I'm honest and say what I'm thinking?"

Jimmy fidgeted. It was a warning. Yet I didn't want my words to back myself into a corner. Everything I said in response could be used against me.

Marcus blinked. "Want to find out?"

I didn't. But with Carper watching, my mind had to rush as fast as an arrow and as steady as a hold around the dead boy's throat. *Think, Pero, think.*

If I ran past him, it'd catch him off guard. I'd avoid having to answer. But I'd be answering in a way. I'd be telling him and Carper that I wasn't an archer or skilled stick-person. When it came to athleticism, I was a runner, and if I had a chance to survive, I had to put my best foot forward.

I let out a breath. *Ready.* What would Marcus do with my

response? Would running away cause more misery? I'd hate to stick around (no pun intended) and find out.

"Lesson one," I said. Marcus could kill me for this. I put one foot behind the other. *Set.* "Don't show your back to the enemy." I looked behind Marcus. As expected, he looked too.

Go.

My heart beat faster before I gained speed. I ducked between Marcus and the girl with bruises, too fast to notice if they'd seen it coming or what they'd do next. Would this accomplish anything? It didn't matter. I had to have all eyes on me. It may be the only chance to show my skill without being killed. If I couldn't use a stick, I'd use my legs. I pressed my feet against the courtyard cement firmly and lightly so I didn't lose momentum. Crowds strolled along a type of farmer's market with stands of produce and flowers and wooden figures that on a quick glance seemed to be shaped like a moon.

A peach stand stood in front of me. Their smell enticed me to pick one up and eat it along the way, but that would reduce my speed. Instead, I leapt over the entire table and landed on my feet. This was not Chosen or Warrior power. This was Pero Moshe, the ordinary.

Moon City citizens—dressed in brightly colored attire—gasped. A man tried to grab me, but I weaved around him. A cluster of people cleared to make a straight path to the front gate. As I neared the city's gates, I saw my end. I slowed and rested my hands on my knees, panting. I looked up at the nearest guard.

"Open the gate." The guard ignored me.

"Open the gate now!"

He didn't move. More was out there, open space, and here I was at a stop, just as I'd been on my daily runs at home. I should've known that everything I chased after eventually ended. I'd gotten past the closet in my room and the forest outside my home, and look at where they brought me. To another wall.

The gate was a few feet taller than me and barred with horizontal, black metal rails. If I placed my foot on the one vertical rail, I could push myself up and clamber over it. As a kid, I'd once climbed a tree about the same height and jumped down with a plastic bag that Dad tried to convince me was not a parachute. I didn't listen then and ended up alive.

I walked to the gate, held onto the rails with both hands, set my foot on the vertical rail, and pulled myself up. The gate rose a couple of feet above me, higher than I'd thought. Circling my hands around one rail, I set my feet against two rails and pulled myself up an inch. My feet slipped, and I fell backward, landing hard. Pain throbbed from my tailbone and up my spine. When the ache subsided, I stood and wiped the debris and dirt off my pants. Just a bruise. I'd try again. If only I had a plastic bag.

"Let her out," a voice said.

I turned around. Carper folded his arms, and his eyes appeared humored. Marcus stood next to him with a scowl. How did they get there so fast?

I turned back to see the guard swinging the gate outward. Beyond the gate was the field, and beyond that was the forest, and beyond that had to be the Lesaries, waiting for the right time to come for me.

"She'll be gone, Carper," I heard Marcus say from behind.

"Will she?" Carper asked.

He knew the answer, otherwise he never would've let me go. Everything I needed was in Moon City. The necklace. Mom. But what he didn't know was that everything I wanted would always be out there. People built walls, and I couldn't trust people.

I didn't glance at Carper or Marcus, only to what was ahead. As I ran through the gates and around the city—the gate guard telling the other guards they could let me go—the tall grass whipped my legs, the sun burned my face, the breeze stung my eyes. I was wide awake to the earth, as if I wasn't stuck inside and hiding any more. It was time to be awake. Whatever the reason I was here, I never wanted to hide again.

Pero, feather.

The voice nearly stopped me. It was deep and very near, like words written across my mind. I ran faster. It had to be Dad's voice in my head, cheering me on. Out of the vibrant blue sky, a bald eagle swooped down and touched the grass. I ran toward it. With every step I took, the eagle flew further away until it reached the edge of the forest. I stopped when it landed on the ground, resting my hand against a tree.

The eagle's enormous wings shimmied and set in place behind its back. Its head twitched and stared at a focal point before moving to another. Its eyes narrowed. How could the eagle not notice I was close enough to see its green eyes blink and the specks of grey on its white face? Close enough for the eagle to be in danger, if I were after it. Was I so insistent on leaving Moon City that I hadn't noticed the dangers around me? Maybe I shouldn't trust Jimmy. Maybe I shouldn't trust Mom. She'd left me. She kept something hidden from Dad. What if she was the enemy?

As swiftly as it had appeared, the eagle launched through the air and into the sky toward the planet Earth. If I could fly on the eagle's wings, would it take me back?

I was alone, my breath the only sound apart from a breeze that whistled through the trees. I knelt and touched a blade of grass with my fingertip. Peace came in moments like this but was hard to keep. As much as I craved to move fast, I also craved rest.

I collapsed under a tree and laid my head against the trunk. The city's walls were not too far away, reminding me that I wasn't entirely free. I closed my eyes and reached for Mom's pendant in my pocket. When my hand grasped air, I rubbed my chest as if the necklace was still there and was a magic lamp that would grant me three wishes. I wished that Carper had never existed. I wished for Mom and Dad and me to be together. One more wish. What should it be?

I didn't know. Maybe my third wish would be to always have a wish. Like never-ending life. Like hope.

Something whizzed above my head and vibrated through the tree. An arrow jammed into the bark and held a folded note in place. My stomach turned rock hard. It could've been my head pinned to the tree. I brought my hand over my eyes to block the sun behind Moon City. A dozen figures stood atop the wall. Carper folded his arms. The girl with the bruises on her legs held a bow in her hand. So, she did have good aim when she wasn't being kicked. What a relief.

I kept myself facing the wall so that I followed my own lesson: never turn your back on the enemy. I guess I turned my back when I ran from Moon City, but I wouldn't risk it now. With one foot against the tree trunk, I pulled the arrow with both hands. It didn't budge. On the wall, Carper had moved his foot to the edge. Was that laughter I heard? If only I could tell the eagle to fly behind Carper, nudge him over just a bit.

I couldn't run back to Moon City without the note. It would mean I failed. How could I read it if I couldn't pull it out? Maybe if I tore the note off. I pulled at it a little. It nearly ripped the whole thing.

Oh, come on.

I pulled off my long-sleeved air-wick shirt, leaving on the tank underneath, and ignored the whistles from the wall as I wrapped my shirt around the arrow and pulled again. The arrow loosened, and I fell backward.

Yes!

I held out the arrow for my audience but groaned. The stick of the arrow was in my hand while the rest was still stuck in the tree. Laughter was definitely what I'd heard the first time.

I threw the piece of arrow to the ground and ripped the paper from the tree. Stepping into the clearing, I held the paper out in victory and bowed. They clapped and hollered.

"Glad you're happy," I muttered. Opening the letter, I held the ripped pieces together.

> *Dinner party tomorrow night. I'll have formal attire ready for you in the mansion at 3pm. Don't be late.*
>
> *Well done.*
>
> *Carper*

On the wall, Carper nodded, then turned and walked away, his followers right behind.

7

———————

לִבְחוֹר

I slammed the fridge and dumped out the leftovers onto the counter. Stabbing a piece of lettuce with a fork, I forced it into my mouth, then spit it out. I stomped over to the bed and fell facedown onto the mattress. Carper had invited me to dinner. At least it was a party and not him and me, unless "party" meant for two. My stomach coiled. He wanted me there in the afternoon, like it took two hours to look amazing. Who was there to impress? Mom?

I lifted my head up from the mattress. Would she be there? No matter what she was like, I'd make Mom proud. "That's my girl" kind of thing.

More than likely, she'd already heard about the new girl who leaped over a booth without knocking over a single peach and ran as fast as the eagle could fly.

When I heard a knock on the door, I pulled a blanket over my head. "Go away, Jimmy."

"I will tell Jimmy you missed him."

I fumbled out from under the blanket as the door clicked behind Carper. I scrambled off the bed. The devil and I were alone.

"Relax, Pero," Carper said. "It's not like that."

The walls seemed too narrow, as if they wanted to squeeze me. Carper leaned against the wall near the door, either to keep a distance or to let me know there was no leaving.

Carper stepped forward. "You were great out there, you know."

"Couldn't we discuss this at your party tomorrow?"

He folded his arms. "If that's what you want."

Why was Carper playing kind? Maybe that was the way he worked: lay down the rules with intimidation, then act gentle to draw me in. I wouldn't take the bait, and I certainly would never let him be my king. "What do you want?"

"Your talent." He threw an object toward me.

I caught it easily. It was the necklace. This had to be a mistake.

"I don't understand why you're giving this to me."

"Wear it," he said. "Never take it off."

"Why?" Then the answer hit me. After seeing me run as fast as I had, Carper would ensure I didn't take off. The necklace might track me if I did. It wasn't a key to rescue Mom; it was a curse to keep me in.

I choked the pendant with my fist, longing to throw it out the window and embrace my fate.

"It seems like you've figured it out," he said. "You're clever."

I'd never considered my big mouth as clever. Dad called it sarcasm. Yet today, maybe because I ran faster than the ginger-bread man, I'd outsmarted Marcus and caught Carper's attention.

"Goodnight." Carper left.

I fingered the mysterious word on the back of the wooden feather. Yesterday I'd wanted it to mean that Mom would return to me, today that I'd return to Mom. Wasn't that why I'd come?

With a grunt, I threw the necklace on the floor and fell back on my bed. I stared above. On the ceiling was a string attached to a cutout. I scurried over and jumped to pull on the string. A ladder unfolded from the ceiling.

Huh.

I checked the lock on the door. Not that it made any difference so far. I grabbed the necklace from the floor, put it in my pocket, and scurried up the ladder like a squirrel, my head popping out into a greenhouse made of clear glass walls and ceiling. Six garden beds held large, green plants that resembled lettuce. Were those the mysterious lì that Jimmy had spoken of? I brought a leaf up to my nose. It smelled sweet, a much better aroma than an average leaf. I let it flutter to the garden bed.

Between glass walls on my left and right were other greenhouses. A Warrior appeared on the roof to my right and picked a handful of plants, shoved them into his mouth, and walked back down. I wiped the hand that had touched a leaf on my pants.

I propped myself against the garden bed, and pulling out the pendant, traced the mysterious word on the back of the feather. The necklace had to stay on. Carper would find out if it wasn't, and getting home wasn't an option without it. "Fine, I'll wear it."

"Never wear what you weren't created for," a voice said.

My heart drummed in my ears. A man appeared out of nowhere and sat on the ground across from me. He wore a long robe and wooden sandals like I'd heard of in the Holy Words. His smile lifted his short white beard and revealed taut wrinkles on his face, the color of oak-tree bark. Acorn eyes met mine and twinkled, as if he were a wise old uncle who never expected to meet me because he was from one universe and I from another.

"How'd you get here?" I asked. "You weren't here a second ago."

"I don't know. Elohim directs me."

Ah. A Lesarie. "Does Elohim often direct you to magically appear?"

He scratched his beard. "Has Elohim made you magically appear?"

I'd somehow appeared in another universe. "I guess so."

I shifted at the silence that followed. He smiled and watched me, as if quiet meant talking and studying faces meant listening.

"Pero Moshe, the chosen." His eyes sparkled.

Henry must've told him about me.

"Are you the Lesarie leader?"

"My name is Hoshea. You can call me Shea."

Henry had mentioned that name. From the sound, I assumed Shea would be a woman, but she-uh was, in fact, a he-uh.

"I bet you wonder why you're here," Shea said.

"To find my mom and bring her back home." That was it. No tearing down walls, no killing doctors.

"You can't escape Elohim's plan for you, Pero."

That's exactly what I wanted to do. "What if I did escape?"

He smiled. "Then He'd bring you back."

I rubbed my temple to stop a headache. Or was it a mind ache?

"You are more important than you realize," Shea said.

"Because I can run fast or because a rich man invites me to dinner parties?" A breeze picked up in the evening air, and I shivered.

When Shea stood, he walked over to me, took his giant cape from around his shoulders and covered me with it. It smelled like pine and felt like a heavy hug. Unlike Dad's sweater, Shea's cape was soft. I shivered again. Not because I was cold, but because I had been.

Shea sat down next to me, his legs nearly double in length

than mine. "Do you realize what it means to be chosen by Elohim?"

It meant that I had to leave everything.

"Whether or not you choose to obey Elohim," Shea said, "if you use the power He's given you for your own gain, you'll only get what you want. But if you choose to use the power for others, you will win many battles. There's a great plan for your life. Elohim has made it known to me."

The lì plants swayed, yet the greenhouse was quiet, as if the evening breeze absorbed all sound.

Just like my distant Grandpa Abram, Shea seemed to be a prophet. What could he see that was so great? So far, my life had involved hiding and being hidden.

"Elohim has chosen a few others. One is in this very city."

"My mom," I said.

Shea shook his head. "Dr. Carper."

"What?" There was no way Elohim would pick someone like Carper to fulfill His plan.

"Carper may not use his power for Elohim, but he is chosen, and you must protect him from harm."

"No." Nausea punched my gut. I only came for Mom. Didn't they have order and pickup parking spots in this city?

Shea remained calm. "You are his guard and are chosen by Elohim to save his life."

Save my enemy's life? I clasped my hands together and squeezed. "I can't do it." I stood up. "And besides, Carper isn't an Abram, is he?"

"Doesn't matter. He's not one of the three chosen to bring power. Elohim's chosen Carper as the first king of the Lesaries."

Jimmy wanted to see Carper destroyed. Kill Carper or save him? Who and which was right?

"How do you know it wasn't your own thoughts?" I asked.

Shea stroked his beard again. "The same way I know I was

in the Lesaries' camp one minute and was here on your roof the next. But why don't you ask Elohim? He may have an answer."

"Elohim doesn't talk to me."

"Are you sure?"

Shea disappeared.

I jumped, and my heart beat faster till it felt like it'd been replaced with a volcano about to erupt. Would anyone else appear, then leave me feeling smaller?

8

לִמְצוֹא

Before the most expensive meal of my life, I lost my appetite. It must've had something to do with standing at the entrance to the mansion without really wanting to be let in.

The door opened, and a man studied me, as if searching for hidden weapons.

"Dr. Carper invited me." I swallowed my nerves. "I'm Pero Moshe."

"He wants you to show me the necklace."

I rolled my eyes and reached for the side of my pants, but there was no pocket. Lifting a finger for the guard to wait one minute, I removed my shoe and tapped out the necklace.

The guard raised his eyebrows. "He wants you to wear it, Miss Moshe. Around your neck."

"Of course, he does." Did guards report sarcasm? I put it over my neck and arranged my hair over the chain. "Is it straight?"

Without a word, the guard opened the door to let me in and closed it behind him. "Wait here."

My entire house could've fit in Carper's lobby. Staircases

trailed up on the left and the right. The theme was white: white marble floors, white walls, white flower paintings, and a white fluffy dog who barked at my heels. I petted the dog, and it settled down at my feet, wagging its tail.

I clasped my hands together. The sound echoed in the quiet lobby. How could someone so terrible live in a nice place like this? The dog was content, the white walls cheery. Carper had built his own happiness while the Warriors killed. Some king.

"Lovely, isn't it?" Carper stepped into the room and admired the view of his own home.

"Very white." I bit my lip.

"I'll show you the rest." He motioned for me to follow.

Every room looked the same, with expensive furniture, dull art, and white walls. The sewing room happened to be pink. At every turn into another room, I expected to see Mom sitting at a piano, standing over a chopping board, ironing clothes, hitting a tennis ball. Was she even here?

I felt disengaged, as if I hadn't entered into an enormous house with a man who treated me like a visiting family member moving in for the summer.

Carper led me into a bedroom with a vanity, an open bathroom, and a view of the city.

"Here's where you'll get ready," he said. "Someone will bring your dress."

He pointed to a corner where a guitar stood on a stand. "I heard you play. Bring it with you to dinner." He turned away.

That was it? "Carper?"

He glanced back, an eyebrow raised.

I opened my mouth, but nothing came out.

Carper put his hands in his pockets. "I took your mom, forced you away from home and into a wall. You wonder why you're here and why I'm treating you like royalty."

Yep. That summed it up. On planet Oregano—or whatever it was called—I was a royal prisoner.

"I'm not telling you anything." Carper shut the door.

I moved over to the bed and sat down. The mattress sunk just right. It was more comfortable than my own at home. What would I need to do to stay in a room like this? Wow them with my guitar?

I picked up the guitar and whistled low. It was a Martin D-28. Solid spruce top. I strummed a C chord. A sweet sound met my ears. I closed my eyes. Only days ago, I'd played in my closet, but it felt like years. Home. Did Dad pace at the kitchen window? Did Henry wonder why he let me go?

Keeping my eyes closed, I played through the chord progression I'd created in my closet when I had the vision of Mom. If I sang it again tonight, maybe Mom would hear, and it would take us home.

A soft rap on the door stopped me. I set down the guitar. "Come in."

The door opened. Draped over a woman's arm was a black sequined ball gown with so much poof that I couldn't see her face.

"You mean I'm supposed to walk in that thing?" At least it wasn't white. I wanted nothing implying that I'd be getting married.

The woman moved around me and threw the dress on the bed. I touched the velvet, form-fitting top, deciding whether I should gag or be excited to dress up.

"I'll look like a poodle."

Tears dripped from the middle-aged woman's face.

"Are you okay?"

She nodded her head, and her mouth quivered.

I saw—really saw—her then. The way her black hair hung down around her shoulders, the precise line of her nose so familiar, the freckles along her cheeks in the exact place I imagined.

"Mom?" My breath caught.

She nodded.

"Woah." I sat on the bed, my legs refusing to support me. Mom was here. My vision blurred, then cleared. My body hung heavy like an anchor in the sand.

She moved toward me. "Don't ruin your dress."

I stood up. All moms had to have said that at least once to their daughters. I'd waited for this moment my whole life, and now that it was here... "Should we hug?"

She sniffled and wiped her face with her sleeve. "I'd like that."

Mom brought her arms around me and squeezed, weeping over my shoulder. As my arms wrapped around her slender frame, I waited for a magic connection to happen, something that would shift inside to show that my life was now complete. Yet I felt nothing but a woman's tears and a thud of frustration. Crying was a good thing, right? It meant she had feelings and wouldn't hurt or hate me.

She loosened herself from the embrace. I spotted a box of tissues on a bedside stand and offered one.

"Thanks." She blew her nose and laughed. "I'm a complete mess."

"Nah. You're beautiful."

She snorted. "You're beautiful! I mean, gosh, Pero, look at you. You're a grown woman." She touched my hair. "Your hair is so long. Did you ever let your dad cut it?"

I smiled. Mom hadn't seen Dad in fourteen years. Did she still love him?

"How is he?" she asked.

What did she want to hear? That Dad hid me well, just as she'd asked? "He's waiting for you."

Her drawn expression seemed pained.

"Well," I said, "he's waiting for two now." We'd go back home. I had Mom. Mission accomplished. Who cared if I had two conflicting tasks? I was done. Onwerto.

Mom grabbed my hand and led me to sit on the bed.

"We're sitting on the dress," I said.

"I don't care."

Neither did I. Not really. All I wanted was to hear what Mom would say, to eat up her words and try to make sense of what had happened and what was next.

"Pero, we have little time before the party. Carper let me see you only for a moment." She checked the clock on the wall, then sighed. "I want you to know that I still love you and your dad very much, and I want to return with you and be a family again."

She watched me as if waiting for approval.

I squeezed her hand. "I want you to return. If Carper gave you back your necklace, we could leave now."

Mom let go of my hand. "Has anyone mentioned our family connection to the Lesaries?"

I nodded. "My friend Henry did. Elohim sent him to find me."

Mom's eyes widened. "You know Henry? He's a wonderful, handsome young man."

And Mom was such a mom.

"He's cool." I shrugged. "For a bodyguard."

Mom gave me a curious look. "Listen, Pero, I'm the chosen Lesarie."

"I was told that I am, too."

"Yes." Mom hesitated. "I can't explain it all right now, but I need you to trust me. Carper wants power to strengthen him. If you have that power, he'll keep you. If you don't, well, we need to hide before he gets rid of us."

"You mean kill."

Mom grimaced. "Possibly."

"Why can't we leave now?"

"Because we need a plan."

"Running fast impressed Carper. That's why he invited me to dinner."

"You being in the courtyard was an initial test to see how you'd respond in a pressured situation."

"You saw me?" Was I embarrassed or pleased that Mom was in the audience?

"I heard you were faster than anyone they'd ever seen, but I don't think that running fast is a prophesied gift. If you're one of the chosen," Mom said, "Carper and I will know because we're all connected."

Mom pulled out her necklace, and I pulled out mine.

"Carper has the third," she said.

"But the Lesaries' leader, Shea, told me Carper isn't the third chosen."

Mom shook her head. "Carper's not a descendant of Abram, and there has been no specific gift he's shown that's drawn our power together."

But if he wasn't the third out of three prophesied, who was?

Mom glanced at the clock. "We'd better get you ready. Have a seat at the vanity and I'll brush your hair."

I sat and watched as Mom grabbed the brush and worked on my tangles. I'd dreamed of a moment like this, when my mom would brush my hair. I savored how it felt. Gentle. Kind. And somewhat painful.

I grimaced when she yanked on a knot.

"Am I hurting you?" she asked.

"Not at all."

"I can't believe you're here. I never thought this day would come." Mom wiped at her face with a wadded tissue. "Once Carper found out about my gift of fighting with the staff, he sampled my blood to create plants with the ability to cure. He became famous, and it drew more people to his strength. Enough followers to grow a city. Carper is who he is because of me. If I were to leave, his potential power would weaken. But if you really are one of the chosen, then his power may increase. He'll want to use your blood for his inventions. We're not free of him until Moon City is destroyed, but I'd rather see us get away before that happens."

Even then, she may not be free if Carper became king. If I saved Carper from destruction, what would it mean for our future?

Mom stopped mid-stroke and looked at me in the mirror. I could stay in that moment for a long time. Mom was alive and brushing my hair.

"Will we make it back?" I asked.

Mom set my hair over one shoulder. It hadn't ever shone as brightly.

"I don't know." She kissed the top of my head.

I studied myself in the mirror. Who should I trust? If I followed Jimmy's request to destroy Carper, I could die. If I followed what Mom wanted and hid, we could get caught. But if I followed Shea's advice and saved Carper, he could hold me captive.

I held onto the pendant.

"Mom?" It was strange to call her name, knowing she'd respond.

"Yes, Pero."

"What does the word mean?" I held out the necklace. "On the back."

Her smile grew. "Koach. Strength. Through the prophet Isaiah, Elohim said, '*My righteousness is near, My salvation has gone out, and My arms will judge the peoples; the islands will wait for Me, and they will trust My arm.*'"

Mom knelt so that we were face to face. "Koach means to trust in Elohim. Not to hope that we will be saved, but knowing that by His strength, we will be."

I held it up. "Why a feather?"

"As we wait for Elohim's strength, we will rise with wings like eagles."

The eagle I'd seen must've been a symbol. Maybe it was Elohim's way of showing me He was real. I tucked it into my shirt. I wanted to wear it, to feel Elohim's power against my chest and let the word soak through my skin.

Koach. Koach.

Mom beamed. "That's why we named you Pero. Your dad wanted to name you after an interesting root word from the English language." Mom chuckled. "And I wanted to remind us that no matter what happened to me in the future, Elohim would watch out for you and bring you koach."

My eyes flickered to the guitar and back to my reflection.

By the strength of Someone I didn't fully understand, I'd sing.

9

לִשְׁמוֹר

The chit-chat faded until every chic woman and spiffy man was studying me. Men wore black jackets over black dress shirts; women, black dresses that clung to their bodies. Mom wasn't at the party yet. I pushed down my growing panic.

Carper scanned my dress and nodded in approval. "You look…"

"Like a cupcake?" My pulse rose. *Don't say sexy, or I'll heave.*

"Stunning."

Gross. I held out the guitar. "Um, where should I set this?"

He jolted from his stupor and snapped his finger.

Jimmy approached, glanced at my dress, and made a face that told me he held back laughter. Great. I was a big bell, or Southern Belle, perhaps.

With only hand signals from Carper, Jimmy leaned the guitar against a white grand piano where around twenty adults mingled. A woman laughed while leaning against a man who looked equally unsteady.

A server stopped with a cart of empty glasses and half full bottles. "Wine?"

"No, thank you." If Moon City allowed teens to kill each other, I supposed they wouldn't care if a seventeen-year-old drank. Still, I'd rather focus on walking without falling on my face.

The crowd fell silent when Mom stepped into the room looking... well, stunning.

Her makeup was natural and lovely, and her hair swirled into a smooth twist. A black dress fit snug around her slim figure and fanned out around her legs. The sleeves trailed down to her wrists. A beauty queen.

Carper kissed her hand. "Lovely as usual."

Mom withdrew. "I'm sure Monica is dying to share an evening with you."

Carper and Mom glanced at the woman whom I'd noticed leaning against the man and now was whispering in a different man's ear.

Carper frowned. "Let's eat."

He directed us to a table long enough to fit the entire party. I sat to Carper's left and Mom to his right. Monica sat at the end of the table. Servers entered with trays in their hands. Saliva pooled in my mouth from the intoxicating smell. A server set a plate in front of me decorated with salad, pasta, meat, and little black things in the shape of pearls.

Across from me, Mom bent her head in prayer. When Carper started eating, I hovered my hand over three forks. Mom lifted her head and picked up the first one to her left and used it for her salad. I picked up the middle fork and went straight for the meat. Tender, but too gamey.

"Bahar." Carper glanced at Mom. "I see your daughter doesn't pray before her meals."

Mom winced. "You know as well as I do that Lesaries on Earth don't always practice the Holy Words."

Would all conversations involve everything I hadn't experienced in life because Mom wasn't around?

I picked at the little, black squishy things with a spoon.

"It's caviar, Pero," Mom said.

Wasn't that fish? I lowered my spoon and took another bite of the meat.

"I'm guessing your daughter also never learned that Lesaries don't eat camel."

I stopped mid-chew, gagged, and spit it into my napkin. Maybe I was eating the hump.

A flush crept along Mom's cheeks as she took a sip of her wine. "I'm guessing, Carper, that you never learned that either."

Wait. Was Mom saying that Carper was also a Lesarie?

"Getting a little snarky, are we?" Carper asked.

"I'm only matching the cards you're laying down." Mom rubbed her napkin across her lips as if they needed a deep scrubbing.

"Are you challenging me?" Carper asked.

"I don't know. Am I?"

Carper's fist thumped on the table and silenced the room.

Mom! Hadn't she learned not to make the hot-tempered man angry? It hadn't taken me long at all to learn that.

Carper stood and pointed to the door. "Out!"

Mom placed her napkin on the table and stood.

A cold sensation iced my body. "Wait! Let her stay. Please. I'll play my guitar."

Mom looked between me and Carper, who sat back into his chair. Everyone at the table was silent, as if anticipating Carper's next move.

At the lift of Carper's empty wineglass, a woman filled it a quarter full. Taking a sip, he lifted his glass again. The woman filled it to the rim. Carper's wine sloshed over his glass and onto his hand, and still he sat in a daze.

"If it's okay with you, Carper," I said.

"Fine."

All eyes glued onto me and Mom as we walked toward the

guitar. Halfway there, I tripped over my dress. The party gasped. I caught myself and waved.

"I'm okay." I smiled and turned around to let out a grunt. It figured the don't-look-at-me sort of girl had to be the center of attention.

"You're doing great," Mom said.

I leaned closer to her. "What was that? With Carper?"

Mom put a hand on my back. "Just play."

I picked up the guitar. Jimmy set out a chair for me that faced the party. When I sat, my dress puffed up. The guitar on my lap settled down the material.

I strummed. Wrong frets. "Sorry," I said to my audience and squirmed in the chair until I was more comfortable. "Is this dress made of steel?"

They laughed.

"Just take it off," the swaying man said.

My face heated.

"We all know you're good at that," another man said.

The men roared with laughter.

Were they referring to when I'd taken off my outer shirt by the tree yesterday?

"Ignore them," Mom said. "They're drunk."

I sat up straighter and strummed. Much better.

"Although..." I picked with my fingers a bluesy tune. "... holding a guitar is a heck of a lot easier than holding a stick."

They laughed harder. Jimmy gave me a thumbs up. Carper perked, leaned back in his chair, and crossed his arms, a wide smile fastened. I had their full attention.

Closing my eyes, I breathed out long and steady. "I'm running after you," I sang.

The room faded from view, and a bright blue color flew into focus. When I stopped strumming the guitar, the room blinked back, the audience waiting. Jimmy nodded.

A vision.

Mom stood against the wall nearby, her face contorted like she might cry.

Carper leaned forward and clutched the feather from around his neck, appearing eager for more.

I played another chord, closed my eyes, and sang. "Won't let any fear in my way."

The same bright blue color appeared on the back of my closed eyelids. It was like I was in a 4-D theater with screens below, above, and around me. I stood on a floor that was also blue. Although I still played and sang, I had shut out all sounds.

My mind separated from my body, like I was in two places at once. My fingers still strummed the guitar, but in my head, I reached out and let the breeze blow against my fingers. A white cloud appeared from the right and drifted by. I touched it. Wet.

An eagle flew across the sky. When a feather fell on my face, I caught it and let the silk-like texture glide against my thumb.

My voice projected, and I wondered if Dad could hear it as he watched another sky from the kitchen window.

"I'm running after you," I sang.

The blue beneath me turned to dirt. Tall grass surrounded me. In a rumble, Moon City rose. The wall loomed above, blocking the eagle, the clouds, the sky.

I ran faster and faster until I was half-running and half-flying. Wings from my back stretched long and wide.

"Comin' home," I sang.

Out from the ground, an army of people young and old marched in silence. They ran until they too were half-running and half-flying. Wings grew on their backs.

We flew around Moon City seven times. The people shouted. The wall trembled.

The notes that I sang rang out pure and long and with passion.

Arrows from the wall rained on our heads. When arrows hit

the people, they faded into the ground until the only one left was me.

The wall stopped its trembling. My wings faded, and the eagle flew away.

The blue sky surrounded me once again with silence.

A still, small voice spoke, "*Under my wings*."

Was that Elohim?

The vision turned black.

I sang the last two notes like someone who'd just stepped off a train to return from a long journey. Quietly. With an ache. With relief. "Comin' home."

I blinked and opened my eyes, the room slowly coming into focus. The once vivid lights overhead appeared dim compared to the blue in the vision. I wanted to go back to that place, to feel warmth and protection, to know that everything was how it was supposed to be—at peace. But there, in Carper's mansion, was the familiar fear. Pulsing in my head, squeezing out my oxygen. Walls felt tighter, closer.

Applause rippling through the room startled me to my feet. Blank faces in the audience made me wonder if anyone else had experienced the same power I had.

Mom approached me and leaned close to my ear. "I saw the vision, and so did Carper."

When I turned my direction toward Carper, I met his fierce eyes, staring me down.

10

מַרְאָה

She pulls back the blankets, and I climb in. She tucks them around me.

"Easy peasy," she says with a smile and hums a lullaby. I never hear the words. Never know if the bough breaks, but I don't ever fall because Mom is there, planting a kiss on my cheek, telling me I'm her girl.

"I love you, Pero," she says.

Those are the words I write for the melody she hums, the ones I hold on to night after night.

I love you, Pero.

I am loved. I am chosen. I am somebody's daughter.

And that is all I need.

ALL THE OTHER NIGHTS, the dream shifted to a nightmare. Mom disappeared, and I cried myself awake.

But not this night. No. Tonight, Mom was real. And after mad Carper kicked us out of the mansion and put us back in the room inside the wall, I needed a real mom.

"You won't leave when I'm asleep, will you?" I squeezed her arm.

"I'll be right next to you all night."

"Are you sure you don't want to sleep on the bed?"

Mom shook her head. "I'm used to sleeping anywhere."

I didn't ask her why. When she was ready, she'd tell me everything, perhaps even all the hurt I imagined she'd experienced. But maybe it was better not to know.

Mom combed her fingers through my hair. The soothing motion made me sleepy, but I forced my eyes open to memorize her face. She had dark brows that matched her eyes and long lashes that would never need mascara. Unlike mine, her skin was an olive tone. There had to be something in her features that I'd inherited. Was it her smile?

I fixated on the ceiling, the light of the moon revealing white swirls in the shape of cotton candy. "Mom?"

Mom stopped humming.

"Did anyone else see the vision?"

"You and I should be the only ones to see it. I don't know how Carper did."

"What did the vision mean?"

"I didn't understand all of it," Mom said, "but the eagle represented Elohim and the safety we can find under His wings."

So it *was* Elohim who'd spoken to me. "He didn't keep you safe."

"He did, Pero. It wasn't the way we would've liked, but He still was faithful. If I hadn't left you and your dad, Carper would've found and taken you as well. I didn't want a captive life for you. Instead, you were safe in your home. Elohim wanted me alive all these years so that I could see you again. And He brought you here safely."

"I guess so," I said. "But He also kept you away for a long time."

"For your safety."

Elohim could've protected me even if Mom had come home sooner.

"It's best not to run from Elohim's purpose," Mom said, "even if we don't understand."

Perhaps Elohim wanted me to rest in His strength. But if I followed Elohim, wouldn't He keep me trapped here? I wasn't sure I wanted to be under His wings if it meant letting go of my chance to be free.

11

לזעוק

Mom sat on the bar stool next to me in the kitchenette. "Headache?"

I rubbed my temples and nodded.

"You need to eat."

I nodded again and rested my head on my arm.

"There's lettuce in the trash," I mumbled in my sleeve.

"Let us end the rash?" Mom asked.

I gave her a quizzical look. "No. There's…" I pointed to the trash can where I'd tossed yesterday's lunch. "Forget it."

"Jimmy's coming with food soon," Mom said.

"How nice of him."

"Maybe I should ask him to bring something for your head, too."

I waved a hand dismissively. What I needed was American artery-clogging food. Like pancakes. And coffee.

"I ought to show you how to use a staff," Mom said. "You may need a weapon, eventually."

The last thing I wanted to think about was how to kill someone or defend myself. So far, doing the opposite of anything violent had been my greatest self-defense. More than likely, Marcus had never trained a Warrior to win by running or playing guitar.

I slumped and rested my head on the counter, my head's throb counting the seconds.

"Mom?"

"Hmm?"

"Just making sure you're still there."

As she rubbed my neck, relief comforted my soul.

A knock at the door pulled Mom's hand away.

Jimmy came in with a tray of three paper bags and steaming mugs.

I perked up at the smell. "Coffee!"

He eyed me. "What happened to you?"

"What? You don't look like this when you wake up?"

"Headache," Mom said.

I held the mug up to my nose and sniffed deeply.

Mom's brow raised.

"Don't judge," I said. "It's been a long time."

"Yeah," Jimmy said, "three days."

"Is that it?" I muttered through the events, counting out the days on one hand.

"She needs food," Mom said to Jimmy.

Jimmy set the bag in front of me and pulled out soft bread, olive oil, cheese, and an apple. I dipped the bread into the oil and shoved it in my mouth. "Is Carper furious with me?"

Jimmy placed a bag in front of him and pulled out the contents. "Carper hasn't come out of his room yet. Usually, Bahar's power improves his mood. Want to tell me how your performance made him so upset?"

I sipped my coffee. How much should Jimmy know?

"Pero saw a vision," Mom said. "The Lesaries are coming to Moon City."

"Was Carper in the vision?"

"No," I said.

Jimmy drummed his fingers on the counter. "Good." He took a bite of bread.

"What's so good about that?" I asked.

"Carper already knows that the Lesaries will come. He must've figured from the vision that it's soon. But he thinks your powers will save him."

My powers would save him if I did what Shea asked and protected him.

"I still don't understand why Carper was upset," Jimmy said.

"It's because of Elohim's voice," Mom said.

Jimmy set down his coffee. "What happened?"

"Under my wings," I said. "That's what Elohim told me right after the walls fell."

"In Pero's vision," Mom said, "Elohim protected."

"What does that mean to Carper?" I asked.

"It means that Elohim's power in you is greater than Carper using your power," Jimmy said. "It means that you are a threat, Pero."

Saliva stuck in my throat. "What will he do to me?"

Mom's face grew ashen. "You need to hide."

I'd become great at hiding, but was that the answer?

"I'm not going with you yet," Mom said. "Not until I know it's safe for me to go."

I jumped off the stool. "I'm not leaving without you."

A thump sounded at the door, followed by keys turning the handle. What was the point of a lock?

A guard barged in. "Pero and Bahar, you're wanted in the training center."

"I'm not ready," I said.

The guard glanced at the watch on his wrist. "Five minutes. I'm waiting out here." He eyed Jimmy's breakfast, then him. He opened his mouth, then shut it instead and closed the door.

"I need to go," Jimmy said. "He'll question where my loyalty lies if I spend too much time with you."

"Should we hide now?" I asked in a whisper.

Jimmy piled the mugs on the tray. "Not yet."

"I agree," Mom said. "It's too obvious right now. We need to think of a place that Carper would never look or a way to hide in the woods."

"I'll see what I can do for you." Jimmy left.

I tried to move myself toward the bathroom, but my feet stayed rooted. "Will he hurt me?"

"You need to get dressed," Mom said.

I forced myself forward and opened the wardrobe. "It's not like anything in here is different from what I'm already wearing."

"Then at least try to look like you didn't just wake up from the dead."

I ran to the bathroom and brushed my teeth, washed my face, and pulled my hair into a bun. When I looked in the mirror, I noticed my complexion appeared drained. How would whatever I'd endure next change my reflection?

"You can do this, Pero," I said to myself.

Mom knocked on the door before entering the bathroom. "Dang it, Pero! Aren't you done yet? Now's not the time to examine your beauty."

"Gosh, Mom, why would I do that?" I threw on shoes. "It's not like I care what Carper thinks of me."

"Keep it that way."

She watched me as I bit into my apple that tasted like toothpaste. What was going through Mom's mind? Did the pain of her past with Carper hurt her so much that she couldn't share?

"You won't tell me what he's done to you, will you?"

"Nope." She hurried to the bedroom door.

I followed. "Why not?"

She sighed and moved a stray piece of hair away from my face. "You're not ready."

THE WARRIORS LINED up around the edge of the courtyard where they trained to kill. Their stance reminded me of wolves ready to charge. Mom and I stood in the middle with Marcus. Whatever Carper had in mind, he wanted a larger audience, and there was no escaping.

Carper and his companions sat on the platform. Jimmy stood nearby. I put my hands on my hips to control trembling. More than likely, Marcus could smell fear and had already sensed it.

"Pero has no training to fight." Marcus' voice echoed off the Warriors, as if they were bricks. "But her power will supposedly show her how."

Were we going to fight the Warriors? Mom and I should've run while we had the chance.

"If Bahar is one of the chosen Lesaries," Marcus said to the crowd, "she will show Pero what happens when we don't follow Carper."

I tried to avoid eye contact with the Warriors. Were they stepping closer, or was my head spinning? I'd heard Mom was skilled enough to fight them all. But even with training, I'd never be able to fight the Warriors. Carper had to know that I was a runner and musician. If this was another test to see what I could do, well, I could tell him I'd lose. Then again, how did I know what I could or couldn't do? The power had surprised me last night. Maybe it would again.

Marcus faced me and Mom. "No weapons. Only your hands."

I pulled my hands tight against my chest. There were only

two of us and many of them. "How am I going to fight all of them?"

Marcus barked laughter.

"We're fighting each other, Pero," Mom said.

My whole body burned. Me fighting Mom? How could I even pretend to know what to do without hurting her?

"Ten seconds." Marcus joined the crowd.

Mom edged close to me and spoke so softly I could barely understand. "Follow my lead."

Mom paced around me. I followed what I observed, slowly circling. I swallowed a lump in my throat. I'd never hurt another person before. Was it natural to fight?

I tried to imagine that this wasn't Mom in front of me but Carper, and let the anger and hatred kindle. Here was my enemy. Here was my chance to show what happens when someone messes with innocent people.

But it wasn't Carper. It was Mom.

Elohim, if you really are the source of my power, show me what to do.

If I could hear His voice, surely He could hear mine.

Mom came at me quickly and punched me in the arm. I fell hard.

The Warriors didn't cheer or respond. Carper's friends made up for the silence with laughter that made their backs hunch.

"Do it again, Bahar!" one man said. "I've got good money on you."

They were betting on who'd win?

I stood and put my hands up in defense as Mom circled around me.

"Punch my face," Mom said. "I'll be easy on you."

My whole life, I had dreamed of Mom's face. I couldn't punch it. Neither could I be a fool.

I swung at her face. Mom ducked and grabbed my arm. She twisted it so that it was behind my back.

"Again," she said.

Pain shot through me from the point where Mom had a hold of my arm to my back. I didn't move until she let go. What was she doing to me?

I punched at her again, and this time she ducked, spun, and kicked my legs from under me. I landed on my side with a bang.

My leg and hip burned.

"Up," she said.

It had to be an act, like the ones I'd given the last few days. She was surviving. And I was the victim. She'd never go too far and hurt me. Unless she wasn't kind after all.

Mom slapped my cheek. The impact smacked like a loud clap. I turned my back to her and put my hand on my face where it throbbed.

This was never the mom I imagined. She wasn't supposed to hurt me, to break me and reduce me to nothing. We were the chosen, after all. Yet I'd left Dad to go somewhere I didn't want to go, in order to find someone who I never knew but who I thought I wanted.

And now that someone had stung me with a slap.

Blood dripped to my fingertips. I lifted my hand to find it bright red and sticky.

Before I could react, the surrounding sky turned black.

The Warriors were gone. Carper, gone. Moon City, gone. Someone had placed me in a virtual reality. A vision.

Mom was there, her form muted as if she were in a picture set to sepia tone.

I saw the silhouette of a throne. On the throne, a man wore a bright golden crown. The crown's brightness revealed the man's face.

Carper.

Mom's voice faded into the background, then slowly grew in volume. "Elohim's power is here. Hit me while you have a chance."

I heard a voice in my head. *Offer your other cheek.*

Elohim. I couldn't doubt His existence any longer. But what would being passive do?

Mom paced.

In the vision, Carper's face glowed until it nearly blinded me. I closed my eyes. The light was still there.

Brighter.

Brighter.

One light flashed an unfamiliar face. He wore a crown and blood trickled down his head. Then he was gone.

I blinked my eyes to focus on Mom. Her image blurred. I blinked again. She came into focus, her face beautiful, tangible, close yet still so far.

Mom's fists were up and ready.

I couldn't fight and wouldn't. Placing my hands behind my back, I planted my feet in front of her, and turned my head to the left so that she saw my right side.

Mom stopped any signs of aggression.

The darkness left. Moon City was back. The people were back. Carper's followers were quiet.

"Hit the other cheek," I said.

Mom did nothing.

"Hit the other cheek!"

Mom stepped back. What was she doing? If she slapped me, she'd be safe.

"No."

Carper's followers gasped.

"What did you say?" Marcus came closer.

Mom glared at Carper and stood solidly. "I said 'No.'"

I should've slapped her. I should've played her game. Now she was in danger. Now she...

Carper pulled out a gun and aimed it at Jimmy.

"Stop," I yelled.

Carper couldn't hear me.

"Jimmy!" I screamed.

Carper pulled the trigger.

Jimmy fell to the floor.

"That's what happens to traitors." Carper snapped his finger. "I want Bahar. Take Pero to her room. I'll ask for her later."

Two guards surrounded Mom.

I reached for her, but Marcus blocked me.

"You can't take her!"

Two guards grabbed my arms.

"Carper!"

He turned toward me.

"I'll protect you," I said to Carper. "I'll make sure the vision happens the way you want it."

"Pero, no," Mom said.

She didn't understand. Neither did I, really. Elohim wanted him as king.

Carper walked away toward the mansion. I had to make him see I was on his side. It was the only way to get us out. I couldn't let Mom be hurt.

Like Jimmy.

"Remember what I told you, Pero," Mom said. "Find a way."

The guards pulled me.

"I can't."

I fought against their hold.

They gripped tighter.

"I can't. I can't." I screamed out her name. "Mom!"

I was three again. She was in the closet, turmoil in her eyes. Except this time there was no last embrace or necklace to save me.

The guards threw me inside my room and closed the door faster than I could reach it. I slammed against it with my fists.

"You have no right! She's my mom! Do you hear me?"

I pounded harder.

"Listen!"

But no one was there. I was nobody's feather. Dropping my fists, I sunk to the floor and cried.

12

מַהֲלָךְ

A spotlight turns on.

"Go!" Mom begs.

I shake my head but obey. I'll run away from Moon City, and no one will stand in my way.

I stop at the edge of the forest.

"I can't go past the line," I say. "It's too dangerous."

The gates of Moon City open, and a mob of people march toward me.

"Keep running!" Mom hollers.

I run, run.

Where are you going, Pero?

I plug my ears at Elohim's voice. They'll find me. They'll kill me.

One step forward, past the edge of the forest, and I stop when something in a bush shuffles.

Carper jumps out, his eyes like fire. Blood trails down his cheek.

Grasping for Henry's hand to hold, I find air.

"Where are you going, Pero?" Carper hisses.

I scream into the darkness.

IT WAS DARK.

Dragging my feet over the edge of the bed, I felt my way to the counter. I didn't want to go back to sleep. Not when Carper waited in my nightmares.

Leaving without Mom wasn't an option. There had to be a way to save her, but without Jimmy, I'd have to rescue her on my own. My heart ached. Jimmy had to be dead.

A loud thud echoed through the ceiling. Someone in the greenhouse... again. I pulled down the ladder and started to climb.

The rail underneath my hands vibrated from another thud above me. Two people. Had Shea brought a friend?

Peeking over the edge, I spied two figures, darkened by the shadows.

"I heard something." The man's voice was low and calm. "Maybe she's coming up from her room."

My arm twitched. Could I climb back down?

"Don't scare her," the second voice said.

Wait. I recognized that voice.

"She shouldn't be surprised," said the first.

"Yeah, but she didn't know when we'd come, and we still need to find her daughter."

I didn't have a daughter. Did they have the wrong place?

"You mean the pretty Pero."

I flinched.

"I never said she was pretty."

Henry! Did I trust him after he handed me off to Carper?

The other chuckled. "You didn't have to."

The other choice would be for me to stay locked up in my room until Carper decided what to do with me. Henry or Carper? I stepped onto the roof.

"Pero!" Henry ran to me, spun me in a circle, then set me down.

I smiled in surprise, then stiffened under his hold. "Are you going to turn me in again?"

He frowned. "You're seriously asking me that? I haven't been able to sleep for days. Imagine trying to explain to your dad that I'd let Carper take you."

"How *did* you explain to Dad?"

"Ha! Not well. I'm surprised he didn't kill me."

I folded my arms. "So am I. Why did you sell me to Carper?"

"I didn't sell you. When I was at your bedroom window, Carper was in the shadows with a gun pointed at my head."

I gasped.

"I didn't have a choice, Pero. I'm sorry. Your dad had me follow you shortly after, but I ended up with the Lesaries instead. I was worried. I didn't know if I'd find you alive. If anything had happened to you, it would've been all my fault. Some bodyguard I am."

I could see why he'd be concerned. Carper was unpredictable and not afraid to kill. Maybe Henry did care and not just because Dad had asked him to protect me.

I placed my hands on his arms. "It's not your fault. I'm alive. You found me. And just maybe I'll forgive you." I grinned.

Henry laughed and nudged his head toward the man who stood in the shadows.

The man stepped closer, appearing younger than Jimmy, but not seventeen either. His fine black hair flipped in the front like a small wave. On the side of his light brown face, a scar trailed from his eyebrow to his mouth. A stubbled beard almost hid the lower part of his scar. His face didn't belong in a magazine like Henry's and Jimmy's. Yet my stomach flipped.

It was his eyes.

Dark brown shone brighter than the moon's reflection from behind me. Something deeper settled there, making my body quiver. As if this look would pull us into a greater realm if we lingered. As if we would surely drown if our gazes drifted apart.

The slight blush of his cheeks and the intensity of his stare told me he felt it, too. Whatever "it" was.

Henry cleared his throat.

I glanced the other way. What was it about this man that drew me? I didn't know him.

"This is Sam," Henry said. "Sam, this is Pero."

"Henry told me about you." He studied the floor.

"I've heard about you, too." Henry had mentioned his best friend often enough that I knew a bit about Sam's likes and dislikes, but he'd never mentioned that Sam would have my head whirling. Was I attracted to Sam like one of those books where the girl falls in love from a wolf-man's psychedelic eye power? Or was I responding to something else in him?

I felt my face heat and stepped into the shadow. "Let's go inside before anyone sees us."

I scanned the roof before heading down the ladder. Henry and Sam followed.

I turned on the bathroom light and left the door slightly ajar.

"Want something to drink?" I opened the fridge. "The pink water's not too bad."

I set three on the counter. They didn't touch them.

Henry scooted a barstool out for me. His hair was shorter; curls sat on top of his head instead of around his ears.

"You cut your hair." I sat.

"Do you like it?"

The cut emphasized his long jaw line and smooth, white skin, making him appear older and more handsome... if that was possible. "It looked better longer."

Henry messed with the curl. "I knew it."

I looked at Sam and found him staring at my face. "Do you need something for your cheek? It looks swollen."

I touched the scratch on my cheek and took in Sam's scar. Would I have my own? "I'm fine, thank you."

When he didn't waver from his gaze, I resisted the urge to pull away. The room stayed quiet for a moment, like we all waited for the heat between Sam and me to cool to a simmer. What was I doing? Henry liked me. At least, it seemed he might. And now I was caught in a flurry of feelings from two dramatic looks between a complete stranger.

Finally, I forced myself away and to Henry, who picked at his nails. "Why were you looking for my mom?"

"We met your mom here a few months ago," Henry said. "Bahar recognized we weren't from Moon City and took us in. She said that she would tie a red scarf to a window for us to find her."

Henry pointed at the room's window. A red scarf knotted around a bar. Mom must've tied it while she stayed with me. Even when she knew she might not escape, she looked out for me.

"Is your mom... okay?" Henry asked.

"She can't come with us. Carper took her. But I think this scarf means she'd want me to go with you."

"I can try to find her."

I shook my head. "She wants me to hide, and there's nothing we can do at this point. Guards are all over Moon City."

I stole another look at Sam. His brows sunk down like he was sorry to hear the news. I took in his bulging muscles underneath a plaid green, button-down flannel, the very shirt I'd picked out with Henry a month earlier. I chuckled inside at his choice of white cotton pants that clashed with the shirt's style. If I'd known that the Lesaries' pants looked like billowing sheets, I would've told Henry to buy some jeans for his friend too.

I averted my gaze when Sam's eyes met mine.

"How'd you land on my roof?" I asked Henry.

"You may not believe us," Henry said.

I smiled. "Shea appeared on my roof. Nothing will surprise me."

"Eagles," Sam said.

The eagle I'd seen in the field hadn't taken me anywhere. "How?"

Henry held up his hand and made a whooshing sound.

I laughed in disbelief. "They flew you?"

"Big ones," Henry said. "They're a part of the Lesarie army."

"Are they how we get out?"

"Sorry," Henry said. "They took off when we landed on the roof."

"Alrighty then." I brought one leg over the other and bounced it at the same time I put my hand on my chin. "What's the plan, Sam?" Was I flirting? Maybe.

Sam smirked, as if amused.

"Well." Sam's eyes popped up to meet mine.

A punch in my gut exploded into a thousand jitters.

"I saw a hose near the lì plants in the greenhouse. We'll climb up the tube that leads to the roof, use the hose to rappel down the wall, and hope you run as fast as Henry says you do. The Lesaries camped a four-hour walk away. We'll walk as much as we can before it's light. Shea will help us with a plan to find your mom. The battle starts in two days, so we'll have enough time."

Sam was the leader Henry and I needed. Someone with a practical and organized agenda. But we'd have to rescue Mom in two days. "Is there enough time to come back for my mom?"

"We'll make it work."

Mom wanted me to hide. There had to be a good reason. I should do what she said. "Onwerto."

Sam arched his brow. "Yes, to whatever you just said."

"My dad says the phrase sometimes when there's a tough choice where we either have to hide or move forward."

"So, you're choosing to move forward?" Henry asked.

"Give me a minute." I headed toward the bathroom and touched the surface of my cheek. If I had makeup, I'd cover up the wound. What could cover up a pounding heart?

13

לִבְרוֹחַ

"We're really gonna slide down a wall on a rope?"

"It's a hose," Henry said.

"Will it hold us?"

"It should." Sam stood underneath the chute in the green-house, the hose wrapped around his torso. If we made it through the chute, we'd reach the rooftop. "Ready?"

"I guess so." I rubbed sweaty hands on my pants. "Oh, wait."

I pulled the necklace over my head. "So Carper doesn't track me." I buried it in the soil.

Sam's posture stiffened. "Where'd you find that?"

"It's mine."

"It can't be."

A wave of heat spread over me. "What do you mean?"

Sam turned away. "Nothing."

Did Sam know who the third necklace belonged to?

Concentrating on the plastic tube, Sam pressed his hands on both sides so hard that his arms shook. He pulled himself up a few inches at a time, then set his feet on both sides of the tube.

"You're gawking," Henry said.

"Am not." I poked Henry in the ribs.

"I saw the way you two looked at each other."

My face heated. "I was studying his scar. Where'd it come from?"

"You were studying more than a scar." Henry smiled.

"Shut up."

Henry didn't show any signs of jealousy. Did Henry have feelings for me? That day in the forest before I was taken, he'd called me beautiful. Later, he'd joked that we held hands. Had I imagined that he saw me as more than a friend?

One careful movement at a time, Sam climbed closer to the top. When he slipped, I turned the other way.

"Pero," Henry said, "your boyfriend is falling."

"He's not my boyfriend." I shut my eyes. *Don't fall. Don't fall.*

"You're closing your eyes again."

"Okay, okay. Wide open." Wooziness swept through me.

Sam made it to the top and disappeared.

"You know he's too old for you," Henry said.

"Would you stop it?" How old was Sam? I didn't really care. *Don't say thirty.*

"You don't want to know how old he is?"

"Nope."

"Okay." Henry whistled a tune.

"Twenty-eight," I guessed.

"Ha! Got you."

"Fine." I folded my arms. "How old?"

"Twenty-five."

"That's it?"

"It's older than seventeen." Henry shrugged.

"He's not old. Just mature, not that you would know what that means." My face throbbed. Why did I say that?

Henry sent me a long, pained look, then broke eye contact.

Thickness tightened my throat. "I'm sorry, Henry."

"Forget it."

I couldn't. Henry was rescuing me again, and I hurt him.

Sam's face appeared. "The rope is secure."

"He means the hose." Henry winked at me.

I laughed.

Sam dropped the hose down the tube.

"Harness yourself first," Sam called. "Tie it in a knot."

Henry grabbed the hose.

I swatted his hand. "I've got it."

I held the hose and froze. The only arm strength I had was from strumming my guitar. I needed help, darn it. "What do I do?"

Henry must've tied knots for fun as a boy. In a minute, he tied the hose into a knot that had two loops and held one loop out. It appeared to be a very secure rubber hose.

"Put your feet through these," Henry said.

I put both feet in the loops and held onto his firm back for support.

"I'll pull you up, Pero," Sam said.

Henry handed me the hose and checked the loops secured around my thighs.

"Go ahead." Henry looked me in the eye, but only for a moment, like he was hiding something from me.

I pulled myself up. The hose was warm and slid through my hands. My arms shook despite me not carrying all the weight while Sam pulled from the top.

"Use your legs, Ro girl," Henry said.

Ro girl. That was new.

When I focused on my legs, my hands slipped from their grip on the hose. I fell a foot before Sam caught the hose again. I let out a breath of relief.

Sam pulled me to the top, and I climbed out.

"You did great. I'll help you down the roof." Sam held the hose and my eyes.

Something was wrong with my heart. My brain. My eyes that couldn't look away.

"Guys," Henry said, "I kinda need the rope. Uh, hose."

Sam cleared his throat and dropped it. Henry was up the tube before I could check how he did. I imagined he'd used his legs.

Sam took the hose over to the edge of the roof and scouted the premises before dropping it down. It plunged below and hung ten feet from the ground.

I studied the drop. *Uh, no, thank you.*

Eagles weren't in the sky to pick us up. Dark clouds formed ahead. A chill was in the air. Rain.

Sam grabbed onto the hose and rappelled without a word. So much for him wanting to help me. He jumped from the end of the rope and landed smoothly. He stretched out his ankles and put his hands on his hips. I couldn't call him a "show off." More a "get-'r-done" kind of guy.

"Want to go next, Pero?" Henry asked.

"Go ahead. That way I have two to catch me if I fall."

"You won't fall." Henry leapt on the edge.

"Wait." I gripped his wrist. "How do I hold on?"

Henry studied the hose plummeting down.

"I think you better cross your legs around it and slide." He nodded to a pair of gardening gloves nearby. "Wear those. Make sure you land in a squat with your legs so you don't collapse at the end. If you're falling, try to land on your side."

Squat, side. Think quickly. I cringed, grateful I'd worn pants so the hose didn't burn my legs.

Henry kept his legs perpendicular to the wall as he walked down backwards like some superhero.

My turn.

I gripped the hose and wrapped my legs around. My muscles only held a good grip for a couple of seconds before I slipped—too quickly. The momentum made me fall at the end of the hose before I knew how I was landing. *Side. Land on your side.* Sam and Henry's crisscrossed arms bent as they caught my back, but my elbow landed on something hard.

"Ouch." Henry let me go to hold on to his nose.

I shivered as Sam took his time to set me on my feet.

"Did I hurt you?" I asked Henry.

Blood poured from his nose that he covered with his shirt. "I'm okay," he said in a congested voice. "Happens all the time."

I cringed when I heard a popping sound as he set his nose back in place.

"That didn't feel good." Henry wiped the remaining blood, snorted, then coughed.

"*You* okay?" Sam asked me.

I held out my hands. "A little shaky and my hands are burning, but no injuries."

"Good." Sam held onto my elbow and directed me to the wall. "Follow my lead."

He crept toward the edge of the wall, peered around, then back. "If we crawl in the tall grass in the other direction, we should avoid the guards. It'll take longer to reach the forest, but at least we won't get caught. Once we're closer, we'll run."

My fingers gripped the ground as we crawled through the field. Rocks and sticks poked my hands and knees. The grass swayed and swished along my legs. If they didn't see us, they'd hear us. A couple of drops hit my head, then warm rain poured over us like a shield. Every few seconds, I wiped my face with my arm and trudged on.

"We can run now," Sam whispered in my ear.

How would I run in the dark?

Sam held onto my hand and lifted me to my feet. He moved closer for me to hear. "Let's go."

Sam ran ahead, and I followed. Henry was out of sight.

The rain whipped my face. It wasn't too cold. Still, I shook. As I approached the forest, my foot landed in a small hole. I fell and stuck to the muddy ground. Pain stabbed my ankle and up my leg. I grunted and dragged myself out of the hole.

Someone knelt by me. "Are you hurt?"

It was Henry's voice.

I nodded and remembered that he couldn't see. "My ankle."

He helped me up.

My right foot seared with white hot pain. My swallowed scream came out as a whimper.

I hobbled with my arm draped around his shoulder.

We'd walked only a few feet when the rain stopped.

"We need to move," Henry said. "Can you walk?"

"No." Where had Sam gone? "Can you carry me?"

"Yes."

Was that hesitation? Sam's arms appeared stronger than Henry's.

"Get on my back." Henry bent down.

I gritted my teeth as I put my hurt foot over his back and held onto his shoulders. An unexpected wave of comfort washed over me. Henry was the closest reminder of home.

Henry ran with ease. "Light as a feather."

I wanted to laugh, but my ankle bumping against Henry's leg hurt too much. Mom said I was Elohim's feather. Protected. Strengthened. Was it true?

Henry ran inside of the forest and stopped when the trees hid us. The forest smelled depressing, as if the short rainfall had layered it with wet wool.

"What happened?" Sam rushed up.

Henry set me down.

"I fell in a hole."

"It's probably a sprain." Henry's breath was shallow. "Let's walk more. We can build a fire and I'll check it out."

"I'll take a turn helping Pero," Sam said.

"I don't mind doing it," Henry said.

"Give yourself a break," Sam said. "I'll let you know if I get tired."

I couldn't imagine how he could.

"Sure." Was that disappointment in Henry's tone?

When Sam scooped me up, I hesitated to put my arms around his neck. With no better way to balance my weight, I held on. Eventually, my heart settled into a steady rhythm, and the smell of leather against Sam's neck became familiar. Not familiar, like Dad's smoky scent, which would've made me ache for home, but kind of like the smell of a favorite blanket.

After a while, the rise and fall of Sam's breath told me he was tired, but I didn't want to be the first to let go.

"What century are we in, Sam? Is it the same as Earth?"

He took a couple of deep breaths. "Origo is old."

"How old?"

"Old enough to cause harm, but young enough to need to be taken care of."

Sam had been hurt. I could sense it in the way he spoke.

Henry stopped ahead.

Sam put me down. I leaned against him to take pressure off my ankle. My wet clothes stung against my skin.

A light flickered. Smoke drifted in the air from a small fire.

"What should we do?" I asked.

"We need to see who it is," Sam said. "If we don't know them, we'll sneak around."

"I can't sneak through the woods in the dark." I pointed to my feet as if he'd see them.

"She's not lying," Henry said.

I resisted making Henry's nose bleed again.

"We can't hide here all night either," I said. "They'll find us, eventually."

"I'll go," Sam said. "You stay here."

Sam was so quiet that it took me at least two minutes before

I realized he'd left. An empty feeling settled in the pit of my stomach. What if it was someone from Moon City?

All I could see through the trees were the flickering flames and rising smoke. No one talked or stirred. Maybe the person was asleep.

Henry huffed. "We'll be standing here all night. Where is he?"

"Patience." I tapped my fingers against my arm. Maybe Sam had left us.

A light shone on my face. I blinked.

Sam held the light up to his face.

"Where'd you get the light?" I asked.

"We're staying here."

"Did you find out who's there?" Henry asked.

"It's a girl from Moon City with orange hair. She said her name is Stone."

My body grew colder, my mind replaying the image of the young Warrior killing the boy during training, the evil glint in her eye when she looked at me.

"We need to leave," I said. "I don't trust her."

"We can't," Sam said. "She has your necklace."

14

לְהָעִיר

Wide awake.

Henry slept to my left. To my right, Sam pulled out a chunk of wood and shaved slivers with his knife. His eyes tracked Stone, who squatted next to the fire and stretched her hands toward the heat.

My clothes were still damp against my skin from the rain. Why hadn't I brought my sweater? It'd be too awkward to lie closer to Henry or Sam.

My foot was elevated on a rock. Henry had wrapped and tied his jacket around my ankle. Sam's flannel shirt was draped over a rock near the fire. His t-shirt exposed arm muscles that didn't appear tired after carrying me.

I watched Sam's dark brows furrow in focus, his fingers cutting with precision, brushing away chips, glancing over the wood to see where he should put his knife next.

When his eyes met mine, I shut them quickly. Nice job, Pero. Like he'd fall for the "I'm asleep" trick. When I opened them, he watched his project and smiled. He wouldn't sleep either, not with Stone nearby.

"I could've killed you, you know." Stone's high-pitched voice brought a chill. "I saw the three of you on the roof from my greenhouse. Can't hide secrets with glass walls. Lucky for me, I watched where you put the necklace."

As much as I wanted nothing to do with the necklace, I didn't want that girl with it, either. If the necklaces really were the key to returning home, I'd need mine. I should've thought of that before I buried the dumb thing.

Sam glanced at Stone, then back to his project. I didn't doubt that the lì Stone ate made her one of the best killers both worlds would ever know. Sam didn't seem to be afraid. Henry couldn't be too afraid. He'd fallen asleep as soon as Sam told us he'd be the watch guard.

But Stone had my necklace. Without it, I'd never go back home. With it, I'd never leave Moon City.

"I don't plan on keeping it." The chain from the necklace hung from Stone's clutched hand. "I don't plan on giving it back to you, either."

I sat up, grimacing when my ankle throbbed. "What use is it to you, then?"

Stone sat crisscrossed in front of the fire. Her orange hair blended in with the flames. "Without the necklace, Carper loses power and I'm safe."

Did I have that kind of power to save or protect a city? Not if the Lesaries destroyed it. If that happened, perhaps all power would be gone and Mom and I would have to figure out how to make it back.

"Why'd you run away?" I asked.

Her green eyes locked on mine. "No point in staying in hell when you have the key."

"You're never safe," Sam said, his chisel increasing speed. "Not without Elohim."

The fire cackled in response.

I'd lived without Elohim my whole life and was safe for seventeen years. Yet I had to hide.

Sam stood and picked up his flannel shirt from the rock. Instead of putting it on, he draped it around my shoulders. My shivering reduced. "Stay warm."

My body warmed more from his closeness. He returned to his wood and knife.

Stone watched me, her form trembling. I recognized her longing for someone to wrap her with care. Stone had no one.

She turned away.

Give her the shirt.

So, Elohim could speak without me wearing the necklace. It didn't mean I had to do what He said. But if He was powerful enough to speak in my thoughts, maybe I should be afraid of what He could do if I didn't obey.

I didn't want to. I couldn't give away Sam's generosity.

The longer I tried to ignore the voice's instructions, the more my stomach rolled. I should share the shirt with Stone. It made little sense. She could be my enemy, but I couldn't live with this increasing pressure growing in my chest.

I tried to stand, but fell back down.

Sam came to my side. "What can I get you?"

I leaned closer, voice low. "Give her your shirt."

He looked at me in surprise and nodded.

Sam took his shirt off my shoulders and walked over to Stone. She eyed him in suspicion, but didn't move. Maybe she figured we were no threat when she had what we needed. Sam set the shirt around her shoulders. Her eyes widened. When I laid back down, I moved closer to Henry, my back against his. He wasn't as warm as the shirt had been, but I was desperate. Sam watched me. I couldn't read his reaction. Maybe he was angry that I'd given away his shirt; maybe he was jealous that I was close to Henry.

"Sorry." I wasn't sorry for the way my turmoil had lifted and in its place a lightness like I'd never known before.

"Don't be." Sam's dark brown irises reminded me of shiny, black agates I'd found along a riverbed years ago.

It was quiet. Stone's head dropped on her chin, and she breathed heavier.

"What are you making?" I asked Sam.

He smiled. "It's a secret."

I smiled back. "You're mysterious."

"How so?"

"When you answer questions, your answer is purposeful, like they're the exact words you intended to say. Few can do that."

His grin stayed on his lips as wood chips fell away from his knife. "Do you answer all questions, Pero?"

"What do you want to know?"

"Why did Elohim bring you here?"

I sighed. "Why does it feel you've asked me something that you already have the answer to?"

He chuckled. "I want to hear it from you."

Sam invited me to go deeper, and I avoided with another question. I moved my head toward the bright stars in the sky that clustered in the thousands like the freckles of a giant.

"Mom would tell me I came here as a fulfillment to a prophecy. Dad would tell me I came for Mom. Elohim would tell me I came to tear down a wall. Shea would tell me... never mind what Shea would tell me."

"Why do *you* think you're here?" he asked.

I waited for the stars to answer, for Elohim to bring another vision.

"I don't know." I looked back to Sam. "Have any ideas?"

"In time, I think I will."

A lump sat in my throat, and I forced a swallow. How could I feel so close to a man who I'd just met and who had said hardly anything? But what he'd said settled. A spark had started, and I wanted it to grow. "Are your parents Lesaries, too?"

He didn't look up from his project. "They're gone."

"I'm sorry for your pain."

Sam's face softened, like he hadn't expected me to sense his grief without him needing to explain. "Thank you."

I studied the scar traveling down the side of his face. "What happened to you?"

Sam touched his cheek. "When I was eight, I fell and cut my face right before my mother left me."

I sucked in a breath and held it.

"My turn to ask you," he said.

I swallowed. Could I answer as honestly as Sam had?

"What happened to your face?" He reached his hand out as if he wanted to touch my scraped cheek but brought it down instead.

"My mom hit me." I grimaced. "Not because she wanted to. I turned my cheek like Elohim told me to, and she stopped. Because she loves me."

"She'll never stop loving you, Pero. No matter where she is."

I smiled. "Yeah." I felt for my necklace, but it wasn't there. Could Elohim bring strength without it? "My mom was gone for most of my life. You may not believe this, but she disappeared right in front of me."

Sam's eyes widened.

"You don't believe me, do you?"

"I do."

"Who watched you growing up?" I asked.

"The Lesaries took me in. A woman named Alexis raised me as her own and loved me."

He'd been loved. That was all anyone could hope for. "I'm glad."

I drifted. I'd pause this moment and let it play in my mind for days to come.

"Sam?" I closed my eyes. The blessing I wanted to give him paused on my lips. "Koach to you."

I heard his smile. "And to you."

When I opened my eyes again, the sky was light, and the air smelled like chicken. Henry slept in the same position he had only a few hours before. Sam held a long stick over the fire with a small animal sizzling. Stone was gone.

I combed back my hair and wiped my teeth with my finger before sitting up.

"Good morning," Sam said.

I yawned.

Sam smiled. "Not a morning person, I take it."

I wanted to hide my face behind a fern. "Not when I only had a couple hours of sleep." I yawned again. "Where's Stone?"

Sam shrugged. "She said she'd be back."

"The necklace!"

Sam reached into his pants pocket and pulled it out. "She dropped it."

How could she be so careless? Unless she'd done it on purpose.

"Her backpack is gone," I said.

"Maybe she's giving us a way out," Sam said.

That didn't seem like Stone. Maybe she wanted to return the favor after I'd given her the shirt.

"Should we leave before she comes back?" I asked.

Sam nodded. "We'll leave. I wanted to make sure you had some sleep before we walk to the Lesaries' camp. How's your ankle?"

"It hurts still."

"Let's wake Henry up, have him look at it and re-wrap. We need to have someone check out your cheek, too. The Lesaries will have what we need to heal any infections."

Sam pulled the stick away from the fire and set the meat on

a leaf. "Ooh, hot." He placed it on a rock near me to cool down. "It's rabbit."

Rabbit. Camel. I'd yet to see chicken in this world. I'd never be able to look at a bunny in the pet store again without feeling guilty.

"You didn't sleep," I said.

"I'll make it." Sam blew on the piece of rabbit he held in his hand and took a bite. Maybe he was one of those people who functioned well on five hours of sleep each night but who died ten years too soon.

The rabbit was mild and sweet. I nibbled. Not bad. I put the rest in my mouth and washed it with rainwater that had been collected in a bucket Stone left behind. If she wasn't coming back, where would she go before Carper found her?

Sam nudged Henry. He didn't budge. What if Stone drugged him? But she wasn't near him, unless Sam had fallen asleep. My heart increased with panic.

Being careful to not move my foot, I hovered my fingers under Henry's nostrils. Still breathing. I looked up at Sam. "Wow. Does he always sleep this hard?"

"What are you doing?" Henry eyed me, then my fingers under his nose.

I moved away. "Waking you from the dead."

His eyes moved down to my lips. "Isn't that usually done with a kiss?"

"Eww."

"Why else would you be this close to me, Ro girl?"

"I was cold last night."

Henry grinned and sat up. "You cuddled with *me*?"

I rolled my eyes. "Don't read into it too much."

Henry stood and stretched. "Ooh, rabbit." He tore off a piece and set it back down. "Hot."

"We need to leave, Henry," Sam said.

Henry picked up the piece of rabbit again and plopped it in his mouth. "Where's Stone?"

"We don't know," I said. "We think she's taken off."

"The necklace?"

"Is in Sam's pocket."

Sam held it up.

"You should wear it, Sam," I said. "So you don't lose it."

Sam hesitated. "Henry should take it."

Henry put his hands up. "I don't want to be held responsible."

Sam fidgeted as he tucked it back into his pocket.

"How'd you scare carrot-top?" Henry asked.

Sam helped me to my feet. "Pero was nice to Stone, and so she left."

"Are you serious?"

As if I'd never been nice before. I leaned against Sam and scolded Henry with my pointer finger held out. "Whatever you're thinking, I don't want to hear it."

"I didn't say a word." He backed away. "Keep that thing away from my nose."

"Gladly."

"Let me look at your ankle." Henry knelt down and unwrapped his jacket, revealing a swollen and purple ankle.

"It's definitely sprained." He touched it gently. "I wish I had something for the swelling."

I blinked back tears.

"I'll re-wrap it," Henry said. "Could you lend me your green shirt, Sam? I think it might stay better and not add as much pressure."

"Can't. Stone took it with her."

"Odd that she would take that but leave the necklace." Henry wrapped my ankle.

Sam winked at me.

I took a deep breath as the pain in my ankle amped up.

Henry tightened the jacket. "Let me know if this slips off, and I'll re-adjust it."

I nodded.

Henry studied my face. "It's okay if you need to cry, Ro."

I wiped at my eyes. "I'm fine. Really." I turned to Sam. "Can you carry me for three hours? You didn't sleep."

"I'll try my best." Sam lifted me off my feet.

"I'll take over at ten," Henry said. "That's when I'm most alert."

"I know," I said.

Henry looked surprised, as if he wanted me to notice him. I hadn't cared for him as more than a bodyguard before and now not any more than a friend. But he said things that made me wonder if he wanted to be more than my friend. I liked Sam. No. I was drawn to Sam—but should I dismiss Henry from my mind so quickly?

After we had been walking for what felt like hours, Sam stumbled.

"Do you need to set me down?"

He lowered me to the ground as if he'd been waiting for me to ask. "I only need a moment." Sam tried to catch his breath.

Henry offered the bucket of rain water he carried.

"I'm sorry to put you through this," I said.

"It's not your fault, Pero," Sam said.

"Yeah, but—"

A whiz near my ear interrupted. Sam yelled out and stumbled backward. An arrow lodged in his shoulder. I reached for him and stopped when I landed on my ankle. Henry caught Sam and laid him on the ground.

I looked up at the sound of a snapping twig.

"You didn't even say goodbye." Carper was gripping Stone's arm.

Jimmy stood next to him, a bow and arrow in his hands.

15

תְּמִיכָה

I crumpled to the ground and put a hand on Sam's side. He held onto his arm and groaned.

"Traitors!" I shouted.

Jimmy's cheeks flamed red. His arms hung limp at his sides, and he dropped the bow and arrow.

"I swear I didn't tell them." Stone backed up. "I don't know how they figured it out."

"The necklace, you idiots," Carper said.

"I wasn't wearing it!"

Carper tapped a finger to his temple with his free hand. "My mind brought me to you. That only happens when you're wearing it."

I didn't understand. I hadn't worn it. Stone had it the whole time until this morning. Sam kept it in his pocket.

"Take them all," Carper said.

"Give us time." My eyes burned into his. "Sam's hurt. We can't go without helping him."

Carper folded his arms. "Hurry, before I change my mind."

"Pp—Pero." Sam sputtered.

I placed my hand on his cheek. "Don't talk."

Henry rushed over. "I need ointment, whiskey, and a towel."

Carper huffed. "Here." He reached into his coat pocket and pulled out a flask.

Stone threw Sam's green shirt to Jimmy. Sam lifted his head.

"Rest." I placed a hand on his chest.

"The—the necklace." Sweat poured down his face as he reached a shaking hand into his pocket and clutched the pendant.

"I didn't have it, Sam. I don't know how they found us."

Jimmy bent down and rested his hand on Sam's. I yanked it off. "You will not touch him again!"

Jimmy watched me. "Trust me."

I let my hand drop. How could I trust him? He was dead but now wasn't. He shot Sam!

My limbs shook, but I let Jimmy take the necklace. He whispered to Sam so low that I barely caught his words. "Not now, Salmon."

Why had he called him Salmon?

Sam's eyes bulged. "You."

Jimmy held a finger to his lips to shush.

Henry held the flask against Sam's mouth. "Drink."

Sam took some, but most dribbled out from between his lips.

I looked from Sam to Jimmy. "You know each other?"

Jimmy eyed Carper and shoved the necklace into his pocket. "I'll explain later."

Jimmy opened his bag and pulled out a jar. "From your mom."

"What is it?" I asked.

"A blessing," Henry said. "It's ointment."

Henry poured the liquid over the wound, and Sam screamed.

Carper plugged his ears. "Is that necessary?"

I glared at Carper. "You're a doctor. Why don't you help?"

He scowled back. "Doctor of science, Pero. There's a difference. And why would I help someone I hurt?"

Without warning, Henry yanked the arrow out of Sam's shoulder. Blood poured from the wound. Sam screamed louder, then passed out.

Henry pressed the green jacket against the wound and leaned his weight on it.

"Where's Stone?" Carper asked, brows furrowed as he glanced from one side to the other. "That sneaky little—" He strode out of the clearing.

"Hand me the ointment," Henry said.

I opened the jar and gave it to Henry again.

As Henry put the ointment on the wound, I stroked Sam's hand and gave the one thing I had. A song. "No need to cry no more. Won't let any tears in my way."

Henry paused, balm dripping from his fingers.

"Comin' home, comin' home, comin' home." The song's meaning had changed. No longer did I sing it for Mom. I wasn't even sure if I sang it for Sam. It was for me. No tears. No fear. I ran after hope.

Henry watched me. "Your voice is a gift from Elohim."

I squirmed. "Will Sam be okay?"

Henry lifted the shirt and swathed Sam with the ointment. Thick, dark blood puddled and glistened on Sam's shoulder. I covered my mouth as bile rose in my throat.

Henry sat back. "We should be careful carrying him, but I think he'll be okay." Henry held the ointment. "Sit down, Pero. I want this on your ankle."

I grinned. "You'd make a great doctor."

"Maybe I will." Henry dipped his fingers into the ointment where Sam's blood splattered on top and spread it on my ankle. I felt instant relief. What was that stuff made of?

"Let's put some ointment on your face. It's not infected, but this will help it heal faster and prevent scarring."

"I don't mind scarring."

Henry dabbed in the ointment and ran his finger down my cheek, pausing at my jaw line. "You're beautiful either way." His eyes sought mine.

I averted my face, and Henry pulled away. Jimmy whistled a tune at the trees.

How should I respond? He knew I liked Sam.

"Jimmy!" Carper called from a distance. "We're leaving. Now!"

"That's our cue," Jimmy said. "I'll take Salmon."

"Who's Salmon?" Henry asked.

Jimmy raised his brows and pointed to Sam.

"His name is Sam," I said.

"Good to know." Jimmy raised Sam to a standing position against him and draped him over his shoulder.

Henry scooped me up and held me in his arms. The place behind my ribs that'd trembled from Sam's touch remained dormant with Henry. Sure, Henry smelled nice and even a mosquito would notice how attractive he was, but his presence triggered something different. I felt relaxed, relieved, at home. Was that another form of attraction?

The sun cast splashes of light on the trees, then the clouds moved over the sun, the forest turning gray and cold. Jimmy was far behind as he struggled to carry Sam. Carper yelled at us to keep up. I laid my head against Henry's shoulder, which was narrower and harder than Sam's. His chest rose and fell with his labored breathing, joggling my cheek against his shoulder.

"Sleep if you need to," Henry said.

I hadn't slept long since I arrived in Moon City, and being held was not the most comfortable way to relax. I tilted my head toward the treetops.

"Is it possible to see Elohim?" I asked.

"We will someday," Henry said between deep breaths.

"How?"

"Keep watching, Pero. You'll see what He can do."

"But I have seen." I'd had visions, Shea had appeared on my roof, Sam and Henry flew on eagles. And yet I couldn't believe.

"You have it all wrong." Henry stopped and set me down, letting me lean against him for support.

"What do you mean?"

Henry lowered me to the ground and untied the jacket from my foot. "When the time is right, Elohim will answer. Now, let's adjust your foot. This pathetic cast is slipping."

"Carper will yell at us."

"He yells at us even when we're moving."

True. The man could never relax.

Just as Henry finished binding up my foot, Jimmy stumbled forward.

"You alright?" I asked.

Jimmy wheezed. "Can't... go...."

Henry rushed to his side and helped lift Sam off Jimmy's shoulders and onto the ground.

"But Carper," I said.

"He hasn't whined yet," Henry said. "I should look at Sam's wound. Jimmy, hand me the ointment after you catch your breath."

I smiled at Henry's doctorly orders.

Henry untied the shirt around Sam's shoulder and addressed the wound with the goop from the jar. I'd have to thank Mom when I saw her—if I saw her.

Sam's eyes fluttered, then sagged shut again.

Henry beamed. "It's worked so well already! He's going to make it, Ro."

"What's going on?" Carper's voice echoed off the trees. "There are no breaks."

"We can't walk any faster." I resisted spitting in his eye.

Carper dashed toward me. I put my hands in front of my

face as a shield. Carper knelt down and pressed his weight into my broken ankle. Crushing. Harder.

I screamed.

"Stop it!" Henry said.

Jimmy's movement toward me was fuzzy.

I was being torn from the foot up. Like I was caught on fire. Ripping quickly. My vision blackened and returned.

Carper let go.

I sobbed.

Carper moved his face toward mine.

I scooted back. "Stop! Stop!"

"You think you can treat me lower than what your vision implied. I'm your king. You'll serve me."

I lifted myself up to sitting. "You may try to control me. But you'll never be my king, and I will not save you."

Did you hear that, Elohim? I will not save him! I will not!

Carper smiled. "We'll see."

I would've thrown my fist to the sky, but I let my blood boil, never breaking eye contact with my enemy.

Every knee will bow to me.

I didn't ask for you! Why do you speak to me, Elohim? Why'd you choose me?

I love you, Pero.

It didn't feel like love. Even if He called me by name, it felt like He had turned His back on me.

"Get up," Carper said through gritted teeth.

I couldn't stand on my own. Not before he crushed me, and definitely not after. "I can't."

"Get up."

I gripped the dirt, put my good foot beneath me, and pushed.

Henry and Jimmy stepped toward me.

Carper snapped his finger to stop them.

I straightened. My foot felt like a million nails were being hammered on my skin. "Happy?"

"For now." Carper turned. "Let's go."

A wind picked up, and a slight trembling on the ground made my good leg unsteady. I collapsed as a low noise filled the air.

Henry knelt next to me and held onto a log with one arm draped around me. Carper looked up at the sky.

"What's happening?" Jimmy asked.

"Seems to be a storm," Henry said.

Jimmy dragged Sam away from a tree. "Let's move to a more open area."

"We're in a forest," Henry said. "There's no open area."

Carper studied the sky. "This isn't a storm."

The treetops swung faster. And in the distance, the low noise grew louder.

"What's that sound?" I asked.

A smile grew on Henry's lips. "Flapping."

A large object flew over the trees. It was an eagle four times larger than the one I'd seen in the field. Two people held onto the eagle, riding on its back. It let out a high-pitched whistle, like a battle cry. Two more joined the first, and dozens more flew past us.

"The Lesaries," Jimmy said.

Carper pointed to Jimmy, his eyes never leaving the sky. "Kill them."

16

לְגָלוֹת

Jimmy sent an arrow soaring through the tree-tops.

"Don't!" I called.

The arrow hit the back of an eagle, bounced off, and landed in the brush below.

"How?" Jimmy's mouth and eyes widened.

Carper kicked a tree. "We need to leave. Now!"

No one moved. Between one passed out, another with a now broken ankle, and an exhausted Jimmy, how could we?

"Jimmy!" Spittle flew from Carper's mouth. "Grab Pero. Leave the rest."

Jimmy watched the birds fly over our heads. The pattern of their shadows against the trees was like a train moving. *Swish. Swish.*

Carper picked me up and flung me over his shoulder. A sharp pain stabbed through my foot.

Carper charged forward in a fury.

"Let me go!" I screamed.

Jimmy and Henry ran to me.

"I'll take her, sir," Jimmy said.

"Don't make me shoot you again." Carper waved his gun in Jimmy's direction.

"You're hurting her." Henry stepped forward.

Carper turned to him. "Do you think I care?"

"You do if you want to keep her. For your power."

"Her power has been useless so far."

Carper was right. I ran and sang and saw pictures in my head that told me things I didn't want to know. I'd walk around the wall in circles, going nowhere. Walls would fall. Carper would be my king. And Mom and I would be... I wish I knew.

I pounded my fists against Carper's back. Pain settled in my gut over the fold of his shoulder. I held back bile.

Latching onto the pendant tied around his neck, I pulled.

Carper threw me. The clasped necklace snapped and remained clutched in my palm. I thumped to the ground and cried out.

Carper's breathing calmed into a steady rhythm. "Pero, your mom's survival depends on your cooperation."

I propped myself on my elbows. "What did you do to her?"

"The faster we're back, the better chance she'll have of living."

Had someone placed fire inside my ankle? "You're lying." My head spun. The surrounding forest closed and opened again.

Carper held out his hand. "Give me the necklace."

What could I do with Carper's necklace? But I had to return. I couldn't leave Mom again. I shouldn't have listened to her when she told me to leave. She needed me.

Carper didn't move. He didn't speak. Had something happened? I tried to sit up but fell back down, my body weaker.

Why is everything so quiet?

Then, the impossible happened. My sight cleared. My head stopped pounding. The pain in my leg disappeared. My ankle snapped back into place.

Was this real?

It was a vision. I stood distanced, like watching a dream. I was not the focus of attention. The vision was not my own. I looked at Carper's necklace in my hand. It couldn't be Carper's vision because he wasn't one of the three chosen. Maybe it was Mom's.

Trees shrunk. The sky grew overcast. Ground dampened. Carper, Jimmy, and Henry vanished right before my eyes. The eagles froze in place.

Sam was the only one in the vision, sprawled out on the ground. His blood-soaked shirt wrapped around his arm.

Sam's body sunk. Deeper and deeper. Down, down, down. Dirt filled him. He was being buried alive.

I wanted to scream out Sam's name but had no voice, wanted to reach out to grab his hand and pull him, but my legs couldn't move.

Then the earth swallowed him. No trace of his body remained. Just dirt.

Wet, murderous dirt.

And I was alone.

By faith. Be strong.

I didn't want to have faith. I wanted a normal life with Mom and Dad inside my home, where it was safe.

The sun rose higher and grew bigger and brighter. I shielded my eyes and turned away. The sun set, sinking lower until there was only a slit of yellow across the horizon. The ground shook. As far as I could see, small sections of soil split. Dirt splattered and broke. Shoots poked their green heads up. Then they grew into trees, and the trees produced fruit. Under the trees grew bushes, and on the bushes grew berries.

From the soil grew a large mound. From the mound, a head popped up, then a torso, arms, legs. Dirt shot in all directions. A figure emerged, and a voice gasped. Dirt fell from his form as he stood. The figure turned toward me, the face scarless.

Sam.

He studied at his hands as if he were the first man created and didn't know what they were. He looked new.

The trees and plants morphed back into the forest. Carper, Henry, and Jimmy re-appeared.

The vision had happened. The evidence laid on the ground. Sam stood, dusted off dirt from his clothes, and walked toward us. Moving his arm in circles, he laughed.

My leg was straight. I stood and leaned on it. Healed.

"What was the vision, Pero?" Carper asked.

"Not every vision involves you," I said.

"Never has a vision caused a physical change." Jimmy examined my ankle. "And Sam. How…?"

Sam gave a shrill whistle using his fingers.

A loud noise swished the trees above. An eagle landed in front of Sam. It lowered its head to let Sam on. He climbed and offered me his hand.

"Come, Pero."

I shook my head. Not without Jimmy and Henry.

"Go, Pero!" Henry and Jimmy shouted.

Then again, maybe it was better to escape Carper while I had a chance. I ran up to the eagle, hopped on, and held onto Sam's waist.

Carper lunged toward me. "The necklace."

The eagle lifted off the ground, its wing hitting Carper. He backed up.

I tied his necklace around my neck. Maybe I could make it to Mom without him knowing. Then we'd be free.

"Pero!" Carper shouted.

Another eagle flew down. Henry jumped on its back. Carper lunged for Henry's leg. Henry kicked Carper in the chest. The man stumbled.

Carper pulled out his gun and aimed it at me.

I squeezed my eyes shut. The gunshot reverberated through

the air. My eyes flew open in time to see Jimmy thud to the ground. Had he taken the bullet for me? "Jimmy's hurt!"

The eagle flew us above the trees.

I searched for Jimmy through the branches. He sprawled out on the dirt. Unconscious. Alone. A tinge of guilt hit my core. Jimmy saved my life.

"Carper ran off." The wind muffled my voice. "We can't leave Jimmy."

"We'll send someone to help him," Sam shouted.

I wanted to fly, yet it felt wrong. I was leaving Jimmy and not returning to Mom.

Henry's eagle met us in the sky. Henry hollered in victory.

Sam motioned for Henry to come closer, directing our eagle toward him. "Jimmy's hurt," Sam yelled to Henry.

Henry glanced behind. "I'll meet you guys later." Turning his eagle around, he whistled to another man who followed.

A burden lifted from my chest. They would help Jimmy.

A woman on the back of an eagle waved at Sam. Her long grey hair floated behind, and cotton pants under her hiked-up robe billowed in the wind. She reminded me of a Greek goddess.

"My mom." Sam waved back.

"The one who took you in when your parents died?"

"Yes. Alexis." He straightened. "My dad died, but my birth mom didn't."

"You said she was gone."

"She is. But she didn't die."

Had she run away? The only other possibility was that she disappeared. But things like that didn't happen to everyone's mom.

"Do you know where she is?" I asked.

Sam didn't respond. Maybe it was too personal of a question to ask.

The eagle flew alongside a storm of other eagles, pointing

forward, its black feathers flickering in the wind. I ran my hand along the silk, letting it sink into the feathers, soft like a pillow.

"Her name is Faith," Sam said. "I've had her since I was a kid."

"She's beautiful."

Below our feet, thousands of people walked through the forest. I shifted a bit for a better look. "Weren't the Lesaries supposed to come in two days?" I raised my voice. "It's only been one."

"I don't know," Sam said.

The air was chilly, the smell crisp. Sam's shirt flapped against my hands. "Sam, are you one of the three chosen?"

"Wait till we land. I can hardly hear you."

He seemed to hear me fine before. "Your scar is gone."

"Is it?" He traced his cheek with his finger.

"You were handsome with the scar."

Sam's hands let go of the eagle.

"Don't let go!"

Sam held onto the eagle again.

"What's your power, Sam?"

In the vision, the earth had swallowed Sam, then spit him back out. Was that really his power or the earth's? Or Elohim's?

"Are you flirting to get me to talk?"

I laughed. "Depends. Is it working?"

"Maybe. But please don't do it again. Well, at least not until I figure things out."

"Like what?"

After an unbearable amount of time, Sam said, "Who you and I are."

Say what?

"Growth is my power," he said.

How could growth be a power?

"I make things grow."

Sam was a chosen. He had to be. But how? The chosen were a part of Mom's family line.

I felt Sam's ribs expand in a breath. "My mom didn't die. She disappeared right before my eyes. If your mom did the same and the prophecy is for the Abram line, and if we both are one of the chosen...."

"What are you saying?"

The eagle dipped down closer to the ground. Moon City came into view.

"If it's all true," Sam said, "then you must be my sister."

17

לָטוּס

Faith landed in the field near Moon City and folded her wings. I jumped off. I couldn't touch Sam. Not now. He couldn't possibly be my brother. I would sense if he were. There had to be another explanation.

A sea of Lesaries moved around us, walking toward the wall.

"We're marching," Alexis called. "You coming?"

"Soon." Sam jumped off Faith and rubbed her head. Faith tucked herself into her feathers and purred.

Alexis came closer. "When you join us, the one rule is that you can't talk. That's what Elohim asked."

Sam embraced her.

Alexis moved toward me and put a hand on my arm. "You must be Pero. Henry told me all about you."

I gave my best smile. "Alexis, right?"

She nodded, then stepped away. "Looks like you two need to talk. You're safe where you are. This is Elohim's battle."

I sat down, Sam next to me. Faith flew away, her wings blowing a gust of wind that pushed my hair back. She joined the other eagles that took off into the blue sky. People bustled around us like a shield. No Warriors from Moon City attacked like Marcus had trained them to. This didn't seem like an ordinary battle.

"I shouldn't have brought it up," Sam said. "I just didn't want you too close. Well, I did. I do."

I turned my head away. "I understand." Lesson learned. Don't flirt until you're certain of family relations. At least he hadn't kissed me. I groaned. "I'm so humiliated."

"Don't be," Sam said. "We don't even know if it's true. Am I right that there's something special between us?"

I stayed locked on his face until the intensity threatened to draw me closer to him.

Sam cleared his throat and looked away. "I want to find out more about the three chosen before we go forward."

"How will you find out?" I asked. "It seems like you and Jimmy know each other, but he can't help if he may be...." I shuddered. "... dead. And my mom's stuck with Carper."

"Well," Sam said, "We should pray."

"I don't remember any prayers. Dad didn't make me memorize them."

"Has Elohim spoken to you?"

"Yes."

"Have you responded?"

"Not with anything He wanted to hear, I'm sure."

"That's prayer."

The last thing I'd said to Elohim was that I wasn't making Carper the king. "Even if I tell Him I'm not following what He says?"

"There's grace even for the angry prayers." Sam stuck his hand out for me to shake. "Meanwhile, can we be friends?"

I couldn't handle being Sam's friend. I couldn't look at him without wishing he was more than a brother. I turned away. "Not yet."

"Makes sense." Sadness rested in his voice.

A knot formed behind my ribs. I was sad too.

Sam stood and pulled me up. "Let's march."

My heart beat faster with each step toward the wall. I wanted to run and find Mom. Could I reach Moon City with no one noticing? I never should have left her.

"I'm going in for my mom," I said to Sam.

"Not now, Pero. That's not what we're here for. We'll talk to Shea later and make a plan to find her."

I rubbed the back of my neck. That may not happen until tomorrow. I couldn't wait that long.

Sam nudged me.

I cursed the fluttering in my stomach at his slight touch.

"It will work out," he said.

What if he was wrong?

Sam eyed me with suspicion. "Just wait, please."

"I will." I spied an open window in the wall with no bars. If only I could fly.

A Lesarie woman handed us white strips of cloth and flasks made of camel skin. I used the cloth to wipe sweat from my face.

Sam smiled.

"What?"

"It's a headdress to protect you from the sun."

Sam blended in with most of the Lesaries in his turban and cotton long-sleeved tunic and pants. Some passerby wore pants I would've seen at an outdoor store at home. One wore a shirt with a picture of an American flag and the words "Land of the Free" across their chest. I chuckled. Did he even know what it meant?

Lesarie women draped the headdresses loosely around their heads, backs, and shoulders. I set mine on my head and let it hang. How would it stay on? I felt more out of place than I had in my black, fluffy dress.

Guards stood on top of the wall every couple of feet. They

spit on heads. Some made crude comments and calls at the women, fighting over which ones they wanted. Others made bets on who'd make it when they did attack and who'd die quickly. Like they could really remember who was who with thousands moving below.

Why didn't they attack? I would've at least expected something raining on our heads besides their saliva.

We approached the wall. The only sounds were our feet shuffling against the dirt, a wheezing man, and the click-clack of a woman's walking stick. Shea led in the front.

As my feet pounded against the dirt, my mind became more focused. A presence lingered in the air. It was the same feeling I had in visions. Like tidal waves shifted us forward. Pain was in our steps for the city. Compassion for the people was in our sweat.

I wasn't afraid.

Maybe I didn't care what Carper would do to me. He'd pressed his weight onto my broken ankle, yet Elohim healed me. No matter what happened inside his city, Carper couldn't really hurt me. Not permanently.

The field blurred, like the background of a photo. A vision pulled me out of the reality of my feet against the ground and into the other now familiar realm.

The wall still stood before us, but the Lesaries had disappeared. Figures as bright as stars grew out of the ground and marched. They dressed in white robes and muttered words, growing in volume. It was not the crowd noise that you'd hear in a busy place with people saying "Where do you want to eat?" or "Stop stepping on my toes!" The noise was pleasant in tone, like everyone wanted to speak with as much enthusiasm and plea as they could.

The crowd chanted. "Koach to you. Elohim for you."

In this frozen time, what would Elohim do for me? In a vision, no one would watch me. Would He let me reach Mom in

Moon City while no one else was around to see? Could I make my own decisions in a vision? I willed my body to move, but it didn't.

Let me move, Elohim. I need to move.

I fixed my eyes on a window of Carper's mansion that rose above the wall. I imagined it was where Mom stood and watched me. Perhaps she saw the vision and asked for Elohim's power to bring me to her.

A figure of light laid a sheer and shimmering hand on my shoulder. He closed his eyes and muttered words I couldn't understand. I felt a warmth of peace pour through me. He opened his eyes.

"Elohim wants you to fly."

It seemed I could put my hand right through him if I tried, yet he was as real as the vision. If I talked, would he hear or would he flicker away?

"I can't move," I said.

"Have you tried?"

"Yes. I...." I lifted my foot. I lifted the other. Had I changed the vision because of my prayer?

"Trust." The figure walked away.

I had to move before it was over and all the Lesaries and guards saw me. More than likely, Sam and Mom could see what shifted. As soon as I'd asked, the vision became mine.

I ran toward the wall, my white headdress floating away. My feet lifted off the ground for seconds. My eyes widened. I took off again. I lifted into the air faster the second time.

I was flying.

I kept my focus on the mansion window and flew upward. Below me, the bright figures faded. Their whispering voices grew dimmer until they were gone. I was close enough to touch the wall. The guards on the roof flickered. I almost flew into one, then swerved to the right and landed on the roof. Running to the nearest chute, I hid. It was clear, but better than nothing.

Like a magic wand had touched them, the guards became fully awake.

Oh, crudmuffins.

I peered down. The Lesaries marched. Sam watched me.

Don't give me away!

Sam marched again.

I licked my lips. Beads of sweat rolled. The sun felt hotter on the roof. Whose idea was it to make a wall out of steel?

At the edge of the roof, the guards watched the Lesaries. I crouched lower. They were close enough for me to hear them talking, too close for comfort. From the roof, I saw the mansion's window. I could jump from this roof to the next. It was risky. But what other choice did I have?

Still crouched, I shuffled on my feet and glanced behind me.

The guard who I'd nearly run into watched the sky.

"Did you guys notice something flying around here a second ago?"

I froze. He'd seen me.

"Yeah. They're called eagles," another guard with a thick beard said.

"No. It was a person who almost hit me." He rubbed his eyes. "Never mind. I've been out here too long."

"Doesn't seem like they're going away soon."

"Why aren't we attacking them?" a woman asked.

"Because we know they'll win," the first guard said.

"Carper's spent years training the Warriors for this."

The bearded guard folded his arms. "He's trained them as bait. If the Lesaries see Carper has built Warriors who can't die when eating lì, there's a higher chance they'll want him as their king."

The first guard sneered. "Yeah, if he actually talks to them about it."

The woman laughed. "What's he going to do? Walk to the

leader and demand that he be king of the people? They'll kill him on the spot."

"The only way he can talk to the leader," the bearded guard said, "is if a Lesarie protects him."

Me.

Shea had asked me to be Carper's protector. If I told Carper I'd protect him (which I wouldn't) and he believed me (which I doubted), then Shea would accept him. In Shea's mind, making Carper the king was Elohim's plan. And I only had six days to do it. But I wasn't going to. I had to reach Mom.

"Why not send the Warriors to attack?" the woman said. "They can't die if they keep eating lì."

She had a point. Why would Carper build an army who couldn't die and not use them during battle?

The guard stroked his beard. "Because it's Elohim we're fighting against. With Him, even eternal beings become mortals."

They were afraid. They sensed Elohim's power. I'd heard He'd split an ocean in half for the Lesaries to walk through and that the sun had once stayed light for a battle as long as one man's arms lifted toward heaven. Did Elohim win in every story?

The woman sighed. "What if Carper doesn't get the Lesaries to join him? Shouldn't we be hiding before we all die?"

Many lives were at stake. Not just Carper's. Shea's assignment didn't feel like such a terrible task. By ensuring that Carper talked with Shea safely, I could save Moon City. But these people who tortured and killed each other daily didn't deserve to live. Even if I saved them, I'd never forgive.

"That's why I have a plan," the bearded guard said. "When Carper comes back, we kill him."

I withheld a gasp. Someone else killing him could solve my problems. Mom and I would have a better chance of making it back home.

"What does that do?" the other guard asked.

The bearded guard folded his arms. "It gives us a chance to run. Carper thinks the Lesaries can save him, but if they accept him as king, then what's the chance he'd want to rescue us when the Lesaries attack? He'll be with them and safe while they slaughter the rest of us."

He was right. They didn't have a chance living as long as Carper was alive.

"There he is." The first guard pointed. "He's hiding at the edge of the forest. See?"

"I see him," the woman said. "So, when Carper gets closer, we shoot him with an arrow, lead the Warriors to fight whoever stands in our way, and then we run."

"Too risky," the other guard said. "I say we kill Carper after he's in Moon City and wait for the Lesaries to take a break. They have to get tired, eventually. Then we escape."

"Fine," the bearded man said. "Either way, Carper is a threat to our survival. If marching around the wall is the only thing the Lesaries plan to do, we have a chance."

I let out a small breath. I could have enough time to find Mom.

I crawled along the glass roof. Below me was a Warrior's greenhouse. They'd only have to turn around, and I'd be caught.

I scurried over a border and balanced on a small ledge. Below were cement and clusters of houses. Ducking my head and keeping my fingers curled along the top of the wall, I dragged my feet sideways a little at a time. If the guards turned around, they'd see the top of my head bobbing and my fingers scooting.

If only the vision hadn't worn off. Then I could fly my way over.

My hands slipped, and my legs trembled. If my mind told my body to fear, I'd never make it.

The mansion's roof was about the same distance as Shea was in height. It didn't seem possible to reach it unless Elohim gave me wings. But it was the closest access I'd seen yet. Ahead, the wall curved around a bend, out of sight and further away from the mansion. Yep. The best place to jump was where I stood. I'd have to turn my body around and bend my knees before jumping. I was sure that's what Henry would tell me. Another ledge of the mansion's roof was in front of me. I could try to land on that if I didn't make it. A balcony was twenty feet below. The key was to land without instantly dying.

"Elohim, is this the way?"

A Lesarie would not doubt. And I was a Lesarie, at least I was born as one. Did I have to know the law in order to identify as a follower of Elohim? But I wasn't a candidate. Not if fear kept me from trusting that Elohim would carry me from here to there. A decision weighed like an anchor in my heart.

Should I jump?

My body swayed in lightheadedness. It was now or never. I bent my knees and leaned forward, preparing to jump.

18

לְהִפָּרֵד

Stop!

My arms flailed. I pressed my back against the wall. Big breath. In. Out.

"Do you always need to be so last minute?" I asked Elohim.

Keep going.

"Fine with me. Jumping mid-air wasn't a good idea, anyway."

Trust me.

"Everyone keeps telling me the same thing. Do I have a trust issue or something?"

Inch by inch, I reached the corner that faced away from the mansion and stopped.

Around the curve, a walkway bridge connected the wall and the mansion. I shuddered that access was just around the corner and I'd been too close to a stupid jump.

I reached the bridge. Hugging the railing, I flopped on solid cement, then kissed the ground.

Crouching, I tip-toed toward the mansion. During Carper's tour, I didn't see Mom's room. I'd have to open every door until I found her. I hadn't thought this through.

Find Carper.

"No." I needed to find Mom first.

Pero. Have faith in me.

But faith meant that I had to let go of my plans. It meant I had to obey what Elohim told me and believe that everything else would work out, even if Mom didn't make it.

Let me mend your heart.

What was wrong with my heart? It had only been crushed, stomped on, lied to. It had only suffered in fear, been alone, confused.

"I don't know how."

But He'd said *Let me*, as if it was as simple as letting go.

So, I sank to my knees. "I surrender."

Something shifted inside, like Elohim's hands had snapped my soul in half to reveal what was really there. A broken heart. A fearful heart. An unbelieving heart. It was like a crushed stone, revealing the sharp and ugly pieces. In my mind, I picked up the pieces and offered them to Him. And in my mind, He took my pieces and put them back together.

"I see you now, Elohim. Give me faith."

I have.

I rested my hands on my chest. The heavy feeling inside lifted. If someone had felt my soul, it would've been soft and light. Elohim had given me a new heart. A whole heart.

I rose.

I needed to find Carper. It was clear now. That's why I'd come.

"Where do you think you're going?" a voice asked from behind.

"Henry!" I crept over to him. "What are you doing here?"

He nudged toward the door that led inside the wall. "Follow me."

"Can't. I have to go that way." I pointed toward the mansion.

"But she's over here." Henry grabbed my hand and dragged

me. He opened a door to the wall. We walked inside a dim and empty hallway. "Your mom lowered a rope for me to climb. She told me she saw you flying here in a vision and that I should find you. Did you really fly?"

"Crazy, right?"

Henry paused in the empty hallway but didn't let go of my hand. I'd held his hand before, but this time it felt different, like I was acknowledging Henry's feelings for me and was unsure how to respond. Yet I didn't let go.

"I… I'm not trying to find my mom now."

Elohim had known she'd be okay and that Henry would help her. I'd worried for nothing, and if I'd looked for Mom in the mansion, I would've gone the wrong way. "I need to find Carper."

Henry tilted his head like he was in deep thought. "We just escaped him."

"I can't explain it all, Henry. I don't understand it myself. You need to believe me."

He stepped closer. His voice and gaze deepened and weakened my muscles. "I believe you."

My face flushed. I tried to escape his stare, but he had me in his hold. I was curious, confused, drowned.

Henry's eyes shifted, lingered on my hair, again to my eyes, and lowered to my lips. A wave of fear passed through me.

In one swift movement, Henry put a hand behind my back, his lips moments from mine. I could feel his breath on my face as he slowly leaned in. My fast pulse told me I wanted to invite him. He hovered when his lips were an inch away. A warm and probing feeling stirred through me and hung in the small space between us. My heart beat in my chest, my neck, my ears. I wanted him to kiss me.

And he did.

I felt everything that I cherished about Henry in his kiss.

Care, gentleness, fun. He could love me, and I'd be happy with a million more kisses like this. But what about Sam?

I put my hands against Henry's chest and pushed him away like he was a leech to pull off my skin.

"I can't." Breathless, I waited until the buzzing in my head cleared. Why had I not expected him to kiss me? Yet I'd welcomed it.

Henry blinked rapidly and backed away. "I'm sorry, Pero. I know you're interested in Sam."

I pressed my hands against my cheeks, wishing for them to cool down. "It's not that." Well, maybe it was.

Henry's bright blue eyes glistened with hope.

"I need to sort things out," I said. "I need time."

Henry averted his eyes and nodded. "Did you want to see your mom before leaving to find the crazy man?"

There were many questions I needed to ask Mom. "I want to see her, but I'm afraid if I do, I'll never leave her again."

"Okay." Henry combed his fingers through his hair. "Are you sure about this?"

"Yeah." I cleared the fear from my voice. "Take care of my mom, please."

"You know I will." Henry slung a bag from his shoulder that I recognized as Jimmy's and handed it to me. "The ointment is in there and some water."

"Is Jimmy okay?"

Henry winced. "He's in critical condition. A few Lesaries took him back to the camp."

"I shouldn't have asked."

"Pero, I'm sorry." Henry reached a hand out toward my face, then brought it back to his side. "I'll do all I can to save him."

I held back tears. Now was not the time to crumble.

"Hey." Henry held his arms out. "I'm going to give you a hug. No negotiating."

I let him bring me close. My head laid on his chest comfortably. This was a perfect place to hide.

He let go. "I'm proud of you, Ro girl." He gave me a boyish smile.

Henry walked to the first door in the hall. After knocking a pattern, the door opened. He stepped in and closed the door behind.

I stayed in place, waiting for Elohim to change His mind. But He didn't. I had a mission to find my enemy and save his life before I lost my own.

The door Henry had gone through opened, and Mom peeked out. She searched around the hall until she saw me. A smile brightened her face as she hurried over.

"Henry said you're wanting to find Carper." She touched my hair and put a strand behind my ear. "By yourself."

"Don't hold me back, Mom. Elohim asked me to do this. So did Shea."

Mom kissed my head. "Are you sure?" Her eyes drank me in like she still couldn't believe that she was looking at her daughter and that she'd let me go again. "If he's angry, I want you to leave."

Carper could hurt me if he didn't agree to talk with Shea. I assumed Elohim would protect me if He wanted me to go, but maybe that wasn't in the plan. Why was I doing this?

I glanced around to make sure no one was around. "Did you see the visions?"

Mom let a breath in. "Yes."

"You know who the third chosen is."

Mom rubbed her head. "Do you know?"

My ears burned. "Yeah." I shuffled my feet and stared at the floor. "I mean, I thought I knew him, but now I'm realizing I didn't."

Mom put a hand to her mouth. "Oh, Pero. Were you interested in Salmon?"

"Who's Salmon?" Jimmy had called him the same.

"The young man in the visions. The chosen Abram line. My...." Mom motioned for me to follow. "We should go inside and talk."

"Your son?"

She froze. "Come on." She knocked on the door in the same pattern Henry had. The door opened, and she pulled me in.

Henry's eyes lit up. "Changed your mind?"

I folded my arms. We couldn't talk about this in front of Henry. It was embarrassing enough that Mom knew I'd fallen for my brother.

"We need some time," Mom said to Henry.

"Of course." Henry looked around for a place to go. He glanced at the ceiling. "Can't go up there right now. Bathroom it is."

I held back a laugh.

As soon as the door had clicked behind him, Mom moved close enough to whisper. "I thought you liked...." She pointed to the bathroom and mouthed his name.

I rubbed my head. "Maybe I do."

"You're falling for two guys?"

"Mom, can we talk about the bigger drama? How about the fact I have a brother?"

"I can explain, but I've hardly had time with you, Pero."

"Does Dad know?"

Mom sighed. "Yes."

I paced. "Great. Just great." I didn't want to be mad at Mom. Each moment with her was one I wanted to treasure. I just hated secrets.

"I didn't know you'd find Salmon. I haven't seen him since he was...." Mom stumbled to the nearest stool. "Every day, I've wondered if I could've kept you both near me." She shook her head. "Even if we hid again, I would've felt unworthy of being a mom and wife. I'm Carper's slave."

Mom's eyes told me the depth of what she must've gone through: the agony, the frustrations, the torture.

"He goes by Sam," I said.

Mom's eyebrows perked. "We named him after his father."

I thought I'd know Mom whenever I'd meet her. That the special things Dad had told me about her would make me bond faster because I would've known that her favorite food was tamales and that she'd accidentally ripped her dress on her wedding day. I hadn't considered another world that she'd come from and that her past would alter my future.

"Sam's dad was a Lesarie before he died," Mom said. "When Carper found out that I was one of the chosen, I became a fugitive until he caught me."

"Why'd you have me? Wouldn't you know Carper would find you again and that you'd have two kids growing up without their mom?"

I choked on the last part. I didn't want to cry. It'd bring back too many emotions that I'd left behind.

"Because I fell in love with your dad."

I didn't want to fall in love. Ever. Not if it pulled people further apart.

The bathroom door creaked, and Henry poked his head out. "Sorry, but we need to join the Lesaries before they head back for the camp."

I didn't turn to Henry. His concerned and I'm-in-love-with-Pero face would've made me want to slap him.

"I'm leaving for Carper." I raised my chin toward Mom. "Then I'll set you free."

"Only Elohim can save us," Mom said.

"He will." I motioned to outside. "In six days, the walls are coming down."

Mom wrapped her arms around me. She gripped her fingers on my back. "Since the first time I held you, I've loved you, Pero Ruth Moshe."

My heart warmed. Where was her love when I'd lost my first tooth, won my first race, bought my first bra? When those closest to us leave, does love remain?

I let go and sighed. I didn't look back until I'd reached the door. Henry's face wasn't the puppy-eyed daze I'd expected. It was the way he'd watched me after he heard me sing. It was in wonder.

"Koach to you," he said.

"And you."

I peeked through the door. All was clear. I ran over the bridge and into the mansion.

I'm running after you, Elohim. I'm unsure if I can love, but I have faith. It's small. I hope it's enough.

Even with a little faith, I can move walls.

Chills coursed through me. "Then teach me how to love."

Even though it hurt, my purpose in Moon City felt clearer than ever. Underneath the monster was a man. Carper may not have deserved to be king of anybody, but he was chosen.

19

לְאָרוֹד

The mansion's hallway was a stark difference from the one I'd just left. Chandeliers lit the white walls every few feet. Shiny marbled floors shimmered from the lights' glow.

Carper, Carper, Carper. Where is he?

My feet echoed with every step. I'd avoid any guards if possible. If they found me, they might kick me out before I had a chance. I'd wait for Carper in the sitting room, if I could remember which direction it was in. Downstairs and to the right?

When a door moved open, I flung myself against the wall. A woman walked out in a dress that looked like it came from the 1920s in my world. Her heels echoed on the floor as she paraded down the hall.

I waited until I could no longer hear her heels before moving. My heart raced at the possibility of another door opening. It was like a suspenseful game where the enemy was hiding and I had to only step on a certain tile for the door to burst open and a creepy creature to pop out with a roar. The silence was scarier than a horror film's soundtrack.

Something in a room crashed at the same time footsteps and voices increased in volume from the distance. I hurried to the door I'd already passed. Locked. The voices came closer, and I strained to hear. None of them sounded like Carper.

Take a chance. Don't take a chance.

Running toward where the crash had come from, I opened the door and closed myself into a dark room.

I rummaged through the bag Henry had handed me earlier and searched for a light. My fingers bumped against something that lit up. I pulled it out. A cell phone. Here? I took a better look at the screen. It was Henry's phone with a selfie of him smiling while I stuck out my tongue.

As I shone the phone around, the light revealed gold coins piled in mounds. My jaw dropped. No wonder Carper was so rich. Why was the room unlocked?

It was tempting to grab a handful before heading out. No one would notice. Except for Elohim. Ugh. It was so much easier when I didn't know someone always watched me. As I turned to head out, the sound of shuffling feet stopped me.

The noise paused, then started again, racing to the other side of the room. Whoever it was had exceptional night vision. My biggest nightmare—the kind children remember when trying to fall asleep—lived in a room no bigger than my family's kitchen.

Something hard slammed into my stomach. I fell to the ground and cried out. The pain in my rib followed.

"Who are you?" I tried to pull in breaths. Although the form was strong, it was also small. No dragon.

A shrill laugh echoed off the walls and made my gut flip like a pancake. *Stone.*

My rising heart beat and her laughter made a horrific duet.

Stone clicked on a flashlight and held it under her chin. Her face glowed an orangish-red that matched her hair. "Hello, Feather."

I screamed. She disappeared, creeping up behind me. She held an arm around my torso and a knife at my throat. My rib shot in pain. I whimpered.

"You say a single word and you're done. Got it?"

I nodded before she changed her mind. My breath felt shallow. Spots of color danced in my vision. She let go, and I put one hand on my rib.

"It's not broken," Stone said.

It felt broken.

"I would've heard it crack when you landed. Probably bruised." Her knife went back into a sheath attached to her pants. She sat across from me and rested her arms on her legs. "What you doin' here?"

I wiped the tears from my face. "I heard someone in the hall, so I hid."

"It was locked."

I shook my head. "It wasn't."

"You calling me a liar?"

I didn't answer.

"I feel sorry for you," she said.

"That's a surprise."

"You and your petty group pacing our city. That's what caged animals do, you know, and all they ever kill is the nicely packaged meat that's thrown at them. Passivity has never conquered a city."

"Neither has standing at the edge of the wall doing nothing," I said. "Are you scared?"

Stone's foot kicked my rib so fast I didn't see it coming. I heard a snap and a cry. It was mine. My vision blackened, and I crumpled to the floor. I was still conscious, but barely.

"We're never scared," she said. "Now your broken rib will remind you."

I would never again underestimate a small girl with a mousy voice.

"Did you think just because you shared your boyfriend's shirt with me, I'd be nice to you? Moon City holding back is part of the game so that Dr. Carper can carry out his plan to get rid of everyone."

I moaned on the ground as I tried to focus on what she was saying. Carper had a plan, but it wasn't to destroy the Lesaries. He needed them in order to become their king. But what was the point of telling her that? She wouldn't believe me.

"Why—?" I tried to catch my breath, then coughed. "Why—you—here?"

Stone's mouth curved up. "The rest of you fools were being pulled around by Carper while I came here to get rich. Carper's so focused on you and the Lesaries marching around the wall like lunatics he won't notice me. But here you are, and I'm gonna have to figure out what to do with you."

How old was Stone? Eleven. Twelve. Maybe she was older than she looked. She was a girl fighting for her life. "You didn't —kill—me."

"Your stammering is annoying. It's only a fracture."

I focused on my breathing. In two days, I'd broken two bones. I could add injuries as another skill.

Stone regarded me with contempt. "I've heard your name means feather. How fitting that your name matches your necklace." Stone stood and gathered gold that had scattered on the floor when she'd toppled onto me. "But a feather is no threat."

Why hadn't my parents named me Bullet?

"You'll—carry—all?" I gestured to the gold and rested my head.

Stone smiled. I hated her smile. "My plan was to take it out a little at a time. Thanks to you, I have a better plan."

I pulled myself onto my elbows. Grimacing, I laid back down.

"You're the plan," she said.

I tried to chuckle but wheezed instead. "Can't help. I'm just a... feather."

She clapped her hands together. "Dr. Carper wants you, right?"

"Doubtful. He's scared."

"Fear isn't in Dr. Carper's blood. If he had you in his hands, he could use you against the Lesaries. If they don't leave, you die. It's as simple as that."

Somehow, she hadn't died when running away from Carper... twice. I closed my eyes. Maybe that would help me forget where I was and why I was hurting.

"Dr. Carper prizes intelligent people like himself," Stone said. "Ones with a plan. I'll tell him I'll turn you over to him and that you can show us where your friends are hiding, including that back-stabbing Jimmy, but only if he gives me my freedom. Once I'm free, I can take off with as much gold as I can carry and no one will stop me. Easy."

"Easy peasy." I smiled. She had no clue what she was talking about. Carper didn't need to find me when I was finding him.

"Your mom used to say the same thing."

I held my breath.

"When Carper brought Bahar to Moon City," Stone said, "she was different, like she had never seen suffering and had everything she wanted. Were you very rich where you're from?"

"Middle class, hard working. No children caged in walls." Only disappearing moms.

Stone picked at her nails. "Bahar isn't the angel of a mom you think she is."

"She told me."

"She killed Warriors. At the annual moon celebration, she threw two Warriors into the fire, including my sister. How's that for nice?"

I cringed. Had they forced Mom to be that cruel? "Carper made her do it."

Stone scoffed. "Carper made your mom do a lot more for him than that."

My neck heated. This was my mom who'd gone through hell. Stone had no right to talk so flippantly about her. "She was a victim."

Stone shrugged. "We are who we are."

Who had made Stone? How could I save her from their hands?

Her name is Cathena.

Did Elohim want me to call her by her name? I could think of many other names to call her at that moment.

"That's not true, Cathena."

Her face fell, her eyes a glistening stone color. She cleared her throat and walked to a corner of the room. "You know my name." If only she hadn't been born a slave. If only she had a chance. But she still could.

"Cathena."

She didn't look up. "Call me Stone."

"Come with...."

"Here it is." She came back with a rope.

I flinched as she pulled my arms behind me and tied my wrists to a pillar in the middle of the room. "That hurts."

"Oh, don't be such a baby. I'm keeping you alive. Be grateful, Feather."

Stone grabbed a pack, stuffed it with gold, and shoved a handful of plants into her mouth. "Want some?" She put the green leaves against my lips.

I turned my head.

Stone laughed. "They're not that bad."

My stomach growled. When was the last time I'd eaten? "How long will you be gone?"

Stone set the pack next to the entrance. "Depends on what

kind of mood Dr. Carper is in when I tell him. If your friends are also sneaking through the palace, it'll be... easy peasy."

"What makes you think Carper won't kill you? He wasn't too happy the last time you ran away."

"I've told you this, Pero. I'm smart." She paused. "Is Jimmy still on your side?"

My heart sank. I wouldn't tell her he was dying.

"Too bad," she said. "He is gorgeous."

I pulled myself against my tied hands. "Don't you dare hurt them!"

Stone faked a sad face. "You're such a cute little feather when you're upset. Oh, I almost forgot." She grabbed a head-band from her hair and tied it over my mouth. "For your silence."

The head-band smelled like sweat and tasted like salt. I gagged. I couldn't think about it. The last thing I wanted was to get sick all over myself. I focused on the pain in my side until my gag reflexes relaxed. When Stone had been gone for a while, I shouted through the head-band. After my throat hurt and saliva covered the band against my mouth, I gave up. It wasn't like anyone could hear me, and I wasn't sure I wanted to be found if it wasn't Carper who heard my screams.

NIGHT HAD to have arrived long ago.

"Get up." My eyes fluttered open. Stone's light shone in my face. She avoided eye contact. She'd probably found out Carper didn't want me and had to decide what to do with me.

Stone untied my hands from the pillar, then re-tied them in front of me. She yanked my chin, gripped it in her hand, and looked me in the eye. "I'm going to take off the gag. You'll stay quiet."

I nodded, eyeing the knife hanging against her hip.

After she took off the tie, I wiped my chapped lips against my shoulder to wipe off the saliva. My chin burned from a rash, and my jaw ached almost as much as the bruise I was sure had formed on my rib. "What time is it?" my voice croaked.

"Four in the morning."

I'd dozed off longer than I thought. "What took you so long?"

"No more questions!"

Stone wound the rope tighter. I refused to make any noise from the pain and chewed my torn-up lip.

"What was that sound?" Stone gripped my hands.

"It wasn't me." I squirmed. "Must you really tighten this so much?"

"Shh."

This time I heard the clawing noise at the back wall, the side that faced outside Moon City. The scraping continued as if someone clawed a chalkboard with their nails. A high-pitched screech echoed, followed by silence.

20

———————

לִרְגֹעַ

y eyes misted as a familiar, heavy presence enveloped me. *Elohim?* The room was quiet, but I felt Him near.

Stone's eye twitched. Her body tensed as if she couldn't believe the screeching was over. "Your people think they're so smart, trying to ruin my plans." She yanked my arm and headed toward the door.

"Pero." My name was spoken the same way it'd been the first time He called me. This time it was clearer, not in my mind but from His voice.

Stone let go of my wrist. I turned.

A man wore a robe that landed at the strapped sandals on his feet. His dark hair curled around his shoulders. I edged closer. The more steps I took toward him, the more I trembled at his power. I stopped when I could go no further and collapsed to the floor. I looked up.

He saw me.

"Elohim." Chills poured through me. It was Him in the flesh.

He nodded. "I'm only here for a moment. It isn't time for me to come. Soon, I will."

"How are you here?"

"I am who I am," He said. "My name is Yeshua, the promised fulfillment. I'll be born through your descendants."

"Mine?" I didn't know if I wanted to love anyone, or have children who'd bring the promised fulfillment. "How are you here now?"

"Time isn't a limitation, Pero. I'm here to take you from Moon City."

"What about Carper?"

"You'll find him." He untied the rope and put His hand into mine.

Stone stared at Yeshua with her jaw hanging open.

"Go away." Her voice was deeper than I'd known possible.

"I've come for you too, Cathena," Yeshua said.

Stone took a couple steps back.

"Cathena." Yeshua's voice held love and authority, just like when He'd said my name.

"Don't look at me!" Her voice was tense and hysterical. She shuddered.

Yeshua stepped close to Stone, His shadow falling over her like a cloak. "Awaken."

Tears poured down Stone's face, her whole body shaking until she sank to her knees. She was like a tree that had crashed to the forest floor. Her head collapsed on her hands at His feet. Planting her hands on the floor, Cathena lifted her head. The piercing darkness of her eyes was gone and in their place was sparkling green. The deep furrow that had defined her face was now smooth. Her smile was innocent and joyous.

"Daughter," Yeshua said, "there are consequences for the pain you've caused. I don't condemn you, but I can't ask you to walk away from your troubles either. I need you to go to the

Lesaries. Find Bahar and protect her. Warn her not to leave the Lesaries until it's time for her to go home."

Stone would help Mom go home? I wanted to hug Yeshua. I wanted to shout out a celebration that Dad could hear across the galaxy.

Cathena nodded her head. "I don't know what happened, but you made me feel alive inside." She sounded innocent, like she'd never had blood on her hands before because Yeshua had washed them with magic soap. "It doesn't make sense, but all I want to do now is please you."

He put a hand on her forehead. She flinched, then relaxed. "Cathena comes from two names: Athena which means goddess of wisdom and war, and Catherine which means pure. Did you know that?"

She shook her head under His hold.

He knelt, His face mere inches from hers. "Your name will have a new meaning. You are now pure in heart because you've seen me. You are a pure warrior for me."

Stone beamed. "Thank you." She gave a stiff bow.

"Come here." Yeshua held out His arm. Stone clung to Him and cried into the fold of His neck.

Yeshua closed His eyes and furrowed His brow as if He were saying a prayer over her. When Stone stepped away from Him, she glowed.

Wiping the tears from her face, she stood straight and cleared her throat. "I'm ready."

"Then go, my child."

Stone ran off, looking far more valuable than the gold she'd left behind.

Yeshua picked up Jimmy's bag and slung it over His shoulder. He took my scuffed-up hand into His calloused hand. His eyes lit up like a smile. "You make me proud, Pero."

Yeshua carried me with Him as He leapt through the wall like I'd seen in a sci-fi movie. We were outside, floating in the air. Golden yellow tinged the cloudless sky, a breathtaking welcome to the new day. Yeshua didn't have wings. He didn't have a pendant around His neck. Yet the tingle in my hand from His hold, told me of His power.

The wind whipped my hair behind me. I caught freedom in my throat and swallowed. I only had His hand to hold, but I didn't hesitate. No fear. Weightless.

We flew past the Lesaries' camp in the field. The tents stood still in the early morning. Smoke from unkindled campfires drifted into the air. I wanted to land there and join Mom, Henry, and Sam.

Jealousy tugged at my heart. Was it as strange for Sam to meet Mom as it'd been for me? I hadn't been the only one who'd dreamed of finding the same woman. I hadn't been the only one who'd cried at night.

One lone figure walked in the distance below. I could tell it was Shea from the white beard that stood out against his black skin. He strolled leisurely, as if accustomed to early morning walks.

Rather than landing with the Lesaries, Yeshua flew over them and into the forest. I wanted to tell Him to turn around, that my family was behind us, but I trusted He had a better place in mind.

A flock of birds flew ahead and led north. When Yeshua slowed around the shore of a small river, He touched down on a bed of rocks like a snowflake. I stumbled when my feet met the ground, then straightened.

The calm and shallow river trickled over big rocks. Birds chirped and flitted among the swaying trees.

"Why'd you take me away? You wanted me to find Carper."

He picked up a rock and threw it across the river. It skipped three times. "You were there for Cathena. Next will be Carper."

My mind boggled at how easily He could change the direction of my course. He took me places I didn't want to go, then set me on my feet again.

"I wish you could stay forever." My breath was steady, everything inside of me at peace.

"I'll stay for a little while." Yeshua's eyes were soft and kind and made my own eyes water.

"What will I do now?"

Yeshua dug into Jimmy's bag and pulled out a cloth with bread and cheese inside. He handed the cloth to me.

"Eat." He reached into the bag and pulled out a wooden cup. After dipping it into the river, He placed the cup on a large rock, then sat beside it. "Rest for a while."

It was the first opportunity to rest since I'd arrived in Origo. I sat down on the rock with the cup and grimaced. My rib still hurt, and my back and stomach twisted in knots. I was alert to sounds around me, like the snapping of a twig or the rustle of an animal in the bushes. They didn't frighten me. Yet I felt more aware now that I wasn't alone.

When I took a bite of the bread, my teeth sunk in and the soft texture melted on my tongue. "This is delicious."

"Alexis made it."

I didn't ask how He knew. As God, He must've known everything. Why did Elohim come as a man? I guess it would've startled me if He'd come as an eagle or a lion. A man was more relatable; He understood what it was like to be human.

"She's an excellent cook." I took another bite.

"Sam made the cup you're drinking from."

I coughed on the bread and used the water to unclog my throat and wondered how long it'd take for me to hear Sam's name and not respond as if I'd been caught kissing another. I examined the cup. It was smooth wood, perfectly round. So, Sam was a skilled carpenter, and I was thinking about him again. What was wrong with me?

"I know," Yeshua said. "I know."

Rather than feeling embarrassed that Yeshua had read my thoughts, I sighed and felt a surge of calm.

"What do you want to let go of?" He asked.

I watched two fish jump out of the water. I was good at holding onto things, like necklaces, but like everything else in my life, the necklace had brought nothing good. Yet it was the only thing I owned that reminded me of Mom. I couldn't let go. It was too hard. I squared my shoulders. "I'm okay."

I sensed Yeshua watch me. My heart tightened, unsure of what to say. It was too much. Since Mom disappeared, I'd never fully trusted people but lived in fear I'd be taken too. I'd fallen for someone who ended up being my brother. I could have a crush on someone else. My life was a mess, but without the messy parts of me, I had nothing.

I glanced at Yeshua. A tear ran down His cheek. He loved me. And more than Mom ever could. It was a beyond-human kind of love. It was a God-kind of love.

"What do you seek?" He asked.

I picked up a rock and threw it along the water. It sunk with a small splash and without a single skip. Figured. That was me. I sought whatever was beyond the forest and the wall and Green Meadow, but I sunk. Maybe I needed to be like that rock and not try so hard to skip along the current. Maybe I could rise only when I fell.

"I seek a human-kind of love," I said.

I took off my shoes that were caked in mud, dipped them in the river, and set them on a rock to dry. Crusted blood glued my blistered feet to my socks. When I pulled off one sock, I yelped in pain as the tear pulled off fresh skin. I put my foot into the water and shivered. I pulled it out, took a deep breath, and set it back in. The current lifted plastered dirt, turning the water brown.

Tears dripped down my face and landed in the water. I wished for my feet to be washed from more than dirt. Elohim had given me a new heart, yet this heart wanted more. If the river could wash away heartache, then I could choose Elohim's love for me and never hurt again.

Yeshua waded over to me and knelt. He didn't seem to notice his wet robe along the hem.

"What are you doing?"

Yeshua picked up my other foot and pulled the sock off gently. It only hurt a little. He set it in the water. I gritted my teeth. He rubbed the dirt off my feet and underneath my toenails with his fingers.

I shook my head. "No, Yeshua. The river will wash me. Please, don't. I'm not worthy."

The little girl inside me was being cared for. It felt wrong that the great Elohim would wash me, but it felt right that He'd clean me.

"A time will come when one will wash me in a river, and then I will be ready for the world. Even when you don't see me now, Pero, I'll always be with you."

His love for me bubbled up like a fountain and threatened to spill out. I couldn't move. I couldn't question. He'd found me in a small town with a tiny family. He'd chosen to bring me all the way to another universe to wash my feet. It was too much love.

"I will prepare you for the battles. Koach is within you." Yeshua took the headdress that was wrapped around His shoulders and brought it to my foot.

"I am life." He rubbed my foot dry and set it on the rock. "I am love."

A tear escaped. Elohim was the love in my heart.

"Come to me when you are tired." Yeshua dug into Jimmy's bag and pulled out the ointment. As He opened the bottle, I breathed deeply the eucalyptus and myrrh that He swathed on my wounds. "I will help you rest."

He placed both feet on the rock and rubbed them with oil.

I should've had many questions to ask Him, but I couldn't think of a single one. My heart beat a slow pace. My stomach loosened its hold. The messy parts of me I'd held onto ripped free. In my mind, I untangled them from around my brain and plopped them into the water.

They sunk.

New words for my song stirred in my mind. I sang the melody in my heart.

> *When you lead me by still waters, you restore my*
> *soul.*
> *Surely goodness and your mercy cover me.*

When He finished anointing my feet, Yeshua placed His hand on my head as He had with Stone. He closed His eyes, and I closed mine too. I couldn't move, even if I wanted to. I had no sense of time or plans or thoughts. Everything was blank and still. Tears moved from somewhere deep inside and were released. I wasn't sad. I'd never been happier. He removed the closet inside and replaced it with infinite space.

I was boundless.

21

לָקוּם

"It's time."

A hand rested on my shoulder, and I blinked my eyes open.

Yeshua kneeled next to me.

I sat up. My back was stiff, my cheek sore from sleeping on a rock. The sun's bright rays told me it was mid-afternoon. "Time for what?"

"For me to leave and you to stay here."

Someone splashed from up the river.

"Carper is on his way," Yeshua said.

When I tried to speak, all that came out was a squeak. I wasn't ready for this. What if Carper didn't listen to me?

I cleared my throat. "Why did you bring me here?"

Yeshua took my face in His hands. "Trust me. Koach is with you, Pero. And I love you."

I tried to pull my face away. "But I can't do this, Yeshua. I don't know...."

He kept His hands on my cheeks and moved my head back toward Him. "Keep your eyes on me, child."

I nodded. Calm settled over me.

Yeshua kissed my head, let go, and waded across the river and through the forest. He disappeared behind a tree right as Carper came around the river's bend.

Carper paused when he spotted me. He was too far away for me to read his expression. Eventually, he trudged through the water. I wouldn't move. My mission was to find him, but now that he was here, I wasn't eager to take any initiative. Either I lacked confidence, or my time of rest had made him seem smaller. Like fear over him was a thing of yesterday and that he didn't require a driving force to plow into him with a sword or stick.

"How'd you get here?" Carper asked when he was closer. He looked around and chuckled. "And by yourself."

Normally, being with Carper with no one else around would've had my knees trembling, but it felt like just another day relaxing by the river. "Doesn't matter how I got here. I've been looking for you. Seems like I've found you."

Dark red blood blotched on Carper's head. Red veins tracked down like spider legs. He slicked his glistening hair, but it flipped back over his forehead.

"You don't seem so classy when hiking through the woods."

He frowned. "No one's out here to see."

"I have some ointment." I fished through the bag.

Carper moved his hand in a dismissive wave. "I'm fine."

"You don't look fine. What'd you do, run into a tree?"

Carper rested on the rock where Yeshua had sat not that long ago. With head tipped back toward the sun, he sighed as if he were relaxed.

"Shouldn't you be giving tours or ranking Warriors on how well they killed each other?"

"You're so much like your mother." His shoulders slumped, and he clasped his fingers in his lap.

Oh, my word. Carper really was relaxed.

"Maybe she learned it from you." I was off to a terrible start.

One more word out of my mouth and he'd kill me for sure. "I'm sorry for being sassy."

Carper laughed out loud. "No, you're not."

"After all I just said to you, you're not hurting me." There was something seriously wrong with this man.

Carper dipped his hand in the river and splashed it on his hair. Blood dripped from his forehead and into the river. He smoothed back his fine hair, leaving a greasy and red-streaked finish. "You're running away, aren't you?"

It wasn't like I could go anywhere. "Should I be?"

"From me, yes." He stretched like a cat.

I held back an eye roll. For the first time since I'd arrived, I wasn't afraid of Dr. Carper. Maybe he hadn't changed. Maybe it was me who had. "Is that why you're here, Carper? Are *you* running away?"

Carper looked stunned that I would ask such a thing. "Call me Calvin."

I smirked. "Are you being serious right now?"

"My first name is Calvin."

"And why would I call you by your first name?" I hadn't even heard Mom call him by his first name.

"Anyone who can confront me is worthy of calling me by my first name." He flicked a water bug off his shirt.

"You didn't seem to feel that way when you smashed my ankle." I cringed, remembering when he'd put his weight on my injury again. The pain had been far worse than a broken rib. But I wasn't afraid that he'd do it again. Strange, indeed.

"I don't care about you and your parading army anymore," he said. "I have better ways to spend my time."

"So, you *are* running away."

"I didn't say that." Carper rubbed the non-bleeding part of his head.

"Does it have anything to do with Moon City rising against you?"

He jerked his head toward me. "How'd you know?"

"I heard the guards talking while I was hiding on the roof yesterday."

"Why were you...?" He shook his head. "Never mind. Why are you here? You said you were looking for me."

"Calvin." The name felt strange in my mouth. "I thought you'd never ask."

He eyed me like I'd gone mad. Maybe I had.

"I'm taking you with me to the Lesaries, and I'm making you their king."

Carper's jaw dropped. "I don't understand."

"Maybe you can't understand my American accent. I said—"

"Oh, knock it off!" Carper said. "Now you're just being an irritating teenager."

"I'm good at that." What had happened during my time with Yeshua? I was out of control. I was acting like... myself.

Carper's eyebrows squished together. "You really are serious."

"So help me Elohim, I really am."

Carper looked the other way. "Who set you up to this? Was it your mom?"

I shook my head. "Elohim told me that this is what I needed to do, and I obeyed."

Carper's eyes traveled to my necklace. "Did He tell you during the vision when I was on the throne?"

That was the vision that made Carper angry because it didn't end with Carper on the throne. It ended with someone who Carper had never met. Yeshua.

"No," I said. "It wasn't in a vision."

Carper cussed under his breath.

"You want to be king of the Lesaries, right?" I watched his face, seemingly perplexed and agitated. "You've wanted it for a long time."

Carper didn't take his eyes off the view of the river and forest. "There are two groups of Lesaries. You know that, right?"

"I know now."

"Then here's a history lesson. At one point, Earth came from Origo. The Lesaries on Origo are on a very slow time while the Lesaries on Earth are on a fast time. Things that happen here in this universe take a very long time to have an effect in our universe. Call it a time lapse. Does that make sense?"

"Not at all."

Carper scratched his chin. "Never mind, then. Let's say that as a Lesarie living on Earth, you didn't like the endless meetings in sanctuaries and following rules."

So, Carper was a Lesarie, or used to be.

"After running away from a people you despise; after hiding for years until you established a plant that would revolutionize the history of mankind; after building a community who worshipped you; after building,"—he stretched out his arms toward what was probably the direction of Moon City—"a magnificent, indestructible city, so that one day when the people who sheltered you your whole life came to threaten everything you'd made, you could rise and rule a people who are disillusioned in their God-following fantasy; after all of that, if a sixteen-year-old...."

"Seventeen."

Carper raised his brow. "A naïve girl who'd establish the power you'd wanted your whole life showed up to say, 'Never mind what you've done. You can have it. The kingdom of the most powerful people on earth belongs to you. No threats needed. No conniving. No ripping necklaces or pursuing visions.' I want to know, Pero, if all that happened to you, what would you say?"

I breathed in and puffed out air. "I'd say that's the longest and most self-absorbed thought I've ever heard."

Carper rolled his eyes. "Seventeen?"

"As far as I know." Any news was possible. I could really be fifteen. Henry could be my brother also. I hoped not.

Carper looked shorter from my angle on the rock.

"I know this is a shock. I'm pretty stunned myself. But this is what Elohim wants."

"That's the thing, Pero. I don't want to be king because Elohim wants me to be. I want to be king so that I can be Elohim. That's why I need you. I need your power."

I shook my head. "My power comes from Elohim."

"Precisely. You are my channel."

"So, you're using the three chosen because you're afraid of Elohim."

Carper sat up straight. The tendons in his neck bulged. "I'm not afraid!"

I nodded once and turned the other way. A crawdad worked its way against the current, but was pulled back. It tried again.

"The Lesarie leader, Shea, came to my roof and asked me to protect you," I said.

There it was. He could do whatever he wanted with it. He could keep taking off and trying to come up with another plan that would lead him right back to where he started. And I wouldn't judge him if he did. Running away wasn't much different from hiding.

"And you said 'yes,'" he said.

"I said 'no.'"

"What made you change your mind?" he asked.

Goosebumps formed along my arms. Yeshua's hands had been against my cheeks only moments ago. He'd told me to focus only on Him. It was love. All of it. He'd already given it to me freely.

"Love," I said.

Carper snorted. "I'm much too old for you."

"Gross." I crinkled my nose. "Not for you."

"One of your many boyfriends?"

Gross again, but not entirely inaccurate. "Love for Elohim."

"I don't like you saying that name." His jaw hardened. Yet he wasn't hitting me or shooting me over it. What had changed?

"You better get used to it if you'll use Him for your power as king."

Carper picked up a stick and swirled it around in the water. "I'm going to be king in your world, not here. The Origo Lesaries have a leader, but the Lesaries on Earth have been begging for one for years."

"Then why'd you come here to build a city?"

"If you had paid attention at all in our world, you would know why." He looked at the sky as if searching for a sign of a third universe. "I was quite famous on Earth."

I searched my memory for his name, for anything I would've heard about Dr. Calvin Carper, the greatest scientist two worlds had ever known, but nothing came to mind. Unease started to creep over me. Maybe I should be scared.

Carper whacked the stick against the rock, threw it in the water, and watched it float downstream. "Let's be going then."

What would the Lesaries say when I brought him? I'd need to protect him if they were angry.

He held out a hand. "I could use some ointment."

I grinned as I pulled it out of the bag. He was asking for help. It was a start.

"Get that dumb smile off your face!" he said.

I handed him the jar in silence. He dabbed some on his head and handed the blood-stained jar back to me.

Carper bent to scoop up a sip of water, stood, settled his backpack on his shoulders, and walked away. I scrambled to pick myself up. I opened Jimmy's bag, pulled out Sam's wooden cup, and dipped it into the river.

I heard a snap and looked up to see Carper's fingers in the air. He'd snapped at me. So, he did still see himself as superior.

At least he was a little more civil. Not that I could say the same thing about myself.

I threw Jimmy's bag over my shoulder and ran to catch up. The wooden cup sloshed water over my fingers. If I was going to be Carper's protector, I'd better be in the lead. But I didn't know which direction to go while Carper did.

We walked for what must've been a couple of hours in silence. My feet dragged against the ground. I kept upright, focusing on the sound of birds in the forest to keep my mind off the pain in my ribs.

"What do you know about the third chosen?" Carper asked.

"You mean you know you aren't the third?"

"I've always known. Somehow I could see the visions, but I never had my own."

"If you aren't one of the chosen, how are you able to see the visions?"

Carper shrugged. "It's a curse I've had ever since I met your mom. It was only when I figured out how to use it toward my inventions that I saw it as a gift."

It was all about him... always. *Elohim, I still don't understand what you're thinking.*

Carper opened up a canister and poured water into his mouth. He closed the lid and looked at my face.

I licked my chapped lips. I'd dropped the last bit of water from the cup over an hour ago.

He sighed and threw the canister over to me. "Only a little. We still have a couple of hours longer."

If only Carper hadn't wandered so far. I wiped off the mouthpiece with my shirt.

Carper humphed. "I didn't even put my mouth on it."

I ignored him and gulped four times before handing it back. "Thank you."

He put the canteen away. "Let's keep moving so we're not here all day."

My ribs ached as we continued walking.

"You never answered my question," he said.

"About?"

"Who is the third chosen? The one you were all emotional about when Jimmy shot him with the arrow?"

I swallowed the now familiar knot in my throat at the mention of Sam. I should be over him. It wasn't like I'd known him that long. "His name is Sam. You couldn't see the vision, could you?"

"There was more power with the three."

I looked at him in surprise.

"How else could Sam heal himself and you? It wasn't just a vision. It was a fulfillment."

The power was stronger with Sam. We could also take over each other's visions, like I did when I flew to the wall. That hadn't been possible before.

"The question is," Carper said, "how can I tap into that power?"

I blinked at his honesty. He was calmer, but who knew how long that'd last? How could he have Elohim's power? I shuddered to think that he might be clever enough to find a way.

22

לְבַנֶס

Hushed voices spoke around fires. Sparks crackled the same color as the setting sun. Children huddled together under blankets. Plates held in outstretched hands were filled. The aromas of soup and bread saturated the air.

"Stay here for a minute while I find Shea," I whispered to Carper.

"Too embarrassed to introduce me?"

I glared. "You don't still have a gun on you, do you?" I should've asked him that a while back, but he hadn't hurt me yet.

Carper held his hands up. "I'm not shooting them, if that's what you're thinking. Can't be king of a bunch of dead people."

"Fine. Just hide behind a tree or something."

He leaned against a tree and folded his arms. Close enough.

I crept up to the clearing's edge and watched the Lesaries through the trees. It'd only been a day since I'd marched with them, but it felt much longer.

Henry talked in one circle, where mostly young ladies gathered. They dazzled him with cheesy smiles. My stomach hardened. Henry had run behind me every day, become friends with Dad, came to my room's roof in Moon City, and trekked through the forest while mending my ankle. He never complained when I brushed him away or closed myself off.

A pretty blonde girl rested her hand on Henry's arm and laughed loudly. A sadness overwhelmed me. After we finished this battle, I wouldn't need Henry anymore. But I was the one who'd turned him down. He could flirt with whomever he wished.

"Pero?"

I startled.

Sam walked over to me and stood two feet away. He glanced over at Henry. "Was I interrupting something?"

My face heated. "No. Why would you be?"

"It's just from the way you were watching...."

"Nothing's going on." I covered my mouth with my hand as if that could hide my lie.

Sam smirked. "I'm happy you're here and safe after that wild vision of yours."

"Thanks." I looked toward the forest where Carper was waiting. "Where's Shea?"

"Somewhere nearby. Is everything okay? You seem worried."

There was no way all these people would accept and understand why I'd brought their enemy with me.

"Let's find a fire to warm you, get some dinner and coffee. My mom—" He bit his lip. Was it because he now had two moms? "Alexis makes the best food."

I'd eaten her bread with Yeshua. I couldn't believe it'd been earlier that morning.

Sam didn't ask about how I'd flown to Moon City from his vision or what I did when I was there. More than likely Cathena had filled him in, if she'd made it. I was relieved. I needed food, water, and sleep before I started talking. But Carper was still waiting. Part of me wanted to make him think I left him there on purpose out of spite. But I needed Carper to trust me.

Shea emerged from a nearby tent. He stepped forward with purpose but stopped when his eyes met mine. His whole face smiled. He crossed his arms and shook his head. "Wow," he mouthed. Then he laughed, his long stride filling in the distance between us. "Come here." He embraced me, and I grimaced from the pain.

"Pero made it, everyone!"

The Lesaries clapped and whistled. Some peeked their heads from tents to find out what was happening.

I grinned. I would've given a bow if my ribs hadn't screamed at me with every bend.

Shea raised his hands to settle them down. "We need to be quiet for Pero's safety," he said. "Moon City may not know she's here and we want to keep it that way."

It seemed the Lesaries had been ready to dance and eat cake for dinner. Instead, people sat to eat their bowls of what looked like chili. My stomach growled. Could Carper wait?

Henry ran to me and lifted me off my feet. I glanced at the faces of the girls he'd left behind. They whispered to each other. The pretty blonde girl looked the other way.

I smiled through a grimace. "Henry, that hurts."

He set me down. "What happened?"

Shea stepped to the side to give us privacy. It really wasn't necessary. I doubted Henry would try to kiss me again.

I touched my rib. "It's not as bad as the last injury. Stone... I mean Cathena broke it."

He scowled. "I knew we couldn't trust her. She insisted on helping your mom."

I put a hand on his arm. "No, you can trust her. It's okay."

"If you say so." Henry rubbed the back of his neck. "There

are a couple of actual doctors here. I'll find one to examine your rib."

I shoved down the disappointment that Henry was no longer my doctor. "I need to talk with Shea first."

Henry whispered in my ear. My head tingled. "Did you find Carper?"

I nodded and scanned the forest.

"I hope you were right about this, Ro girl."

"Me too."

Henry nodded toward Shea. "I'll let you two talk."

Henry tousled my hair before leaving and joining another group. I wasn't sure what he saw in me. In his mind, I had to be the sad little sister who didn't shower enough or wear deodorant. I patted my hair. It was tangled and gritty. I probably had circles under my eyes from lack of sleep. My back and neck ached from sleeping against a pillar the night before. I felt weak from little water and food. It was more than my hair that was a mess.

Shea put his large arm around me and directed me toward the circle nearest us. Alexis opened a spot for us to sit. The fire blasted warm and welcoming heat. A flame shot sparks into the sky, exploding with tiny popping sounds.

Alexis handed me a plate. "Better eat before you fall asleep in your bowl."

I wanted to devour it, but I also didn't want Carper to come out and surprise everyone. "Shea, I need to tell you something first."

He set down his bowl and waited. I leaned close so only he could hear. "I brought Carper."

His eyes widened. "Here?"

I nodded and motioned my head toward where he hopefully still waited.

"Well done, Pero. I'll take it from here."

Shea walked toward the woods, his robe billowing behind

him. I was relieved to have the responsibility lifted but concerned that if anything bad happened, it would be my fault for bringing him.

I shoved chili into my mouth.

"Easy there." Alexis sat.

I slowed down. "This is amazing."

"Family recipe."

Even something as simple as hot liquid pouring down my throat was heavenly.

"We'll talk more later," Alexis said, "but first we need to find you a place to sleep. You're losing color."

I glanced at her, then back to the forest. Shea was twice the size of Carper. Was that enough defense if Carper threatened him? When Alexis put a hand on my knee, I focused on her.

"It'll be all right. Shea will know what to do."

Would he? Or had Carper pretended to be gentle so that he could bring Shea into the woods to kill him? Did Carper still have his gun? I should've checked before bringing him here. There were children. But what could he really do as one man against thousands of us?

Us.

Since when had I identified myself as one of the Lesaries of Origo? Around me, children laughed and adults chatted—all ages, all colors of skin. There was love here, like a family. This could be my home. But what about Dad and Mom? They needed me back in Green Meadow. Was it possible to have two families?

Alexis helped me to my feet. "What you need, dear, is a bath, but since we're sparse on water, that will have to wait. Tomorrow, I'll take you to your mom. She's sleeping now. Cathena is doing a great job looking out for her."

I smiled. Cathena had joined the Lesaries and was welcomed. Maybe I could be too.

"I'm glad my mom's being taken care of," I said. "She needs it."

"So do you," Alexis said. "You know, Pero. I learned a long time ago that nurture doesn't come only from who we're born to. Elohim brings family to the lonely."

"I see that. I just wish I would've known you all a long time ago. Dad hid us well, so we never had many friends, and we hardly attended Sanctuary. Wouldn't want to be too close to anyone in case they were dangerous, including other Lesaries."

Alexis brought me in to her side for a hug. "We're here for you now, and I'll join with your mom and love you like a daughter. Elohim has brought you into our care."

I'd only met her days ago, and yet she felt like a close friend. Was this how all of Elohim's people loved? With acceptance, with grace?

"How's Jimmy?" I asked.

Alexis sighed. "He's not doing well."

"Then I need to see him tonight."

———

TWO LESARIE GUARDS blocked the entrance to the tent where Jimmy stayed.

"My friend is in there." I pointed toward the tent. "Can I see him?"

"I don't think that's a good idea." Sam came up beside me.

"He is a guard for Carper." The tent guard looked from Sam to me and back.

"Jimmy saved my life." I clinched my fists. "He's on our side."

Sam held my eyes until I wanted to pull away. "I'll let you see him, but I'll go with you."

I almost disagreed, but I couldn't judge Sam without

knowing what he was keeping from me. From the sound of it, they weren't on the best of terms. "All right."

"Jimmy isn't who you think he is."

Sam hadn't been around Jimmy in the last week as much as I had. I trusted him. He took a bullet for me.

Sam nodded at the guards, who reluctantly let us pass. The tent was large, so we stayed standing as we walked in. Jimmy lay on a mat on the floor underneath a pile of blankets. His eyes fluttered open. "Pero. Glad to see you made it."

"Hi, Jimmy." My voice squeaked like a little girl's. I sat on the floor by him and rested my hand on top of his. It was way too hot. Jimmy looked like he had a hard time swallowing. "Do you need something to drink?"

"Please."

I brought a nearby cup to his lips. He drank a sip, then laid his head back down. "There are things you don't know about me, Pero."

"You've been nothing but kind to me, and that's all I need to know."

"You've been a good friend," Jimmy said.

I squeezed his sweaty hand. "You need to make it. Okay?"

Jimmy's face looked pained. "I'll be around, Pero."

He glanced at Sam again. "Salmon is a good man. He'll take care of you."

I shook my head and whispered. "He is a good man, but we're not together."

"Not yet," he whispered back.

I chuckled. I couldn't tell him that Sam was my brother. I couldn't tell him that Carper was nearby. When Jimmy was better, there'd be plenty of time. "I'll come back tomorrow and visit you. Okay?"

"I look forward to it."

I kissed his hand and stood up. I waved him goodbye as Sam escorted me outside.

"He won't make it."

Sam sighed. "I don't think so."

An emotional wound punctured my heart and lodged there. Jimmy was my first advocate in a new and scary place. He'd protected me many times. He was dying because of me.

"Sam, what happened between you two?"

Heavy footsteps and labored breathing came from behind us. We turned around.

A Lesarie guard from Jimmy's tent ran up. "Sam."

I touched my throat. "Is Jimmy okay?"

"Yes." He stopped, catching his breath. "Sam, Jimmy wants to talk with you."

Sam raised a brow. "Did he say why?"

"No. He just said it was urgent."

Sam looked at me. I shrugged. "I'll wait for you outside the tent."

"You should sleep, Pero."

"I'm fine." I yawned.

Sam nodded and ran ahead with the guard. As tired as I was, I couldn't sleep. Jimmy could die any moment, and I had to know the story. I'd wait outside the tent all night.

"Psst." The sound cut through the silence.

It was quieter as many people had retreated to their tents. Lights shone through some. A couple of snores came from others. Carper peeked through the doorway of a tent. A large white bandage covered his wound. Two Lesarie guards stood in front of him. He motioned for me to come closer. Two guards blocked my way.

"Pero, right?" one guard asked. "You'll need to back up, please."

I was the fulfilled prophecy, so they must all know my name. And soon everyone would know I'd brought Carper. Would I be famous in a good way? Probably not.

I took a step back and sat on the ground so I could see Carper between the guards' legs. "Is this okay?"

One guard turned around so that he faced Carper. He held out a sword. "You have two minutes."

"Is the sword really necessary?" I asked.

Carper smiled. "Still trust me now, huh?"

"Why shouldn't I, Calvin?" I crisscrossed my legs and held myself up to avoid pressure on my rib. "Or should I call you 'Your Majesty'?"

"Shh." Carper eyed the guards. They didn't show that they cared what I'd said.

I lowered my voice. "We're still keeping secrets?"

"For now. Shea wants to hide me until the walls come down."

"That's not for another five days. Rumors are going to spread by then."

"Yeah, thanks to you."

I threw my hands up. "Hey, I'm the one who saved your life."

"How is inviting me to be with your people in another universe saving me?"

I laughed through my teeth. "I saved you from having to run and hide all your life, which, believe me, is kind of like dying, especially when those you love are taken from you." I picked a piece of grass. "Not that you'd understand."

Carper fidgeted. "Just because I'm heartless doesn't mean I've never been hurt."

"You admit that you're heartless." I waited for his remark. But there was none. Carper had feelings? I'd thought he was as hard as his city's wall.

"I'm forgiving you," I said, "and you better accept it because there are few who'd forgive after what you've done."

"What have I done?"

I scratched my brow. "Hmm. You hurt my mom, me, my dad, Jimmy, my brother."

"What brother?"

I gulped. He would find out eventually. "Do you remember the name Salmon?"

Carper nodded. "Salmon was your mom's husband."

He said it so casually, as if they'd been friends or good acquaintances. Did he not remember that Mom had a son and that he had driven Bahar away from Sam as he'd done with me? Did he not remember that when he had Bahar, he took advantage of her, making her his slave? The truth of Carper's callous heart settled like the night's darkness. Could I really forgive?

"I didn't kill Salmon," Carper said.

"Wait. What? I thought Sam's dad died because he was sick."

"Jimmy killed him."

His words were another punch to my ribs.

"Pero?" I barely heard Sam behind me. He beckoned me from a distance. "We need to talk."

23

לִלְמֹד

I stared into the fire's flames. Ours was the only light left in the quiet, sleeping camp. Mom sipped coffee. Sam carved a piece of wood.

The chirp of the crickets lulled my eyes closed.

"Would someone please say something before I fall asleep?"

Mom cradled her cup in her hands. "We should wait till morning."

"No," I said. "We need to talk now."

Mom dropped her head. "Salmon, you start, then."

Sam blew woodchips that landed in the fire and kindled a splash of sparks. "I'll be leaving for Earth after the battle."

I looked at him. Would he be in my home as my new brother? I couldn't handle the awkwardness of him becoming a part of my family. "Be sure to buy some jeans when you get there."

Mom and Sam laughed.

Sam's smile wavered. "Are you sure you want me to be the one to tell this, Bahar... Mom?"

How much had they bonded while I was being kicked in the

ribs by Cathena and walking through the woods with Carper? It wasn't fair.

"Pero needs to know," Mom said.

My pulse rose, ready for Mom to bring another slap to the life I thought I knew.

Sam set the rough carving on his knee. "My dad worked for Jimmy's dad on a farm in exchange for living there."

"How old was Jimmy?"

"He was a teen," Mom said. "A nice boy. It was his dad who was the problem."

Sam nudged his head toward Mom. "You remember more than I do."

Mom pursed her lips. "One day when Jimmy's father, Dan, was gone for the week, there was a fire in the barn, and Dan's colt tried to jump a fence. He didn't make it. We got the fire out, but the farm was a wreck. When Dan came home, he became a bigger problem. It started with harsh words, then he became violent toward Salmon, picking at everything he did wrong." Mom held her shaking hands together. "There was an accident."

I closed my eyes as if that would shut out the pain I expected.

Mom cleared her throat. "This is too much for you."

I opened my eyes. "I want to know."

Mom nodded. "Salmon and Dan got into a fight. Punches were thrown. Nasty words said. Jimmy was there. He tried to stop them. But they wouldn't listen. So...."

Mom put her hands over her face. I wanted to wrap my arms around her, but I was glued to the log that I sat on. I didn't know that every time I'd cried for Mom, she'd cried for more than just me.

Sam paused his knife against the piece of wood. When he looked up, grief had taken over his face. "Jimmy shot my dad."

I ran my fingers through my hair. It wasn't the Jimmy I thought I'd known.

"The part I remember," Sam said, "is running up to my dad and crying and Jimmy yelling 'I didn't mean to' over and over. And then Jimmy ran away. I didn't see him again until recently." Sam rested against a tree stump. He folded his arms, looking to the stars as if searching for comfort there. "After my mom disappeared, Alexis took me in. When I turned seventeen, I discovered I had an ability to make things grow."

"Without the necklace?"

Sam nodded.

Every time I sang in the past, did I not realize it was power from Elohim? Had my gift always been powerful?

"Alexis was concerned for my safety," Sam said. "She told me my mom had left because of her gift and that I needed to be careful. For a while, I stayed with some relatives on Earth, but once my uncle discovered I had the gift, he told Carper. I ran back to Alexis. We joined a group of Lesaries who kept us safe. With all our traveling, no one ever found me."

"Until now," I said. "Because of me."

"Don't say that," Sam said. "The prophecy had to be fulfilled. We would have never been brought together if it hadn't."

"What was the point of us finding each other if we're all going separate ways?"

"What do you mean, Pero?" Mom asked.

"I mean, we've all been apart for so long that we'll never be together. Mom doesn't belong with Dad. Just as Sam doesn't belong with Mom or me. What was the point of having a prophecy that'd bring us all together if we're divided?"

"I believe it will unite us," Mom said.

I thought of Yeshua's caring hands washing my feet. One word from Him and we'd be united.

Sam threw wood chips into the fire. "Jimmy's parents gave their property to Jimmy when they passed on, and he just gave it to me."

I gasped. Not because of the offer, but because two memories flashed across my mind. In Carper's limo, when I'd first met Jimmy, he'd mentioned that his parents owned a farm that wasn't much different from ones around my house. And just minutes ago, Sam said that he was leaving for my world. Did that mean Jimmy's property was near my home? But that would mean that Mom and her first family had lived near me too.

"Where is the property?" Mom asked.

I gazed at Mom in confusion.

"A place called...."

"Green Meadow?" Mom and I both asked at the same time.

"That's the farm where we lived," she said.

"It is?" Sam's eyes bulged.

"That's my home," I said.

They both looked at me.

"What?" Mom asked.

"That's where Dad and I moved, when you told us to hide."

A chill traveled down my spine. Out of all the places we could've moved to....

"Huh," Mom said.

My stomach tightened. "What was that for?" I asked.

"Nothing." Mom set down her cup, clasped her hands, and leaned forward toward the fire. "I just think that this was all part of the plan."

"What plan?" I asked.

"That we'd all three go back to Green Meadow. That we'd start again as a new family."

"I don't think...." I rubbed my head. Sam couldn't join our family. Wouldn't it be hard for Sam if Henry and I ended up together? And what would Dad say? "I think that Sam living with us in our house would be a lot for me to get used to."

Mom shook her head. "I didn't mean that Sam would live with us. He'd have the property he could live on. It would be the same town, so we'd all be together."

Sam could use his gift to grow plants. It was a good fit for him, but where did it leave me? I'd finish high school, maybe find a job at some boring place, and Sam would probably come over for dinners at least once a week. It was too much. Too weird.

Mom looked at Sam with intense focus. "It's time," she said to him.

Time for what?

"This will be a shock," Mom said.

It wouldn't be the first time someone had shocked me with news. Nothing could be bigger than Sam being my brother.

"Mom just told me two days ago," Sam said.

There it was again. Sam knew some family secret from my mom before I did. I didn't want to share her. Sam had Alexis. I had Mom.

"Pero," Mom said.

My stomach flipped with each passing second.

Sam put his hand on mine.

I pulled away. "What are you doing?"

"Come with me," Sam said. "We'll claim the property together. I'll make you happy, Pero."

Was he proposing? I was only seventeen. And brothers didn't marry their sisters. "What do you mean?" I put my hands on my hot face.

"I'm not your brother."

The heat in my cheeks traveled down my whole body. "I don't understand."

Sam looked at Mom.

Mom took a deep breath. "Pero, you were adopted."

My head spun. I couldn't focus on one thing. "I'm adopted."

My voice whispered like it spoke through a cloud. Words tossed through my brain at high speed.

Dad never told me. Who are my birth parents? Who's turning the lights off? Where is my strength?

My koach.

24

———

סָפֵק

It was dark when I woke yet light enough to see silhouettes of trees cast on the tent. I sat up and touched the colorful wool blanket covering me. I blinked and took in the mat I slept on, the purple tapestry that hung next to the mat, and a basket full of herbs, jars of oils, and bandages. My blue pack from home was across from me, and Dad's sweater laid out over the blanket. Hugging the sweater up to my nose, I breathed in a hint of Dad. How many times had Dad watched the time, wondering if I'd ever come back? An ache grew inside. I missed Dad as much as I'd missed Mom.

But I was adopted. Dad was not my dad.

Laying aside the white robe that had been set out for me, I put on the yoga pants and tank top from inside my pack. I pulled on Dad's sweater and laid back down on the mat.

Surely Dad would still take me back. Did Mom consider me as her own, or had I been replaced by her actual son?

Next to the basket was a bowl of water, a cloth, and a bar of soap. I dipped the cloth into the water, dabbed into the soap until there was a lather, and scrubbed my face and pits. Inside my pack, I found deodorant and mouthwash. At the bottom of my pack was a brush.

A stirring from the other side of the tapestry made me pause and lift the edge of the purple cloth. Mom laid on a mat, her back turned. I recognized her shoulder-length black hair that I'd not inherited and thought back to what Carper had said about me having Mom's eyes. That, too, could never be true.

Letting go of the tapestry, I brushed. I'd never known Mom. She was gone nearly my whole life, and nothing about me came from her. My breath stalled. I felt around my neck and clung to the pendant. I had one thing that was Mom's: Abram power. But I was not an Abram. Then whose blood did I have, and how had I become one of the three chosen?

I heard more stirring behind the tapestry and the sound of feet shuffling.

Mom's head peeked around the edge. "You're awake." She sat on the cot and felt my head. "Temperature's good. You look better. Is that...?" She sniffed near me. "Mouthwash?"

"Found it in my bag."

"Can I have some?" Mom grabbed the wash, dumped it into her mouth, swished and spit into the washing bowl. I wouldn't be washing my face again anytime soon.

"Ah. My mouth hasn't felt that clean in over a decade." She eyed my brush. "Would you like me to brush your hair again?"

Moms brushed hair. Women who pretended to be my mom didn't.

Why, Elohim? Why bring me to Mom only for me to learn she's not who she says she is? I risked my life for her.

"I don't think so."

Mom sighed. "Can I get you something to eat? You must be hungry. You slept a whole day."

Wow. So, it was day four of marching around Moon City.

Good. The closer we were to being done, the sooner I'd go home.

"I guess I'm hungry." Maybe she'd get the clue and give me some space.

"Okay, but, Pero, we need to talk at some point."

"There's nothing to say. I came all the way here for you, and I don't even know you."

Mom blinked back tears. "But I've known you since you were a newborn. I've loved you every day."

"Yeah, for three years."

"No, Pero." A tear ran down her chin. I wanted to wipe it; I wanted to smack it. "For seventeen years and eight days."

I looked up. "You remember my birthday?"

She nodded. "Of course, I do."

If it really was my birthday.

I folded my arms and held them tight against me. "But how can you claim to love me as a mom and love Sam in the same way and expect me to fall for him? It's too strange."

She placed a hand on my knee. "Honey, you don't have to fall for Sam. It's okay."

Mom was always alive in my mind, yet I'd never imagined there to be a Sam. Sure, there'd been a connection between us, but it had faded the moment I learned Mom was alive for him too. Yet, no matter who this woman was to me, I loved her.

I hesitated, then curled up next to Mom, laying my head on her lap. This was where I wanted to be. "How am I one of the chosen?"

Mom rubbed my head. "I don't know. Elohim loves you, Pero. I'm sure of that."

"Who are my parents?"

Mom stopped rubbing my head. "I don't know that either. I was at our old house not too far from Moon City and looking for Salmon when I heard you cry. You were swaddled in a blanket and inside a hollow of a tree that was tall enough for me to stand in. I picked you up. Right when I held you in my arms, I ended up in the hallway of your dad's apartment."

I sat up. "Are you serious?" She had closed one chapter of her life and opened the next. "You never went back for Sam?"

Mom put her hands up in a question. "I couldn't figure out how. I tried the same closets that had gotten me there before, but none worked, and I couldn't go back to where I first started traveling when I was seventeen."

"Where was it?"

"I'm... you.... I can't tell you. It'd be too dangerous." Mom pinched her bottom lip. "Some are hunting for us, the chosen three. But don't worry. They're far enough away from you whether you stay here or return home."

"Are you coming home with me?"

She turned away as if she hadn't heard. "I'll find you something to eat."

"Never mind food, Mom. Are you coming with...?"

"We can't. I've tried Carper's mansion, the rooms in Moon City's walls, and I've looked for the tree with the hollow where I found you. It's not here."

"I thought the necklace would bring us back."

"I thought so too, but when Carper had the other necklace for me, it still didn't work."

"Maybe it will, now that all three of us have the necklaces."

Mom shook her head. "The doors open up randomly and for different people. Carper and Jimmy have traveled between worlds twice. The first time was to find me, and the second time was to find you."

I scratched my ear. "How do I get back home?"

"If you're supposed to go back home, it will happen. When I found you in the tree, that tree hadn't been there before."

"What do you mean?"

Mom shuddered. "It grew right before my eyes. I think it's Elohim who brings the doors."

My heart beat faster. There was one who I'd seen make things grow in an instant. "Do you think Elohim's using Sam to grow them?"

Mom's brow furrowed, then her eyes widened. "The vision! Pero, I think you may be onto something."

"But how would Sam grow the opening you disappeared through when I was three?"

"You're right. He wasn't there so couldn't have grown it. Unless it's Elohim's power that causes growth, no matter where Sam is."

"Do you think Elohim could've used Sam's gift to grow things before he was even born?"

"It's possible," Mom said. "Elohim once said to a Lesarie prophet, 'Before I formed you in the womb I knew you, before you were born, I set you apart; I appointed you as a prophet to the nations.'"

"Could the same be said about you and me?" I asked. "Did you ever have warrior skills before you learned you were one of the chosen three?"

"I did. It was weak, but the gift was always there." Mom smiled. "It was in you, too. Whenever I sang a lullaby, you sang along. Even as a baby."

We were born with gifts. Why had my birth parents not wanted my gift? Why had they given me away? Would my dreams of Mom be replaced with the parents I never knew?

Mom hummed.

"That tune sounds familiar," I said. "Is it the lullaby you used to sing me?"

Mom nodded. "It's an old song that's been passed down about Elohim. Some call Him Yahweh. It's a name so holy and sacred that we don't address it to Him out loud. It means 'I am who I am.'"

"Can you sing it?" I asked.

"I'll try." She cleared her throat. "I am who I am. Do not

worry about tomorrow. Don't you worry about today. My child, I love you, and I am your King."

Elohim was our king, not Carper. Hadn't Elohim directed me so far? Then why choose Carper when we had all we needed? Carper didn't come close to Elohim. But maybe it wasn't about who we were or who we came from. Maybe Elohim chose out of love.

Mom sang. "Even in your suffering, even in your pain, even in your discomfort, I am who I am."

She was quiet after.

I smiled. "Mom?"

"Hmm?"

"I like that song, but your voice isn't how I imagined it to be."

Mom laughed. "It's better?"

"Oh, no, it's terrible. But it's better because I hear it."

She rested her head against mine, and in that space, I couldn't be mad at Mom for not telling me the truth. I couldn't be mad at Dad, either. They loved me, and that was enough.

"I'm sorry—"

"Hello?" Sam's voice from behind the tapestry cut me off. "Can I come in?"

Oh, no. I wasn't ready for another proposal. I shook my head at Mom to keep her quiet.

She gave me a disapproving look. "In here. Pero's awake."

I groaned. Perhaps I wasn't sorry for my anger toward Mom.

Sam peeked his head around the corner. His eyes sparkled when he saw me. I looked the other way.

"I brought food for both of you," he said.

"Thank you," Mom said, "but I was just about to grab some myself. I think Pero could use what you brought."

Thanks a lot, Mom.

On the tapestry, two black rings circled around a purple

background. In the center was a deeper purple that mesmerized my senses, allowing my body to relax.

Mom left. Sam set down a plate of food on the floor next to me. From the corner of my eye, I saw Sam sit on the floor. I picked up the plate of bread and grapes and took a bite. The bread was soft. I washed it down with a cup of water.

"Are you going to look at me?" Sam asked.

I set the cup down. My gaze landed on his. Brown and deep like a chocolate ocean. His mouth curved into a sly smile. He'd shaved his beard, his cinnamon skin smooth with no scar. I couldn't deny the fast pitter-patter in my chest. I turned back to the tapestry. "No, I'm not." I took another bite of bread and looked away.

Sam cupped my face in his hand and turned it back to him. "I'm sorry." He let go.

I chewed and swallowed. "For what?"

"For jumping on you like I did. I was excited we weren't related, and when Jimmy offered me the land, I wanted you to be a part of it. I couldn't imagine leaving without knowing you more."

Panic escalated. I melted from one look at Sam, but that couldn't determine whether I should marry him.

Sam tucked in a knee and circled his arms around his leg. "I need to know, Pero. I... this is difficult for me to ask, but I want to know that our feelings for each other are mutual, or if... if you are interested in someone else."

I gulped. "Someone else?" He meant Henry.

"Yeah. Is there someone else?"

I should tell him that there was nothing between me and Henry, but was I sure there wasn't? When Henry kissed me, I wanted more time to think about how I felt about Sam. And here Sam was in front of me, and he wasn't my brother, and he was handsome and kind and patient. And he was one of the chosen. His land would be so close to my house. Yet while I was far away from the place I lived, who made me feel more at home?

The answer slammed against me like a heavy weight.

Henry.

I looked at Sam. His eyes darkened to damp mud. As he scanned my face, I let my eyes answer.

I'm drawn to you. I'm one of the chosen with you. But I cannot love you.

Sam's nod confirmed he'd understood.

I tried to make sense of my feelings. Maybe I'd change my mind. Maybe if I left with Sam, I'd forget all about Henry.

Never. Henry was not the type to be forgotten. In a day, the feelings I had for Sam had already lessened.

"Sam." I reached my hand out and placed it on his arm. "I'm ready to be friends."

"Okay." His unsteady voice told me otherwise.

"Ro girl!" From behind the tapestry, I heard Henry enter the tent. "Your mom said you're awake!"

Sam and I stood on impulse, as if to finalize that whatever had been between us was over.

Henry's long feet stuck out from under the tapestry. "Can I come in?"

I walked around the tapestry.

Henry's grin reached his ears. "I'm so glad you're okay. I need to tell you something important."

"Is it about Jimmy?"

"No. Nothing has changed."

Sam stepped out from behind the tapestry.

Henry's countenance grew grim. "Oh."

25

לֵאמוֹר

"Hey, Henry," Sam said. "I was just leaving."

"No, stay." Henry backed up. "I should've realized Pero would have company." He turned.

"Don't go," I said.

Henry turned back around. "As awkward as this is, I can't leave because I need to tell you something."

Sam bolted toward the exit without a glance. "I'll see you two for the march soon."

He was gone before I could tell him "I'm sorry" or "Goodbye" or "I didn't mean to hurt you".

"Are you alright?" Henry asked.

My face must've looked grieved. I turned it into a smile. "What did you want to tell me?"

"Carper's gone."

"What?"

"He must've left last night because he isn't in his tent. The Lesarie guards are both unconscious. It just shows Carper's true nature."

Carper had no place to go, and he wanted to be king too badly to leave. "He didn't run away."

Henry gave me a questioning look. "What makes you think that?"

"The guards in Moon City were after Carper. They want him dead."

"You're sure?"

"Yes, I'm sure. That's how I found Carper in the woods. He was hiding from them." If something happened to him, the prophecies wouldn't be fulfilled.

"You want us to find him, don't you?" Henry asked in a voice that said it wasn't something he wanted to do.

"Yes."

"Why do we need him?" Henry asked.

"It's not about if we need him or not. Believe me, I'd survive without Calvin Carper."

"His name is Calvin?"

"Listen, Henry. Elohim chose Carper to be the king of the Lesarie people in my world. The Lesaries on Earth have asked for a king, and this is Elohim's way of making it happen. Don't ask me what good it will do, but I think that Carper's changed."

Henry put his arms up in surrender. "Hey, I follow you, remember?"

"You follow Elohim."

Henry scratched his chin. "Something's different about you, Pero. You were asleep for more than a day and wake up to be all Shea wise."

I shrugged. "Yeshua's changed me."

"Who's Yeshua?"

"Right." I fidgeted. "No one I know."

Henry gave me a quirky smile. "Will you be ready to leave in ten minutes?"

"Yes, but I think we should invite Sam and my mom. A vision may help us find Carper."

"Do you think they'll be okay with us finding Carper? Especially your mom."

From the strain in Henry's voice, I would've guessed he didn't want Sam to come along. "We need them."

Henry chewed his lip. "I've seen powerful things with the three of you using your gifts, but I want you to remember that Carper's life isn't dependent on your talent but on Elohim's strength. It's Elohim who'll tear down Moon City in two days."

But Elohim had chosen the three for a reason. "You think they shouldn't go?"

Henry shuffled his feet. "Bahar's trauma with Carper and Sam's emotional ties to you may be more of a distraction than help."

I blinked and took a step back. "Distraction? You're the one who kissed me when I tried to find Carper the first time. Are you sure *you* can handle being next to me?"

"I've never been able to handle being next to you, Ro."

His grave tone told me it was a compliment. No, more than a compliment. Perhaps desire.

"You make me weak," Henry said, "in a good way."

My stomach fluttered. I wanted to tuck his words into my heart and let them simmer for a lifetime, but I couldn't forget that Henry liked to flatter. Sam and Mom were the key to us finding Carper and leaving Moon City.

I lifted my head. "Can't have weak people search for an unpredictable king, now, can I?"

His face darkened. "Fine. Take Sam. He *is* stronger."

My heart shrunk. "I didn't mean it that way. It's just when I'm around you, sometimes I say the worst." I dug myself into a deeper hole, and my words were burying me with him. If I didn't stop, he would be too hurt to return.

Tears welled in Henry's eyes. "You think because you're a special chosen that you're more privileged than some pathetic bodyguard. That's all I've been to you."

I shook my head. "No, Henry. You're more than that. I need you."

Emotion stuck in his throat and came through his voice. "Well, I can assure you Elohim loves me just the way I am without needing something from me."

Henry turned toward the exit.

What had I done?

"I ended it with Sam," I called. That had to mean something to him.

Henry stayed with his back toward me. "It seems you've ended it with me, too."

"Henry, wait!"

"You're on your own, Pero." He stomped out and turned his head over his shoulder. "I'm sure it will please Calvin that you and your two companions fed his thirst for power."

My breath hitched. I covered my head. What a fool I was!

Henry stormed away. He was gone, just like that. The last careless word thrown at him because I thought I was more privileged. I massaged my aching heart.

"Elohim, give me a second chance. I can't lose everyone."

Give Carper a second chance.

Could it be that Carper needed someone to show him love just as much as I did? But could I do that at the risk of losing everyone?

Lonely. So, so lonely.

Shea ran up to me. "Pero."

What now?

He stalled. "Are you okay?"

"Why does everyone keep asking me that?" I wiped stray tears. How'd those get there? "Of course, I'm okay."

Shea knelt so that his face was near mine. "Carper's gone. I need you to go with Henry to find him. Can you do that?"

I crossed my arms. Henry would never forgive me.

Shea put his hands on my arms. "Be strong and courageous. Don't be afraid or scared. Elohim, your God Himself is who goes with you. He will not fail you."

I believed him. Elohim was with me, and He was my God. But I couldn't do this. Relationship repair was too messy.

Shea watched my eyes. Connecting. Giving. "Koach to you, daughter."

I shook off his hands. Done. So done. "I can't stand that phrase." A few people peeked their heads out of tents. I didn't care. Let them all hear me.

"What should it mean to me?" I shouted. "That I'm some wonder woman as soon as there's a necklace around me? What does that mean for those who don't wear it? That you're not chosen? That you're weaker?" I took the necklace off and threw it on the ground. I stomped on it and grunted. "There. That's that. I'm Elohim's chosen, but I refuse to be *the* chosen. I'll never wear a symbol if it means that I'm better than who I really am. My name is Pero Ruth Moshe. I'm adopted, used, labeled, but unashamed. And I'll never hide again."

People around clapped.

"We love you for who you are, Pero!" someone yelled out.

I took one look into Shea's wise, compassionate eyes, and I ran.

I ran through the forest, my feet trained to tread on tangled branches and packed, wet dirt. I was done with the attention. Why would they look to me when it was Elohim who'd win for us? It wasn't me.

"I don't want it to be me."

Then be weak.

I stopped and held onto a tree for support. I crumpled under the tree and panted.

"I am weak. Do you hear, Elohim? I can't be strong. I don't want to be."

Peace, like a current, came from the soil and into my whole being. I laughed in His presence. "Is this what weakness feels like? Is this dependence?"

Run home, Pero. I am your home.

I set my forehead on the ground and stayed there. Humbled to nothing. Rising to someone. I sang. "Comin' home, comin' home, comin' home."

The weight of my past shook off like torn up roots. It was as if Elohim's hand reached into me and pulled. Roots of abandonment, gone. Roots of hiding, gone. Roots of heartache, gone.

After a long time in the fetal position, I moved and pushed myself from the ground. I flipped my hair back and brushed wood chips from my face. I felt new. Awake.

I let out a long breath and stopped it when I saw Henry sitting under a tree. His eyes were closed, and he muttered to himself. I recognized his prayer posture. As I stood slowly, his eyes fluttered open.

"How long have you been here?" I asked.

"Shea pointed me toward where you ran. He asked that I follow."

Did he want to follow me, or had he been forced?

"I'm not used to actually stopping on a run with you," he said. "It was a nice change."

I tapped my foot against a log. "I'm sorry for what I said."

"Thank you."

"Will you forgive me?"

He avoided my eyes. "Maybe."

"Maybe, yes?"

Henry went from sitting to up on his feet in one jump. "I'll forgive you for what you said, but I need you to prove to me you mean it."

"I turned down Sam for you, stupid!" I felt a blush travel up my neck.

Henry raised his eyebrows and held back a grin. "You have leaves in your hair."

I brushed my hair and flung a couple of crumpled leaves to the ground.

Henry walked toward Moon City, his smile still lingering. "Let's go find Carper."

That was it? No bringing me into his arms and telling me he adored me? No teasing?

"Are you coming, Pero?"

I scurried to reach him but didn't cut in front. This was *his* journey.

I laughed.

"What's so funny?"

Okay, Elohim. Got it. I'd remain humbled by following. I needed humbling as much as Carper. "Nothing."

"Well, stop messing around and keep up."

I laughed harder. "Do you want to borrow some earbuds? I've got some lit music." I took a deep breath before I snorted.

"A far better sound," he said.

I lost it, bending over in waves of hysterics.

"You keep laughing like that and you'll for sure scare away Carper's kidnappers."

I laughed until I cried at the idea of Carper being kidnapped. Talk about being humbled. "Nope. I'm not doing anything. You're leading this one, baby."

"Did you just call me baby?"

"It fits you." I exploded in laughter. My stomach cramped. I could hardly breathe.

"Hilarious, Ro girl."

"Have I proved that I'm sorry yet?"

"No," he said. "You've proved that you're a very peculiar little lady, and I can't believe I let you lead me all these months."

"Well, I *am* faster." I wiped tears from my eyes and settled my breath.

"We'll see about that." Henry ran fast.

"Hey! No fair!" I sprinted forward until I was a few feet behind him. "What'd you put in my pack? Rocks?"

"Steel."

"Ha!" I panted. "I bet you have feathers in yours."

"Nah." He re-adjusted his pack. "I'm done carrying feathers."

We arrived at the Lesaries' camp and jogged through crowds of people stretching and packing waters and head-dresses. They were getting ready to march.

"Where are you going?" The pretty blonde girl who'd been close to Henry the other night watched us pass by. She looked me up and down and smiled as if she approved.

Henry waved. "We'll be back soon, sis."

"Sis? You have a sister?"

"Yeah, who'd you think she was?"

"Just a very pretty girl," I said.

"You were jealous."

"Very." I emphasized the word, a smile on my lips until we passed Sam. He put water in his bag and glanced at the sound of our pounding feet. His eyes met mine, looked at Henry, then back at me. I smacked into Henry's back. Sam turned away. I rubbed my nose. Henry walked.

"Why'd you slow down?" I asked.

"Because you did," Henry said.

"Sorry." I turned my head one more time. Sam put his pack on and walked the opposite way toward Moon City's wall without a glance.

WE EDGED CLOSER to the side of the wall that wasn't guarded.

"You're sure Carper's back in Moon City?" I asked.

Henry shrugged. "Where else would they take him?"

"Uh. To the forest to kill him? Honestly, we're probably too late."

"Then why are we doing this?" Henry asked.

"Elohim told me to find Carper," I said.

"Well, did He tell you where to go?"

"Nope." I twiddled my thumbs.

"You're a big help."

"I also make a lousy leader," I said. "I don't have any idea what we should do."

"Let's wait for the Lesaries to march and join them."

"Please, no. I can't stand the thought of being next to you when I see Sam again."

"There'll be eight thousand other people, Pero. You probably won't even see him." He kicked the dirt. "Besides, Sam should be used to seeing us together by now."

"Yeah, but now it's different."

"How so?" Henry smiled playfully.

"Oh, come on. You know."

"I have no idea what you're talking about." His expression turned serious.

I put my hands on my hips. "I'm not telling you again. Last time, you laughed at me and said I had to prove myself."

"What do you need to prove?"

"That I...." That I wanted to kiss him. That I didn't want him to leave me. That I might love him.

Henry smiled. "That you what?"

"I...." I couldn't say it. "Dang you, Henry!"

Henry laughed.

"Hey!" a man called from the top of the roof.

I jumped. Henry stepped in front of me.

"Why are you the only Lesaries today?" The man on the roof crossed his arms. No visible weapon. "Did the rest run away?"

I cupped my hands and shouted. "We're looking for Dr. Carper."

Henry covered his ears. "Too loud," he whispered. "And you forgot to say Calvin."

I elbowed him.

"Aren't you Pero?" the man asked.

"Nope." Yikes.

"Way to go," Henry muttered.

"No matter," the man on the roof yelled. "Without Carper, you're nothing."

"What do you mean without Carper?" I shouted.

Henry covered my wrist with his hand as if I were being arrested. "Where is he?"

"Carper's dead."

26

רְחִימוּ

Dread and joy bolted through me at the same time. Was Carper really dead?

"How?" Henry asked the man on the roof.

"Why would I tell you?" He shooed us with his hand. "Now go away before I decide to hurt you."

Henry pulled me from the wall, his fingers moving from my wrist and to my hand. With Carper dead, no one else in Moon City would survive when the walls fell. And I couldn't just let the Warriors die.

What do I do, Elohim? There must be a way to save them.

"I think we need to help the people of Moon City leave," I said.

Henry shook his head. "They won't come. I've been to battles before. They never surrender."

"But they're hiding from us. Isn't that surrender?"

Henry squeezed my hand. "Hiding is defeat."

All those years that I'd hid, was I really living as if I'd already been caught? Dad's best intentions to keep me safe lasted for fourteen years, but how much did I miss because I hadn't fully lived?

"What if Moon City could get away?" I asked.

"Then what's the point of a battle?"

We wouldn't fight this battle to destroy lives but to bring peace. Mom, Cathena, Jimmy, and Carper were rescued, but thousands would die. It wasn't fair.

In the distance, the Lesaries marched toward Moon City, starting on the opposite side of us.

"Let's join," Henry said.

"Don't you wonder?" I asked.

"Wonder what?"

"If the man was lying about Carper. Elohim wouldn't have told me to find Carper if he was dead."

"Maybe it wasn't Elohim who talked to you."

Elohim's voice was distinct from my own thoughts, like coherent words spoken from an inner voice that was not my own. "I think it's Elohim. And Elohim chose Carper. He has to be valuable for something."

"He's good at killing," Henry said.

Ahead, a flash of red swept from tree to tree. I blocked the sun from my eyes and squinted.

"What are you looking at?" Henry asked.

I pointed. "There. Through those trees. I saw someone."

"It's probably a Lesarie."

"I've never seen a Lesarie wear red, and this is the opposite side of the camp."

The same red figure darted to another tree. Two more figures followed. "Look! There's more."

Henry followed my eyes. "I don't see anyone."

"I'm going to check it out." I walked toward the forest.

Henry put his hand on my arm. "Ro."

"I'm done waiting. I've been waiting my whole life."

He sighed. "I'm right behind you."

"Don't be."

Henry put his hands up. "What do you want from me, Pero?

You've proved you can let me lead, and honestly, I love it when you lead because you're fearless. But tell me where I belong with you? Do you want me to follow or stay behind?"

Fearless. He called me fearless. Oh, how I wanted to be!

"I want you to go with me." I squeezed his hand. "To be beside me."

He pushed my hair back with his hand. "Okay. But can you go with me sometimes?"

"It depends on where you want to go."

Could this work between us if we both wanted to go different places?

"I'm following those invisible people in red over there." Henry nudged his head. "And I want to help you find Carper. Then I want to tear down a wall. And then I want to take you home."

I swallowed at what he might be implying. He'd drop me off with Dad and leave, just like Mom. "You'll stay in Origo?"

Henry brought my hand up to his lips and kissed it. When he sighed, his breath on my hand traveled from my fingertips and up my arm. "My family's here. I've already been away from them for so long, and you have one more year of high school to finish."

A fate I didn't want to remember.

"But I've found a way for us to communicate," he said. "A code on our phones lets us call extra-long distance. I tried it a couple times when I was on Earth, and it works. When the year is over, I'll return to you."

I turned my head, a familiar feeling rising in my throat. "You won't come back. My mom never did. You can't promise something you don't know."

He cupped my chin in his hand and turned my face toward him. "You're right. I can't. But I can promise that no matter the distance between us, I'll always be by your side." He placed my hand on his chest. "Right here."

His heart beat an unsteady rhythm that dysregulated my own.

"Okay, Ro girl. Let's go save Cal man."

I beamed. "You're good at coming up with nicknames, Hen."

He winked. "You're lousy at it."

I laughed.

We ran toward the woods, ducking our heads to hide ourselves in the tall grass. When we were at the edge, I hid behind one tree and Henry behind another. *This way*, I mouthed and pointed.

We scurried between trees and took breaks to hide behind each one. Just as I was about to step out again, Henry motioned for me to stop and put a finger to his lips. I peeked through the branches of the tree.

Carper walked into view, another man in red holding onto his arm. His hands were tied behind his back, his face covered in bruises. I sucked in a breath. Part of me was glad to see payback for the pain Carper inflicted on far too many. The other strange part of me wanted him to be okay.

"We've been over here already, Carper." I recognized the man in red as the Moon City guard with the beard who wanted to kill Carper. "If you don't find it in the next five minutes, you're done."

"I swear it was over here," Carper said. "Let me focus so I can think."

The female guard who'd been on the roof came into view.

"I think you've done enough thinking. You're just buying time."

The first guard held out a gun. "Where's the door, Carper?"

A door? Why would they be looking for a door in the woods? I covered my mouth. The door to the other world. Carper searched for the hollow tree that Mom escaped through with me.

"It doesn't work that way." Carper gritted his teeth. "I told you it may not be here. The door is only available at certain times. I don't know why."

"You mean it just appears randomly?" the woman asked.

"Exactly."

The bearded guard holding Carper grabbed his ear and twisted while pulling down. Carper groaned. The guard held him there. "I don't believe you. Nothing grows instantly."

Unless you possessed a gift for growing things. At least Carper couldn't see Sam's vision. But wait. He did see Sam healed.

"I've got it! I've got it!" Carper shouted.

The man let go. "Got what?"

"I know someone who can make it grow."

No! Don't say it. I eyed Henry. He shook his head to warn me not to intervene.

"Talk faster, Carper," the bearded guard said. "Your time is up."

"It's Pero's boyfriend," Carper said in a hurry. "I think she said his name is Sam."

Henry raised his eyebrows. I put my finger to my lips to keep him quiet.

"And how does this Sam make things grow?" The guard scratched his beard.

Keep your mouth shut, Carper. But of course, he wouldn't. He cared more about his own life. Why had I saved him only to see my friends' lives threatened?

"I think it's his power," Carper said. "He's one of the chosen."

I closed my eyes. It was over. It was all over.

"Can we trust him?" the woman asked.

"We'll find Sam and see for ourselves," the bearded guard said.

"I suggest you move quickly," Carper said. "The walls will fall in two days."

The man lowered his gun and slapped Carper. "Shut up."

Carper spit saliva and blood on the ground. He looked at the man as if he did not feel threatened in the least bit.

"Come on," the woman said. "We need to find Sam."

I should bring them to Sam. Then Henry could run off to warn him and it would buy Sam more time to figure out a plan or hide. I motioned to Henry that he should leave.

He shook his head.

Go, I mouthed. *I'll stay*. I pointed my finger at myself. *I'll find Sam*. I pointed to them.

What? he mouthed and put his hands up in a question.

I shook my head. This was ridiculous. My last moment with Henry would be spent playing charades.

I put my hand on my chest, made my fingers walk in the air, and pointed to them. I pointed to Henry and made my fingers walk away, then pointed toward Moon City.

Henry shook his head at me, his eyes wide. *No*.

I shrugged. *It's the only way*.

No, he mouthed again.

I should listen to him. Maybe Henry's plan was better. I crossed my arms. Waiting was so hard. I laid my head back on the tree. An acorn fell and landed at my feet.

Uh-oh.

"What was that?" the woman asked.

"Probably a stick or something," beard man said, "but check it out just in case."

I looked at Henry.

Nice going, he mouthed.

I was getting good at reading lips, but I was terrible at staying quiet. My drumming heart and chattering lips confirmed it to be true. And the acorn hadn't helped. We'd have to go through with my plan. There was no use in having both me and Henry caught.

Henry slowly dropped his pack. I did the same. He pointed

at me and put his hand out for me to stay and pointed at me again and then at them. He pointed to himself, then the other direction, and he made his arms move swiftly as if he were running. Then he held out three fingers.

I gave him a thumbs up. We would countdown from three, then I would expose myself while Henry ran away. *Brilliant, Henry. If only I'd thought of a plan as great as that one.* I should give him the credit.

I love you.

Did I imagine Henry's mouth formed those words? But his eyes confirmed what his lips said without a voice.

Did I love him? I thought I did, but when it came to forming the words, they stuck on my tongue until they dissolved.

Henry broke our trance with three held out fingers.

Two.

One.

Go.

"I'll take you to Sam!" I stepped out of the clearing with my hands up in surrender.

The man aimed his gun at me.

Henry ran off in a flash.

The man turned his gun toward Henry.

No. No! I love him!

There it was. I loved Henry Beggs. But during the split second between the gun being aimed at me, then at him, my chance to tell him was shot down.

Two explosions filled the air. Carper screamed like a girl. So did I.

27

לְהַצִּיל

Henry ran out of view. I turned around to find the two guards on the ground, dead. A different man with white hair aimed his gun at me.

I screamed again, my body trembling. Who was this man? Where'd he come from?

"How'd you get here, Rose?" I could've sworn I heard a tremble in Carper's voice. The guards felt like jokes compared to this man who didn't resemble or smell like a rose but whose gray eyes were as sharp as thorns. From one look, I could sense this man didn't just threaten to kill but took action. And now my company included a killer and supposed ex-killer.

Rose held out his gun toward Carper, his muscles steady, his aim well-rehearsed. "Hǎo jiǔ bu jiàn."

Was that Chinese?

"Put down the gun, Rose, and we'll talk."

Rose aimed the gun at me. "Not until you tell me who this is. She's pretty, Carper. A little young for you, though, don't you think?"

"You'll leave Pero out of this," Carper said.

He was protecting me! I could hug him. But then I noticed

the slight shake of Carper's head, as if he was ashamed that an unruly teen took over his spotlight.

"Pero, huh?" Rose's lips curved into a slight smile. "Congratulations on finding her, Carper. But I've got to say, she doesn't look anything like her mom."

Thanks for the reminder.

"The guy who took off before I shot these two clowns," Rose said. "Was he the third chosen?"

So, this mysterious, older man knew Carper and his agendas well. Had he helped Carper capture us?

"That's none of your business," Carper said. "And you still haven't answered how you're here. When we left through the portal from your home on Earth, you weren't there. We both know the door's never opened for you."

"Relax." Rose lowered his gun as if that would show Carper he'd relax, too. "You always were uptight. I've been on Origo for years, waiting for this moment. Not everyone believed you were dead on Earth. Thanks to the very detailed notes you left behind in the lab, I found you quite easily."

Carper growled. "What do you want, Rose?"

Rose's intense stare made me think I'd see thorns shoot from out of his eyes after his next blink.

"The same thing these fools were after. I want the chosen."

He turned his icy stare at me, and I shuddered as if thorns pierced my skin.

"You're not scared of him, are you, child?" Rose asked me. "Your mom wasn't either until she became one of Carper's many girlfriends."

Carper took a step forward. "I said to leave her out of this."

Rose lifted his gun again, and Carper took two steps back. "I'm in charge now. You hear? You've made your fame and fortune, and now that your mighty Moon City is under some strange ring-around-the-rosie attack, it's my turn."

Rose pulled my left hand behind me with the strength of

someone who could rip a book in half. Could he rip people? There was no need for him to pull so hard. I'd thrown myself at his feet, begging to be tortured.

He tied my hands tighter than Cathena had. I bit my lip and closed my eyes on tears that fell. Rose's fingers scraped at my skin around my neck. I yelped from the sting.

"Where's the necklace?" he asked.

"I don't have it." Good thing I threw it on the ground during my fit with Shea.

He mumbled something in an unfamiliar language, then knelt at my feet. "Give me your foot."

I struggled to balance while Rose pulled off my shoe and shook it. He threw it on the ground and pulled off my sock. So detailed. He held his hand out for me to offer my other foot. I set my bare foot on the cold ground. He threw the other shoe and stood. "Where is it?"

"I got rid of it."

Rose pushed me to the ground, hard. "You're nothing without your power, just like your mom."

Tears now dripped down my chin. "You're right. I am nothing without power, but it's not my own. It's Elohim's."

Rose laughed hard and loud, then lifted the gun and pointed it toward me. "I don't care where you get the power. I need you to take me to the other two chosen."

I no longer cared who took us next. It didn't matter when Elohim could do much scarier things than whatever power Rose hoped to gain through us. And besides, walls were about to fall. Surely Elohim stirred some big plans.

"I'll help you find them," I said. "But only on two conditions."

Rose raised a brow.

"You will untie my hands and you will release Carper."

Rose scratched his head. "I'll untie you, but I'm not releasing Carper."

Rose pulled out a knife and sawed at the rope. My hand burned as the knife grazed against my skin. The rope pulled away, and I rubbed my wrists. The slight cut stung.

"Get up!" Rose said.

I wiped the tears from my face. Why was I so upset about this? I'd seen a gun in my face on more than one occasion in the last couple of weeks. Perhaps exhaustion set in from being pushed around with no deliverance. Two days could not come fast enough. "I'm getting my shoes on."

Through my tears, I tugged the shoes toward my feet, but I hesitated when my wrists burned at every slight movement.

Rose huffed. "Carper, get her shoes on!"

Carper rushed to my side and nuzzled my feet into the shoes, as if I was the precious little girl he'd longed to care for.

"You're taking too long," Rose said.

Carper left my shoelaces untied. Lifting my hands, Carper examined them, made a soft clucking sound, then pulled me up. More tears threatened to spill. Did Carper really care for me?

"I see," Rose said. "Pero's not scared of Carper because he's softened. How sweet."

His tone of voice told me he'd use Carper's weak persona against him. He'd better toughen up to his normal lovely self or we'd all be dead.

"Carper's not my friend. He's hurt me too many times." That could be true.

"The Lesaries are marching around Moon City now," Carper said. "Sam and Bahar are with them. I suggest we wait at the camp for them to return."

"My necklace is at the camp," I said.

"Fine," Rose said. "We'll go there first."

I sure do hope I was hearing you, Elohim.

The flop of my untied shoes was the only reply.

THE LESARIES' absence in the camp brought an emptiness I couldn't figure out. Did a place become full of energy because of the life people brought to it?

"Get your necklace," Rose said to me.

I bit my lip. "I don't know where it is."

"You're the one who took it off."

Glancing at Carper, I braced myself for a laugh. "I threw it on the ground somewhere over there." I motioned with my head. "It's completely smashed."

Carper didn't laugh. In fact, his face grew dimmer, like his old self waited to emerge.

"You know, that was your only chance to escape," Rose said. "I guess you're not going back."

I guess he didn't know that Elohim took me places, not a wooden feather. "Guess that means you're not going through any doors. Can't have visions without all three of us wearing the necklaces."

"Carper caught you, and I found my way here."

"I wore the necklace," I said.

Rose kneed Carper in the groin. Carper doubled over. Why be punished for my bad news? Wait. Maybe I could live with this.

"Look for it, Pero." Rose put a hand on the gun attached to his belt. "Don't try anything that Carper would do."

Carper groaned on the ground. He'd hate me later. Not that he didn't already.

I thought of Jimmy. He wouldn't be marching with the Lesaries because of his injury. I should bring up that he'd been here. Never mind. Bad idea. But I could go to his tent to "find the necklace" and warn him. If he looked well enough, maybe he'd know what to do.

"Shea probably has the necklace in his tent." I pointed toward Jimmy's tent with a shaky finger.

"Then go!"

I walked into the clearing. Dry grass fluttered against my feet. I heard the snap of a twig and turned. Rose followed from a distance. I imagined his fingers creeping up like spider legs, crawling onto my neck and sinking into my skin.

Focus, Pero. Koach.

I picked up my pace. The sooner I left Rose, the better I'd breathe. Unless he followed me inside.

I arrived at Jimmy's tent. "I'm searching for the necklace." Could Rose hear the tremor in my voice?

"Five minutes." He shifted his head back and forth like the eagle.

I nodded and stepped in. Jimmy's mat, gone. Jimmy, too. Maybe he hadn't made it and the Lesaries buried him. My eyes watered. I couldn't jump to conclusions.

"Stop!" Rose's voice said from outside. "What's your name?"

"It's Sam."

Great shrimpers! What was Sam thinking?

"Sam Nesim? Is that really you?"

Apparently, everyone but me knew Mr. Rose.

"Good to see you too, Uncle," Sam said. "I hear you're looking for me."

"Right. We'll save the hugs for later."

Some family reunion.

"I want to trade," Sam said.

Trading for me wouldn't work when Rose wanted all three of the chosen. *Why'd you come, Sam?*

"You can't have her," Rose said.

"Not Pero," Sam said. "Carper."

"Nope. I'm keeping Carper."

"What's Carper to you? He won't get you where you want to be. If you take me and Pero, I can use my gift to grow a door to

Earth and then we'll be on our way and Carper will suffer by himself with a destroyed city."

Maybe Sam was on to something. With a trade, we could go home and Carper would get what he deserved. But without Mom? And Elohim wanted Carper to come with us.

I heard the click of a trigger. What an uncle! "I need all three of you for my plan to work."

"Let go of Carper, Mr. Rose," Mom's voice said, "and the three chosen are all yours."

Mom knew Rose also. When all of this ended, I needed one long backstory. Now, I just wanted Henry to pop out from behind a tent and volunteer to join, but his voice didn't come.

"Pero!" Rose called.

I stepped out of the tent with my hands out as I'd seen in movies. Did the actors shake as much as I did? Mom and Sam were there. I didn't need to be so nervous. Maybe my nerves came from a gun pointed toward me, or because going home might not be as smooth as tapping my untied shoes together.

Mom stood at attention, her fighting stick ready at her feet. Sam stared at me as if he thought me more beautiful than his memories told him. I wanted to apologize for letting him down.

"Without you," Rose said, "Carper is limited. And thanks to Carper, I have access to all of his lab. But what about the necklaces?"

Sam took off a necklace. "Here's Pero's." A piece of the feather pendant hung in the other direction. It was mine, for sure.

"Give it to her," Rose said.

Sam held out the necklace and dropped it into my outstretched hand. He looked at me. His eyes didn't look pained like earlier that day. Instead, they were confident.

"Show your necklaces." Rose nodded toward Sam and Mom. They showed their keys to a place I didn't want to go without Henry.

"Your power exceeds Carper's." Rose's smile traveled up on one side of his face. "Deal."

The reality of the transaction punched me in the gut. We were being taken. Again. Who knows what he'd do to us? I wouldn't see Dad, nor Henry. Maybe I wouldn't want to if it meant their lives were in danger. I'd go back to Earth but not home. I'd been sold to Mr. Rose.

28

לָשִׁיר

ose kicked Carper in the stomach. Carper crumpled to the ground. His chest heaved in and out in big breaths. What a way for the Lesaries to find their king! Maybe it would soften the news to see him curled up and surrendered. But how would Carper be king of the Lesaries in the other world if he couldn't get there?

Rose looked in the distance toward Moon City. The Lesaries marched around the city. I strained to hear the pattern of their feet. *Thump. Thump. Thump, thump.* Scattered, not uniform.

"We need to move," Rose said. "Quickly."

"Where would you like me to grow a door for you?" Sam asked. "I can grow one anywhere."

How could he be so sure?

"Doesn't matter where," Rose said. "Just do it before the Lesaries come back."

"The thing is." Sam scratched his forehead. "I need the other two chosen in order for it to work."

That couldn't be right. While I played guitar in my closet, Sam grew all kinds of entrances and exits to universes. But did I play guitar at the same time he grew things? Even without the necklace? And did Mom practice her jumps and kicks with her stick at the same time?

"No surprises," Rose said. "You already ran away from me once."

This must've been the uncle who Sam talked about before, the one Sam ran away from when threatened.

"You have my word," Sam said.

Mom's eyes darted in my direction. She gave a slight nod. If Mom could trust Sam, so would I.

"I need to grab a guitar for Pero," Sam said. "Bahar will need your permission to use her staff." Sam raised his hands up to emphasize caution. "She won't hurt you. I promise."

"I believe you," Rose said. "I've known Bahar for a long time. Get on with it, then."

Mom picked up her stick and balanced it on her hands. Closing her eyes, she let out a deep breath.

Sam ran to a fire pit. The last of the ashes trailed a thin line of smoke into the air. He grabbed a guitar propped on a log. Sam ran to me and handed it over. The guitar weighed more than what I was used to holding. It was made of rough, dark wood. Rustic. Beautiful for its simplicity. I plucked a string. It had recently been tuned. The sound made a throaty growl.

"Where'd you get this?" I whispered.

Sam dropped his eyes. "I made it."

My mouth flew open. "It's gorgeous. Do you play?"

I wrapped the leather strap over my shoulder and held the guitar's body against me, readying my fingers on the bar.

"I made it for Henry." Sam's face turned light pink.

I felt my cheeks do the same. Sam and Henry were good friends for a while, and I'd ruined their friendship.

"I didn't know Henry played." If we still had a chance together, maybe we could go on a real date to ask each other twenty questions. But after I left, we'd have to resort to extra-long-distance phone calls. Would I have a phone wherever

Rose took me? My lungs constricted. Would I have anything at all?

"What should I play?" I asked.

Sam cleared his throat. "Focus on Elohim. Sing to Him, and you'll know what to play."

I'd written a few songs, but never in front of an audience or spontaneously.

Sam leaned closer so that only I could hear. "It's not the necklace that brings you power."

My eyes widened. Elohim was the power. It must've been more than three who were chosen to display His power. Weren't all of Elohim's people chosen? And Carper could see the visions because Elohim allowed him to. It had always been Elohim.

I hovered my right hand over the sound hole, as if it could tell me what to play. My mind played out a melody. *Da-da-da.* The notes resembled Mom and Dad calling out my name, Jimmy begging for a longer life, Henry telling me he loved me. *Da-da-da.* Like a baby's first words. Like learning a new language. Yeshua's language.

"Yeshua."

His name was all I needed to sing. Yeshua: the beginning of strength, of hope, of the greatest rescue I'd ever known. He'd pulled me from hiding and into a light so marvelous that I could only taste it and savor its goodness.

The sky darkened. Fire burst into flame on the fire pit. I puffed out a breath when my body recognized an enveloping presence.

Elohim was here.

Mom opened her eyes—her hands still balancing her stick —and smiled.

I played full chords and focused on the melody of the guitar as I hummed and sang, "Ye-shu-a, Ye-shu-a."

Rose dropped his gun and covered his ears. "You can't say that name!"

The darkness and fire evaporated, like someone slurped them up into the sky with a giant straw.

Carper still laid curled up in a ball, covering his face with his hands as he wept. "What have I done? What have I done?" he repeated.

"Enough, Carper!" Rose shouted, but the hold on his gun weakened as his hands shook like a billowing storm.

"It's the only way," Sam said.

"Fine!" Rose put his hands over his ears again.

What power! What intense, wonderful power that came from His name!

Pero.

And yet He still called me.

I let go of my guitar and let the strap carry it around my shoulders. With hands raised to the sky, I reached for Yeshua.

I only wanted to say His name. All I knew was that I loved Him.

"Yeshua," I sang. "Yeshua. I love you."

Learning a new language started out simple. Syllables joined with sounds, and I found my heart connecting the words. My soul longed to learn them before my mind did. The words stirred.

What do I sing to you, Yeshua?

You've told them who I am. Now watch what I'll do.

The darkness settled; the fire lit up. Sparks flew into the sky like fireworks, His presence exploding. I played hard on my guitar, and Mom threw her stick into the feair and caught it. With acute focus, she moved her legs and arms to the twirl of the stick in a kind of dance. A tear appeared on her cheek like dew on the morning's grass. She resembled the eagle, soaring, flapping, reaching, longing. The heartache stirred in her swing. The pound of her staff on the ground thudded in praise. She stomped it again, and the earth shook. I beat my guitar as a duet. The heavy sound of the guitar roared like thunder; the strike of Mom's staff bolted like lightning.

Boom. Boom. Boom. A perfect storm had awakened.

The staff landed. A crack in the ground moved swiftly, right underneath where Carper laid. He jolted and eyed the crack until it stopped where Sam waited on his knees.

"What happened?" Rose asked.

Sam's empty hands cupped on the ground. "An offering. I need an offering."

Give him your guitar.

That's what Sam waited for. But why? I lifted the strap over my head and brought it to Sam.

Sam touched the guitar. "Perfect." He moved it aside and dug into the crack in the ground with his fingers.

"What are you doing?" I asked.

"Planting a tree." He gripped the dirt with his fingers, and it moved and sputtered at his touch.

Why would Elohim accept carved wood to open a door? Why would He let the door open if the enemy would lead us through?

Mom rushed over to where Sam knelt and dug.

I knelt next to both of them. "Let me help you."

Our fingers worked. Scooping, digging. The moist soil stuck to our fingers. Rose watched us work as if we sculpted something never previously seen. In a way, we did.

Someone else's fingers entered our cluster. Carper wiped his eyes with his sleeve and snorted up snot. His bloody bandage matched the smear under his nose. Mom moved away from him a smidge. Carper looked at her with sorrow, like a murderer at his own trial, begging for a second chance. Would she answer? Or did it hurt too much? She met my gaze for a few seconds, then dropped her focus to the ground. A second later, she scooted back over to where she'd been and brushed arms with Carper.

"Carper, get out of there!" Rose called.

Carper stopped digging and stared at the hole. More tears dripped on the mud. Had he changed so much?

Sam looked up. "Let him help us. It'll make this go faster."

No one spoke. Carper glanced at Sam, then put his fingers back to work.

With our tears moistening the soil, we dug without a word. Our hands made a deep and long hole.

Sam placed the guitar in the hole. I wanted to mourn. The ground would swallow a beautiful instrument and form a portal I didn't want to go through.

We buried the guitar, clustered around the mound, and waited.

"What if it doesn't work?" I whispered.

"Faith, Pero," Sam said.

I thought of myself on the wall's edge, ready to leap onto the roof of the mansion. I'd stepped forward in the most obvious direction and believed an answer would come. Elohim stopped me before my fall. Was that faith?

The mount shivered. The ground spit out dirt.

"Move!" Rose shouted.

We scattered back.

A sprout shot out of the ground. White, then tan, then green. Small. Insignificant. It grew like a plant filmed in time lapse. The leaves blossomed and multiplied like butterfly wings. Up. Down. More leaves. Up and up. Bark formed and grew strong. Branches traveled like tiny spider legs. When it had matured, the tree stopped its rapid growing. It was not a hollow tree like Mom had walked in on the day she found me. Light emanated from the tree in the shape of a door.

"Open it," Rose said.

Sam paused, then pushed it open. Bright light poured on our faces.

Carper backed up, then ran away toward Moon City. Rose charged toward Sam and pushed him through the door. I shielded my eyes. Sam disappeared. My turn.

My gaze set once more toward Moon City. I'd never see it again. I never wanted to. But would I ever see the Lesaries again?

"Come on, Pero." Mom pulled on my hand.

I yanked it away. "I don't want to go. The battle hasn't ended."

"It will end. Even if we don't see it."

"Henry hasn't come."

"We'll find him," Mom said. "This is our way back home. The door doesn't open unless we're supposed to go through it."

I shook my head. "This can't be the way, Mom. I refuse to be locked up in another cage."

I planted my feet. My eyes searched for Henry. In the distance, the Lesaries marched back toward the camp. They'd be here soon, but not fast enough.

"He's dead!" someone called from a distance.

Who's dead?

When I turned toward the tree, my eyes adjusted to the light. Only Rose remained.

"Now!" Rose grabbed my arm and pulled.

Elohim, this can't be the answer.

"Henry!" *Where are you?*

I leaned my whole body back. My shoes skidded on the ground. I fell and grimaced at the pain in my tailbone. Rose grabbed my ear and tugged.

My cry lessened as I saw him. So did my hold. "Henry."

He ran faster than the eagle flew. "Ro!"

"I don't want to go!"

Rose pulled me closer to the door.

Henry grabbed my arm, held onto me, and leaned back. They played a game of tug-a-war with me as the rope. We staggered from Rose's hold. My knees scrapped along the ground. He stood on the threshold. I narrowed my eyes. So bright. His hand loosened its hold on my arm, and Henry and I fell. Rose grabbed hold of Henry's foot and dragged him toward the door. Before I could call out his name, it pulled Henry away from my hand, into the light, and through the door. Rose reached for me, but the light faded in a flash, and only a tree without a door remained.

I touched the tree.

The ones I loved, gone.

29

———

לְהַחְלִיט

I placed both hands on the tree and closed my eyes. Maybe I could pray them back. Maybe I could pray myself there. Henry came to rescue me, and then left.

I looked at the clear, blue sky. "I sang your name, Yeshua! You said to watch what you would do."

A normal-sized eagle flew across the horizon.

"Is that a sign?" I yelled to the sky. A symbol of me as a feather? Stuck? Powerless?

"I'm sorry," Carper's voice said.

I moved my head back down and examined the bark that my hands still pressed against. No light.

Sorry, Dad. I tried.

I turned to Carper. His expression softened, and he sighed. Was it just my imagination or did Carper feel sympathetic?

"They're all gone." Carper's voice broke. "It's all my fault."

I leaned against the tree and folded my arms. "Don't be so dramatic."

Carper's shoulders drooped. "Your boy... your friend..."

Thank you very much.

"He told me right before he ran off to save you that the

Lesaries carried Jimmy on a cot around the wall. Jimmy wanted to march with them. He died during the march."

The world slowed down to smash my heart. He couldn't be. He had to be okay.

"Pero?"

Carper came back into focus.

"Will you forgive me?" he asked.

Carper—the man who'd killed Jimmy, made Mom his concubine, broke my family, hurt me and many, many more—asked for my forgiveness. I thought I could forgive him. I'd said it so easily before.

"I can't." My tone was deep, my teeth gritted. "You killed him."

Tears sprung to my eyes at the image. The Lesaries supported Jimmy through his last breath. After so many years as a prisoner, he was finally free.

"I understand." He squatted and put his fingers together, deep in thought.

I watched the Lesaries walk closer. It didn't matter. Henry was gone, Jimmy dead.

After a long and uncomfortable pause, Carper spoke. "I told your friend—"

"His name is Henry."

"Okay," Carper said. "I told Henry that there may be a way to save Jimmy."

My eyes flew up to his. "Don't mock." A tear fell then. Quickly, as if taking off before more followed.

"I'm not mocking, Pero. That's why Henry ran after you. In one room in the mansion, there's an opening to a dark hole that can take you to the other world. Usually, the door is locked. But one time it wasn't."

"Is that the time you came to find me and ruined my life?" I couldn't hope again or handle more dying dreams. Even if Carper spoke in a gentle tone.

Carper's throat bobbed up and down. "Yes."

I shook my head and smeared my tears away. "Leave me alone, Carper. You've taken enough."

"Let me finish."

I tugged at my necklace. Had I not left through the door because Carper needed a friend?

"The door opened because of your mom." His eyes searched mine. "Her necklace brought me to you."

I shook my head. "Elohim must've done it. My mom doesn't have that kind of power."

"I think we can get you home, Pero."

Maybe we could, but the necklace wouldn't fit the lock. "Why help me?"

"Because it's where you belong. And we'll bring Jimmy with us."

I grimaced. "Bring his body? Don't you think he deserves to be buried here? Why drag him somewhere he doesn't belong?"

"Because his old body waits for him on Earth."

I gasped. "You don't think he'd be alive again."

"I do think so."

"How?"

"That's the way it's always worked. When we leave one universe, our bodies are left behind until we return. And that's the way we'll find your mom."

"But my mom wasn't in Green Meadow."

"She's in another part of Earth," Carper said. "That's where Rose is headed. I'll lead you to her. We'll get your mom back and your boyfriends."

"Please, don't start that again."

"I meant your friends who are boys." He put his hands up. "I won't judge."

"I'll go with you, but I won't need the necklace."

"Why not?"

"Whenever I worship Elohim," I said, "He makes things happen."

"So, we need to sing?"

"We need to worship by doing what He has given us gifts to do. What's your gift, Carper?"

He crinkled his nose. "I don't know. I guess inventing things."

"Okay then. Maybe you can worship with your inventions instead of killing. But if we are to worship with our gifts before Moon City is gone, we better get on it. Only one day left."

The Lesaries came trickling into the camp. Some eyed us and the new tree in suspicion.

"Aren't you Pero?" one boy asked. Three other kids stood behind him with wide eyes.

"Uh, yeah."

"Where'd the tree come from? Is it true that you can really fly?"

"Uh—" I'd never babysat. What do you say to kids? Isn't it best to tell them the truth? I would've liked to have known the truth about myself as a kid. At least I could've spent my life wondering about my birth parents.

"Leave her alone now." Carper shooed them with his hand.

Okay, don't answer the children. That's one way.

"Who are you?" the boy asked Carper. "Did you plant this tree?"

A large hand rested on the boy's shoulder. The boy looked up at Shea. His eyes bulged, and he ran off, his friends in tow.

"Do you always scare kids away?" I smiled.

Shea's face was grim.

My smile faded.

"Both of you, come with me," Shea said.

Carper and I glanced at each other and followed Shea to his tent. Shea bent his back so that his head didn't hit the top and pointed to two mats nearby. "Have a seat."

Carper sat with a groan. I lowered myself carefully to avoid pressing on my sore ribs and tailbone.

Shea sighed as he plopped on the mat. He grabbed a cloth and wiped sweat from his neck, face, and beard. Picking up three wooden cups nearby, he poured water for each of us from a wooden pitcher. I looked for a symbol or signature that'd mark it as Sam's work but found nothing.

"I saw Henry without Pero," Shea said. "Bahar and Sam left with him."

Intricately designed rugs covered the ground. I studied the red and blue pattern.

"Where'd they go?" Shea asked.

He didn't ask about the tree. There could be money growing from the branches, yet it seemed he wouldn't ask.

"Did you see the tree out there?" Carper asked.

Shea took a drink of water, never pulling his brown gaze from Carper. He held it in his hands and waited.

"They're inside the tree." Carper sipped from his cup with his pinky out, as if he were having tea with the queen. "Two Moon City guards took them instead of me. It was Sam's idea."

"Elohim grew it?" Shea looked at me.

I stared back but didn't try to speak. I didn't want to cry or have another necklace-stomping fit, and Carper didn't seem to mind doing all the talking.

"Yes," Carper said. "With Sam's gift of growing."

"And Elohim changed you?" Shea asked Carper as he patted his heart.

Tears sprung to Carper's eyes.

"I see." Shea looked at me again. What did he see in my eyes? Unforgiveness? Pain? I'd met with Yeshua Himself, yet I still squeezed bitterness with a closed hand. That's how it felt inside, like a hand pulsed a large lump of play dough underneath my rib. I didn't want to let go.

Shea looked to the ceiling and nodded his head as if I'd read him my diary. "What's your plan?"

From my peripheral vision, Carper waited for me to talk. My ears burned.

"Tell him, Pero," Carper said.

I sighed. "Carper and I will take Jimmy to a room in Carper's mansion that could lead us home. Jimmy will live because his body is in the younger universe." Another breath. "I will be home with my dad. Carper will establish himself as king of the Lesaries."

"You forgot the most important part," Carper said. "We're not going to Green Meadow. They're in China."

I sneered. "I don't believe you."

"It's the place I made the lì plants."

"Everything is made in China," I said.

Carper picked at his nails. "If you watched the news at all, you would've already known I'm telling the truth."

"If you hadn't taken my mom, I wouldn't have been sheltered and could've watched the news." I didn't dare look at Shea. His calm face would surely tell me to relax.

"We'll find Pero's mom and friends," Carper said. "It'll work out."

"You don't know that."

"Yes, I do," Carper said. "A great power will be at work."

I pulled the necklace off and held the pendant. The feather dangled by one piece of wood. Only a minor break, and it'd be ruined. "This necklace is a joke. I have no power with it. I'm nobody special." I snapped it in half. "Still want me to tag along?"

Carper shook his head. "Not that power, stupid."

I jerked my head in surprise. "You should be nicer now, Calvin."

"And you should forgive me now." Carper stared at me. "Pero."

I swallowed. An immature, murderous man compared me to him. "I need time."

"So do I."

We entered a staring contest. Carper blinked first. Ha! I won. Yet it didn't feel so good.

"Maybe you shouldn't go with me if you can't trust me," Carper said.

"I do trust you, at least at the moment. I just don't know if I like you yet."

Carper chuckled. "I don't know if I like you yet either."

"You'll both leave tomorrow morning." Shea stood, ducked his head, and took giant steps for the door.

My head spun toward him. "What?"

"Shea, with all due respect, we need to leave now," Carper said. "Before the walls fall."

Shea looked back and forth between us. "If Elohim provides an open door, there's time. Right now, you need food and rest and a good scrub." He turned on his heel and ducked out of the tent. "You leave tomorrow."

I folded my arms and sniffed my arm pit. Yep. I needed a bath badly.

Carper rubbed his temple.

We had to leave! Henry, Mom, and Sam were stuck with Mr. Rose and no one to help. Was Shea really that wise?

"We won't make it on time if we don't go," I said.

Carper fixated his gaze on the rug.

I stood and left him alone.

30

מַסְוֶה

Did someone call my name?

"Pero."

And again.

"Pero, wake up."

I jolted with a snort, rubbing drool off my clean chin. The day before, Alexis had found enough water and a basin for a cold, small bath. She'd cleaned my wounds, rubbed olive oil on my chapped lips, and fed me. I'd gone to bed early. Part of me felt relief that Shea insisted we wait. The other part of me complained that we could've missed our chance to leave. But if Shea was right and Elohim opened a door, then being late wasn't possible.

A stranger knelt next to me, a lantern in his hand. I jerked back. He wore the Moon City guard's uniform. His long brown hair pulled back into a pony, and a bandanna tied around his neck. His face seemed familiar. I rubbed my eyes and looked again. "Carper?"

"It took a minute for you to recognize me. That's good." He threw a pile of clothes at me, another uniform. "Get dressed. We're leaving."

"It's still dark." I shivered and pulled on my sweater's sleeves.

"We have a better chance getting in if we leave now."

I stood and staggered. Carper caught my arm.

"I'm fine." I picked up the pants. They looked like my size. "Where did you find these?"

"Doesn't matter."

I sniffed them. "You didn't kill for these, did you?"

"Just put them on."

I pulled at the edge of my sweater and paused. "A little privacy, please."

"Right." Carper stepped outside.

I shivered my way into the pants and shirt. I picked up my sweater. There's no way I could get away with wearing it. I swapped my sweater for a hat as yellow as a street lamp.

"Seriously?" As if a bright yellow hat wouldn't call attention.

"Done?"

"Almost." I tucked my hair into the hat. Good thing there were no mirrors around, or I would've pulled it off in a second.

"Ready now?"

"Need to find my shoes."

Carper brought them from the opening of the tent. Never did I think Carper would bring me my shoes. Then again, he rushed, and I moved slower than a sloth.

His eyes widened.

"I look stunning, don't I? Like as good as I would in one of your black, puffy dresses." I patted my hat. "If you're trying to make me an easy target, I think it will work."

"They'll be so distracted by your head, they won't even notice your face."

"That's one way to look at it."

"You should pull it down more so I can't see your face."

I adjusted the hat. "Yeah, because who needs to see where they're going?"

Carper nodded. "Better."

"What about Jimmy?"

"He's outside of the tent," Carper said.

I shivered again. "You left a dead man outside of the tent?"

"Does it matter where I put him? It's not like he cares."

I didn't like that we talked about my friend as if he were today's trash. "What if this doesn't work?"

"You're giving up before you even try."

I put on Jimmy's bag. "Maybe I'm not used to things happening just because I believed they would."

"That would make two of us." Carper guided me to the entrance.

Jimmy laid on a cot with handles on both sides. In the moonlight, his skin appeared lighter, his lips blue. I shivered. "I don't know if I can look at him all the way to Moon City."

"It's dark, Pero, and it's only across the field."

I blew my cheeks up like a blowfish and puffed out air. "Let's get this over with."

I bent down and set my hands on the handles. Dirt clung to the bottom of Jimmy's shoes near my face. Carper faced forward and held the front handles.

"You won't drop him that way?" I asked.

"Better than walking backwards."

I gripped the handles. "On the count of three."

"One, two, three," Carper said in a rush.

We lifted the cot. Not too heavy. But how would we move Jimmy through the city unnoticed?

Carper took off, and I propelled forward to match his stride.

"You should've counted down again. I wasn't ready."

"All we're doing is walking." He shifted his hold. "There's nothing to count down."

I bit the inside of my cheek. Would the mocking ever end? Okay. I'm sure my sarcasm didn't help.

The camp stayed silent. The moon grew dimmer as the sky turned a light gray.

"Oomph." Carper dipped down a little. "Watch out for the hole."

"It's probably the same hole that broke my ankle."

I circled around the area where Carper fell. As if I could see the hole in dusk light.

"Didn't *I* break your ankle?" Carper asked.

"Technically, yes, but I wasn't going to bring that up again."

"Does that mean you've forgiven me?"

"Choosing not to bring up memories of when you were a jerk isn't the same as forgiving."

He cleared his throat and didn't snap back.

I was being mean. "Keep your mouth shut, Pero," I muttered. Sweat pooled in my hands.

"What's that?"

As my hands slipped, the cot fell. Jimmy slid down and slumped forward, his head landing on the mud. I wanted to throw up.

"Oh, come on!" Carper set down the cot and pulled Jimmy back into position. Jimmy flopped onto the cot with a thud.

"Great. Now he's going to wake up with a concussion," I said. Was there such a thing as worse than dead?

Jimmy's head sagged to his shoulder and lower than possible if he'd been alive. Acid burned my throat. I covered my mouth and looked the other way. We could've at least put a blanket over him.

"Now," Carper said, "let's try this again." He picked up the cot.

I wiped the sweat from my hands onto my pants and picked up the handles. When I lifted my head, we were at the entrance of Moon City. Only two guards stood at the gate.

Carper set down his end of the cot, and I followed. He adjusted his scarf so that it hid his mouth. I adjusted my hat so it hid my eyes.

"Has Dr. Carper returned?" Carper asked the guards in a lower octave.

A laugh stuck in my throat.

A guard jerked his eyes open, like an alarm had just gone off.

"Uh, no," the non-sleeping guard said.

"How come there's only two of you?" Carper asked. "If Carper were here, he'd kill you."

Such permanent consequences Carper once had!

The other guard stood up. "Well, Carper's not here. Last I heard, he ran away. I guess the pressure of the Lesaries got to him."

A cloud shrouded Carper's face. "Or a guard tried to kill him."

Careful. Wouldn't want to be too close to the truth.

"Nah," the non-sleeping guard said. "That was the rumor, but I don't believe it. No one's brave enough to kill Carper."

Carper snorted. I kept my mouth shut. The guards kept looking at my hat as if a swarm of bees had built a nest. Maybe it's what kept the guards from noticing who they were talking with.

"Who do you have there?" the sleeping guard asked as he looked toward the cot.

My stomach was like a spatula flipping a pancake.

He stepped closer. "It's Jimmy!"

Relief waterfalled from the top of my yellow head.

"Where'd you find him?" the guard asked.

"In the forest," Carper said. "Dr. Carper asked that I find him after he killed him. I guess he felt guilty enough to see him buried in Moon City."

"Well, if Carper doesn't come back with the three chosen

—" The sleeping guard pushed a button on the side of the door that opened the gates. "—we'll all be destroyed."

"It's not too late to join the Lesaries," I blurted.

Carper's eyes burned at me.

I bit my lip.

The guards laughed.

"I'd rather die than join those lunatics," one said.

Lunatics. Carper and I jumped through appearing doorways while the Lesaries marched around a wall to see the city destroyed. Both were unusual. But didn't this nonsense challenge me to live by faith?

"Do you need help carrying him?" the non-sleeping guard asked.

"I think we can handle it from here," Carper said. "Thanks. If Carper comes back, tell him we've got Jimmy. We're his guards at headquarters, just in case you don't remember."

Nice.

"Sure thing," sleepy said.

We picked up Jimmy and walked through. The guards shut the gate behind us.

"And that's how it's done," Carper said.

"Extraordinary."

"That's the nicest thing you've said to me, Pero."

My stomach coiled. *Should I forgive him, Elohim?*

Of course, Elohim would want me to forgive. That's why it was so hard.

When movement caught my attention, I placed my finger against my lips. Ahead in the courtyard, Marcus set out mats and weapons. The light gray sky told me it was around 5:30. Time for training.

"Let's move through the shadows," Carper said. "Marcus will recognize me."

Carper led me along the wall, stopping every few feet to pause behind a tree, a bush, an empty food cart. When we reached a door leading inside the wall, Carper set down Jimmy and pressed his hand against a sensor. The door opened, and we scurried into a dimly lit hallway. A half-smile formed on my lips. I'd been kissed at the end of this hallway.

"Pero!"

I twitched.

"Get your head on. You'll see your boyfriend soon." Carper walked forward. "Whichever one he is."

Was I that readable?

"His name is Henry."

"I don't care." Carper walked a few more paces. "The fast runner?"

So much for not caring.

"I thought you liked that Sam guy."

Okay. I belonged on some bachelorette show. Got it. Let's move on.

"I thought so too at one point. Then I found out he was my brother."

Carper sputtered a laugh.

What did he think about Mom having another child? Did she have more children through Carper? I didn't want to know.

"It's a long story you don't want to hear," I said.

"If this door is open, we have a long journey ahead of us. There's plenty of time to listen."

And to forgive.

We arrived at the end of the hallway in front of Mom's room, where she'd escaped with Henry. Carper peered around the corner that led to the bridge connecting to the mansion.

"Clear," Carper said.

We walked to the door and passed the exact spot where Henry... enough of that.

Carper set down Jimmy and pressed his hand on the sensor. How come the door opened for Henry and me before?

When we were halfway over the bridge, something moved below me.

"Why'd you stop?" Carper asked.

I studied the cot, Jimmy's hand, his finger. Maybe it was like when you think you feel a raindrop on your head, but it's really dew falling from a branch or bird turd.

"I thought I...." Jimmy's cheek twitched once, then nothing. No movement at all. I was paranoid. Stressed. Jimmy's dead. He had been for a day.

I shook my head. "Nothing. Let's keep moving."

The sun peeked its head in the sky. We'd wasted more time.

With another press of Carper's hand on a sensor I'd never used, we walked inside and down the quiet mansion hallway. By the end of the day, the Lesaries would wipe all these perfect rooms and marbled halls out. Goosebumps chilled my arms. Would we escape in time?

Carper stopped at a room, set down Jimmy, and opened the door.

"Why is this unlocked?"

I peered inside. Shimmers of gold sparkled in the hallway light. "That'd be Cathena."

Carper gave me a questioning look. We stepped in and laid the cot down. The door shut behind us with a click. When a light turned on, a hand met my cheek, and I staggered. Pain radiated through my face. When my body leaned back, Carper grabbed me by the shirt and set me on the ground. He dodged a punch and plowed into the opponent. They both landed on a mound of gold coins with a pleasant-sounding crash.

Carper rushed over to me. "Are you okay?"

I pressed my eyes closed and opened them. Blurs, colors whirled.

Still, I saw the opponent rise.

"Carper, watch out!"

Too late.

31

לַהֲרוֹג

Carper's feet were swept from under him. A head collided into his short torso and plowed him to the ground. One punch to the face. Two. Three. Blood spurted.

"Leave him alone!" I shouted.

When the action stopped, the throbbing in my cheek started. I blinked again. The face came into focus.

"Jimmy?"

Carper groaned. Jimmy released his leg's hold over Carper's stomach. He panted. I shuddered at the fire that roared in his eyes.

"Traitor!" he said.

"What are you talking about? You were dead. Again. We brought you here to save you."

Jimmy's eyes watered. Or had my vision blurred? I blinked rapidly, then saw him. Clearly Jimmy.

"I protected you from Carper. All I asked was for you to use your power to destroy him." Jimmy pointed a trembling finger at Carper but kept his eyes on me. "I asked Sam to kill him, too.

He's dangerous. A monster." His body heaved. He shot a lethal look at Carper. "He ruined my life. Why'd you save him, Pero?"

Good question. Elohim wanted me to, and I trusted Elohim. Then why hadn't I been nicer to Carper—willing to forgive—when he'd obviously changed? I felt like a traitor, but I hadn't hurt Jimmy. I'd hurt Carper.

I stepped forward. "Sam chose to release Carper. Sam took his place."

Jimmy's gaze went distant. "Why would he do that?"

"We watched Sam grow the tree that turned into an exit. Sam vanished. Somehow, I'm still here. That's why Carper and I are leaving and we're bringing you with us."

"You didn't answer my question." Jimmy placed a foot on Carper's hand and stepped down. Carper groaned.

I stood up. "Let go now!"

"He nearly killed me, Pero! He took your mom, abused her. He killed children. Countless children." Jimmy smashed harder, and Carper called out in pain. "Why save him? Tell me, or I will kill him myself!"

Carper's diaphragm expanded, up and down. His eyes searched mine in desperation. My mind replayed what he'd done. Taken my mother. For years, I blamed myself. Because I wore the necklace. Because as a chosen, I'd be taken by Carper to be tortured, to see terrible, dark, murderous things that I never wished to relive in nightmares to come.

Carper. Monster. Pompous scoundrel.

With one long exhale, the tightness in my stomach eased.

I had one choice. Love or hate. Should I save my enemy again?

Yes.

"Because I forgive him!" The strength behind my voice surprised me, as if a bottle inside my lungs broke and a pleasant smell filled the room.

Carper glanced at me with his one good eye and smiled.

Jimmy squeezed his fists. "I don't understand."

I lifted my chin. "I forgive Dr. Calvin Carper."

Jimmy's scowl distorted his handsome face. "I thought you were better than this."

His words were like glass against my swollen cheek.

"I'll never forgive," he said.

Jimmy reached underneath the bottom of his pants and pulled out a knife. Before Jimmy could thrust the knife into Carper's chest, Carper kicked Jimmy's legs. Jimmy folded over. The knife flew and stabbed into the wall. Jimmy crawled toward it. I ran and reached for the knife. Jimmy jumped up and grabbed my waist. I screamed. When my hair whipped around his face, he grabbed it and pulled. I yelped. He tightened his hold, and I bit his forearm. Hard. The taste of bitter flesh filled my mouth. Jimmy let go and doubled over. I spit out blood and gagged. Carper threw a long hook under Jimmy's chin. Jimmy crumpled to the floor.

He was out.

I put my hand against the wall and took a deep breath. I'd be okay.

Carper threw himself on the floor and dug his hand into a pile of gold coins.

"What are you doing?"

He pushed the gold away. "Digging."

I tucked my hands under my arms to stop the shaking. "No 'thank you?'"

"For what?"

"I don't know." I stopped to catch my breath. "That I saved you again. That I forgave you."

Carper moved more gold aside. "No time, Pero."

I squatted next to him and dug my fingers into the pile of gold. They felt cold and hard, a vast contrast to the dirt I'd dug only the day before.

"Why are we digging?" I asked.

"The door is on the floor."

"The door?"

Carper looked up. "Yes, the door."

The door was on the floor.

"Gotta dig," Carper said, "before Jimmy wakes."

A thundering sound echoed through the mansion's walls.

"What's that?" I asked.

"Has to be the Lesaries."

The sound grew louder, an unsteady rhythm of marching feet.

"Why are they here so early?" I asked.

"We need to hurry." Carper dug furiously.

"How much gold is here?"

"Too much."

I spotted wood, then a crack in the shape of an opening.

Carper picked up a string from the floor and pulled. Nothing moved. Carper swore.

"What's wrong?"

Carper pulled one more time, then dropped the string. "It's not opening."

"Is it stuck?"

"No." Carper put a hand on his head. He grimaced and put his hand back down. "We're stuck here. Forever."

Carper slammed his fists against the wall. I stayed kneeling by the pile of gold. As I picked up the string and pulled, the door stayed put.

Elohim, could you open this door? Please? I tucked my legs in and hugged them.

"We need to go," Carper said. "Before Jimmy wakes and the walls fall."

They're all gone, Elohim. All the ones I love are completely gone.

My whole heart had crushed like the wall would soon, and still the Lesaries marched on.

You're under my wing. Elohim's voice rang calm yet deep, peaceful yet dangerous.

I closed my eyes and imagined that an eagle flew into that very room. The eagle paused time. The eagle opened his wing. I ran there and felt his warm, soft feathers. Like a pillow to sink into. He closed his wing over me. The walls would fall, but I wouldn't fear.

I was the King's feather, and I found safety under His wings.

"Pero." Carper's hand rested on my shoulder.

I let him help me to my feet and pulled the string one last time. The door stayed shut.

"It will be okay," I said to myself more than Carper. "Elohim's here."

Outside of the room, shouts came from down the hall.

32

———————

לְהַצִּיל

"Pero, it's not a good time to go into shock." Carper opened the door. "They're after us."

"They're after me?" I stared at Carper, my brain sitting in fog.

When Carper shook me, my eyes blinked, then opened. More shouting drew closer. Carper ran out of the room. I quickly followed.

"Stop or we'll kill you both!" The voice came from a guard. There were at least five.

I ran faster. An arrow whizzed past my ear. Across the bridge, through the door to inside Moon City's walls, Carper pulled me into the nearest room and locked the door behind him.

"Locks won't stop them," I said. "They never stopped you."

"Nice try, Carper!" a man shouted through the door.

Carper shoved me into the bathroom and shut the door behind him. The lock clicked as the outer door slammed open and knocked off the picture of Carper onto the floor. Carper opened the bathroom sink cupboard.

"Get in," he said.

"You're not thinking clearly. We can't both fit under a sink."

A fist banged against the bathroom door. "We know you're in there!"

"Now, Pero!"

"Fine!" I crouched down and crawled inside. "There is no way—"

"Push against the back wall."

"I don't understand."

"Your hand! Push the moon-blasted wall!"

I pushed against the back of the cabinet, and the piece fell flat. I gasped.

"Don't just stare at it!" Carper pushed my backside forward.

I crawled inside of a tunnel, my hands and knees wet against the damp floor. "Where are we going?"

"Shh."

I crawled blindly forward.

A high-pitched scream sent a shudder through my body. "What's that?"

"Don't know," Carper said. "Sounds like it's coming from inside these walls."

Eeeeeeekkk.

I sensed a darkness in the air, thick and tangible. I stopped and held out my hand but couldn't feel anything in the way. My throat constricted. Screams rose in volume. The unseen drowned me in panic. I sat and put my arms around my head.

"Call out to Elohim." Carper's voice wavered. "I don't think the screams are from people. They are monsters brought on by me."

"Did you invent creatures underneath your city?" I shouted above the noise.

"No, they're invisible."

"Demons aren't real, are they?"

"Maybe they are," he said. "But I think they'll go away if Elohim's here."

"Why don't you call out to Him then?"

"What makes you think Elohim would rescue *me*?"

A sound rang past my ear like a ghost whooshing by. I shuddered. "If I would choose to rescue you, I'm sure Elohim would also."

I sensed more than heard Carper's sigh. "Elohim?"

"You'll need to be louder than that."

Carper grumbled. "Can't He hear me, no matter how loud I am?"

"I suppose."

"Elohim!" Carper's voice cracked.

I held in a laugh.

"Rescue us!"

The noise tapered into quietness. Too quiet. Like an empty tomb. It was still dark inside the tunnel, but the spirit of darkness had left and in its place was nothing. No worlds. No closets. No me.

Only emptiness.

How could I sense the spiritual as much as I had always known the physical?

An explosion brought my hands over my ears as fast as lightning. Up ahead, sunlight poured into the tunnel and blinded my eyes. A part of the wall had broken off, leaving a large enough opening for us to escape.

"I can't believe that worked," Carper muttered.

"Hello?" came a girl's voice. "Is anyone in here?"

"Cathena?" I asked.

"Pero?" Cathena peered into the tunnel. "What are you doing in here?"

I tilted my head back and laughed. "I'm being rescued."

Cathena reached her hands into the darkness and pulled us to the light where we fell into step with the Lesaries.

WHEN PEOPLE MARCH for something they believe in, they speak it, not with words or painted signs alone, but with their feet. Each step felt holy. Each pound of foot on dirt meant war.

I didn't wear a hat. If they spit on me, I wanted to feel it. If they used their weapons, which they hadn't, I wanted to go down, having fought in full view. No hiding.

Eight thousand Lesaries marched. Elbows poked and hips bumped, but I didn't mind. I felt secure with more Lesaries around me. Even if Moon City tried to destroy us with explosions or abusive words, unity in multitudes brought strength.

Shea said we were to march around the city seven times. It could take all day. In our packs, we carried water. We carried sweat, tears, the years we'd wasted not trusting a bigger cause, the time we'd spent holding on to fear more than Him. We felt the weight of it all, the burden of ourselves, and we shed it as we walked. We watched it fade with every prayer in our minds. The prayers called out to Elohim for deliverance from ourselves, for peace in our hearts, for the walls to knock down our selfishness and limitations. We asked to be humbled to dust. We asked to be nothing so He could be everything.

The guards didn't call out to us this time. I should've hated them. I should've wanted them destroyed, but I felt the weight of their pride and grieved it was heavy enough to knock them down.

My feet numbed as I kept walking. The sun fully awoke, but a cloud partially hid it, giving us relief. I entered the inner part of my brain, the part where my thoughts connected to Elohim. I sensed Him more.

Thank you for protecting me.

I sensed His pleasure in my gratitude.

My awareness of self faded. I forgot about Henry, my family, my home and only remembered Yeshua and His hands washing my feet. I remembered His care. I remembered His love.

I cried then. I cried for Moon City, I cried for Dad, I cried for Mom, for Henry, for Sam, for Jimmy and Carper.

Do you see? Do you know? Believe in Elohim, and He will win your battles!

As I cried, the earth trembled beneath me. I stopped marching and waited.

I strained my eyes toward Shea in the front. He searched the sky, and I looked too. An eagle soared and called above us. I recognized the call as Sam's eagle, Faith. She didn't wait for me to follow. She only flew.

I grabbed Carper's hand. It twitched. Should I let go? Holding his hand felt like the right thing to do. I wanted him to know that I cared for him as a friend, that I was sorry that we couldn't make it to Earth, that it'd be all right because Elohim marched with us.

Carper squeezed my hand.

We'd made it. Carper's city would be destroyed. But there would be a new beginning, somehow, somewhere.

I believed.

An empty feeling fluttered in my stomach. I believed, didn't I?

Shea turned to the Lesaries with trumpets. Bringing the trumpets to their mouths, they blew out their first notes. They played a melody so pure, so beautiful, it echoed off the walls. It wasn't long before people around me sniffled and wiped tears. I understood their response as the same one that had brought me to my knees in front of Yeshua.

Yes! This is you, Elohim! When even music played makes the soul tremble.

A breeze picked up and tossed my hair. I had no vision. I didn't play my guitar or sing. Yet power permeated my very being.

The trumpeters finished one last note that stretched on for as long as they could let out breath, which for a trained trumpet player was a long time. After, it became so quiet that I thought maybe I'd entered a silent film.

My heart skipped a beat.

One woman blew a note through a horn louder and lower and more triumphant than the trumpets. The earth trembled with it.

Above the noise of the waning horn, Shea called out, his voice echoing off the city's walls. "Shout! Shout! For Elohim has given you this city!"

Shea shouted; the Lesaries joined. One-hundred, four-hundred, double, and more.

Eight thousand people shouted. It was the sound of a stormy ocean, of an avalanche, of a stampede of wild horses. As the shouting grew in volume, so did the ground increase its movement.

There was a significant release inside as I shouted. Yeshua had healed my wounds; He'd untethered my fears. But with this shout, I went beyond being free. I soared. Like my vision. Like the eagle. I flew away from it all. There were no walls.

A sound came deeper than the stormy ocean, like somewhere in the middle of the earth. That kind of deep. The guards on top of the wall fell over. Some tried to run, but the wall—like a monster—pulled them back until they held on tightly to whatever or whoever they could. We shouted. Carper wept. A roar of sadness and fear came from Moon City's mouths.

With one final deafening shake that started as a tremor and moved into the largest quake the world had ever known,

the walls

fell

down.

A wave of dust shot into the air and cleared to reveal piles of pieces, as if the ground itself had turned to steel and yet still exploded to nothing. What Carper had once thought indestructible now lay dead and buried along with the very ones who built it.

We stood like statues. Somehow, by Elohim's power and our faith, it had happened.

The Lesaries walked through the rubble, coughing and covering their mouths. Some cried. Some stayed still with stunned expressions.

No one clapped or hollered or chanted their victory. We were all too solemn. The place that had been a prison transformed into a grave.

Dust billowed along the ground like dirty clouds as far as I could see. Even the sky had turned brown. Ahead, under a field of dust and debris, I saw a shimmer.

I touched Carper's arm. "Look." I pointed toward the sparkle. "Let's go check it out."

Carper wiped the tears from his face and followed my lead without a word. Every once in a while, he'd stop to lift a piece of steel from a body and would say the name of the one who'd been buried, and he'd cry. For many more faces, he said, "I didn't know him," or "Her face is unfamiliar," and he'd cry again.

I stopped where I'd seen the shimmer. The walls of the gold room were in debris around our feet. No room remained. Gold coins scattered. Most were buried and dull, as gray in tone as the rest of the mess. What once sparkled in splendor now dulled from the dust.

The shimmer I'd seen still lingered, but it came from a crack along the floor in a rectangular shape.

I shuddered, swallowed, staggered. "The door."

Carper's eyes widened. "Open it."

I tightened my hand around the dirty twine and pulled. Bright light flooded our faces, and we coughed from the dust that flew into our noses. When I let go of the string, the door crashed against the floor and an opening in the shape of a circular tunnel slid into darkness.

Carper laughed. "He did it. I can't believe Elohim did it."

I wanted to say I told him so. That I knew Elohim would make a way, yet I hadn't been certain either. But one thing I was sure of. A door opened, and Carper and I would walk through it, with Elohim leading the way.

Shea watched us from a distance, threw his head back, and laughed. He placed his hands on his chest, then turning toward Carper, he bowed. He raised his head and hands toward the sky. To Elohim.

I followed Shea's lead and bowed my head toward Carper.

"Oh, get up!"

I straightened. "Why?"

"You're embarrassing me."

"Dr. Calvin Carper gets embarrassed?"

"Enough of that. Let's go home."

Home. Well, closer to home. Closer.

Carper held out his arm toward the slide. "Ladies first."

Sitting on the edge of the slide, I peered into the dark, then clutched the broken pendant in my fist.

Mom.

My mind echoed with her scream, just like I'd heard every night for fourteen years. Yet this time it sounded quieter, as if she heard my lullaby and held onto the hope that I was on my way.

The ones I loved most were out of view.

But not forever.

DID YOU ENJOY THIS BOOK?

One of the best ways to support an author is by leaving a review. It doesn't take much, just a sentence or two, or a star rating. Please, leave an honest review of *The King's Feather* here: www.amazon.com/dp/B0C31QG7DS/.

And if you're on Goodreads, please leave a review at goodreads.com/authoramyearls.

Thank you!

DISCUSSION QUESTIONS

1. In the first act, Pero considered whether to follow Henry and rescue her Mom. Have you ever had to make a difficult decision that involved sacrificing comfort? How did that make you feel? How would you feel if Elohim called you on an adventure that took you outside of your comfort zone?

2. Pero had a difficult memory about her mom disappearing when she was three. When was a time that you experienced grief? What was it like for you? Did it get better over time?

3. Pero's name comes from the root word for *feather*. The necklace symbolizes being under Elohim's wings. Psalm 91:4 says that God "will cover you with his feathers, and under His wings you will find refuge; His faithfulness will be your shield and rampart." What does it mean to be covered by wings? How do *you* respond when being cared for?

4. Pero doesn't know if she can love Henry. What would be good reasons to wait or to start a romantic relationship? What would you do if you were in Pero's situation?

5. Yeshua saved Pero from inside the wall and took her to a river to rest. Describe a time when it felt like you were trapped in a wall. Who helped you out? Do you believe the same thing can happen today?

6. Pero learned that Elohim's invitation to life in Him was for everyone, even Dr. Carper. Is there someone in your life who you find difficult to love or forgive?

7. Pero learns that she is no more valuable of a person than Henry. Describe a time when you felt pressured to be great. How did that make you feel?

8. Toward the end of the book, Henry, Sam, and Bahar disappeared without Pero. Have you ever been left behind? Has a difficult circumstance left you feeling alone? Share your story with your group or with a friend.

9. Were you expecting a door to open for Carper and Pero in the end? When has life taken you in a different direction than expected? How did you cope?

10. Pero had a musical gift. What is your gift? How can your gift benefit others?

ACKNOWLEDGMENTS

Buckle up for possibly the longest acknowledgments section ever! I can't believe how many helped me toward my dream of publishing!

Jesus Christ, thank you for choosing me, for loving me. Yeshua, I love you.

Eric Earls, love of my life, thank you for listening to me brainstorm nearly every day for the last four years! You are the right one to release me to flow in all God has planned for me.

Haven and Sadie, thanks for letting Mommy write and believing in me. Yes, it's finally a real book. I love you, my silly girls.

Karen Grunst, where should I start? I'm tearing up just thinking about you. God knew what He was doing when He brought you into my life. Thank you for your friendship, weekly calls, prayers, edits. You are a treasure.

Ginny Yttrup, thank you for believing in me and the calling on my life before it had come to completion. I learned a lot from my internship with you. What a wonderful advocate you are for pre-published authors!

Stef, as soon as I stumbled upon your designs at Seventh-star Art, there was no better choice for me! I was eternally grateful when you said you'd do it. My covers couldn't have turned out more fantastic.

Okay, you incredible author friends, your advice, encouragement, and prayers are the reasons I made it! South East Clancy (yep, I really just wrote that in my book. So, go write a meme!), Susan Sage (white rice is nice and so are you), Lisa Bogart (still can't believe you drove all the way to my house just to cheer me up), Shadia Hrichi (I finally got to meet my spiritual mother!), Tara Johnson (let's go watch Broadway), James L. Rubart (awesome blurb writer, way to shock my broca!), Thomas Umstattd (my novel started with an idea; my career started with you), Hannah Curry (my inspiration of all things royal), Jannette Fuller (your encouragement is everything), S.D. Howard (how many times did you pull me out of publishing ideas that weren't the greatest?), Katherine Barger (oh the laughs!), Kandi J. Wyatt (you are a connector!), Hannah Muldery (umm, greatest character drawings ever!), Teddi Deppner (lucky me has been to the beach with you twice), Rebecca Meek (thanks for reading at the beginning!), Josh Kilen (you were right about self-publishing being the way to go), Christina Nelson (sorry I ate your birthday present), Karen Barnett (the solid spruce top is for you), Heidi Gaul (Wa's up?), Quanny Ard (you're my greatest cheerleader and info of all things in the publishing world), Erin Taylor Young (thanks for thoroughly editing my sad first draft that hopefully will never see the light of day again), Linda Howard (yep, God brought us together), Marylin Furumasu (thanks for the awesome graphics and support!).

To my oh-so-talented critique group—Christina Suzann Nelson, Heidi Gaul, Karen Barnett—I'm blessed by our friendship, and my waistline is blessed by the restaurants we've visited.

Gina Cornelius. You are an AMAZING friend and website, tech, marketing guru. I'm thankful God was up to something grand when I stuck my phone number on your front door. Hi, Matt. Miss you guys!

My many beta and proof readers for Drafts 1, 2, 3... thank you for your input and direction on where the heck to go next. Teen beta readers, thank you for believing in Pero.

Mom, Dad, Bethany, Katie: I love you. I cherish you. Karen and Victor, your support means so much to me. Uncle Dan, write on.

To mis amigas: Jessica, Josh, Stephanie, Paul, Charmaine, Joel, Kristy, Krista. Thank you for listening to me go on about everything word-nerdy and for your prayers.

Thank you, Christ Church community group, for our rich discussions of Bible stories, one of which led to this book.

John Orton, thank you for listening to Jesus and preaching to the Church. Hannah Orton, two words come to mind when I think of you and how you've shaped my life: honest and constant. Those alone define a forever friend.

Tiffany and Monica from my Confluence family at Radiant Church, you may not remember me introducing myself at a church leaders' conference in tears because your message on Proverbs 31 about God releasing creativity in women changed my life. You both prayed and had a vision of me sitting at my desk and God writing His hand over me very slowly. I held onto this vision throughout my writing process.

To my readers: You are strong, loved, and chosen. Thank you for responding to my virtual letters. Onwerto and koach to you!

Want to know what happens next? Go to amyearls.com/forbid-denreignbook or scan the QR code below for Book 2. And read the first chapter of *Forbidden Reign* on the next page.

FORBIDDEN REIGN
CHAPTER ONE

A fall doesn't last forever. Yet as my hand clutched air and a scream lodged in my throat, I wondered. How hard would I crash?

I smacked against a body. At least it felt like a body. The crunch of bones, the bend of flesh. I searched my way through the dark and found what felt like a finger. Cold and still.

With a scream that would've woken the dead, I scuttled away, my palms pressing into carpet, as I collided into another body. A grunt sounded, and I leapt back.

"Watch where you're going, Pero."

I found Carper's arm and hugged it. "I think I killed someone."

"Don't be so dramatic," Carper's voice said. "You only landed on yourself. You left a dead version of yourself in this universe, and now you're returning."

"That makes no sense."

"Has anything you've been through in the last month made sense?"

"Fair point."

When we left Earth a month earlier, the last I remembered

was being drugged, thrown into a limo, and waking up in the older universe, Origo. Now that I'd returned to Earth, had I restored to my old self? My soul felt lighter, as if I'd transported back as a different Pero Ruth Moshe: brave, fearless, a chosen girl full of faith.

Carper wiggled his arm from under my squeeze. "Where's the light?"

A quick pressure and pain dug into my foot. "Ouch. Be careful."

He stepped off.

"You could apologize." I reached my hands forward and met what felt like empty clothes, then hangers.

"Why would I do that?" I heard Carper's feet shuffling.

"Right. Because you apologizing a million times while we walked through the debris of Moon City wasn't enough. *I'm sorry. I'm sorry.*"

"I never said that."

"Ha!" Past the hanging clothes, I touched a wall, then bumped against something light but solid with my feet. Were those shoes? "And I suppose you don't remember crying your eyes out either."

"I definitely did not do that."

As much as Carper had changed for the better in the last week, his moodiness still exposed its annoying head. Or was that just his personality?

"Sometimes I wonder."

I heard Carper's hand meet the wall and brush against it. "About what?"

"If you're really a kid trapped inside a sixty-year-old's body."

"Watch it. I'm only fifty-six. And there are far too many stilettos in here."

"Say what?"

A light shone. I turned my head and blinked. A large closet held coats, dresses, and an impressive supply of heels.

"Oh, yeah," Carper said. "I forgot about him."

I turned to where he gazed behind me and gasped.

Jimmy lay unmoving on the floor. Carper had said Jimmy's body was left here on Earth when he was transported to Origo.

"Maybe you landed on Jimmy."

"Not myself?"

Carper shrugged. "Jimmy's body died here too while he was in Origo. But he's not returning."

"It feels so final now," I whispered. "You know, Jimmy helped me survive a lot, including you."

"Don't forget he also tried to kill us."

I recalled Jimmy in Moon City's mansion, a knife in his hand as he charged over to Carper. Somehow, we'd survived. "He wouldn't have killed me."

Carper raised a brow.

Without Jimmy, would I have come back? Would Carper have come with me, humbled?

Carper's lips tightened. "It should've been me." He didn't take his eyes off Jimmy.

"Perhaps. I mean, you *are* a murderer."

"I suppose I am."

I shrugged. "Should've been me, too."

Carper pivoted.

"Mom, Sam, and..." I swallowed. "...Henry are missing because of me."

"Doesn't mean you should've died."

I shook my head. "You don't know who I was before you found me. I was scared all the time. I can't trust that kind of heart. I'm not sure if it ever really beat at all."

"Getting effusive, are we?"

I smiled. "That's a big word for you."

"You underestimate me." Carper held his hand out to display the door ahead. "Shall we?"

"What about Jimmy?"

"We'll bury him later." Carper cleared his throat. "I'd like to take him to his homeland. I think he lived somewhere in the States."

"He's from a farm. In Green Meadow, actually."

Before he died, Jimmy gave the farm to Sam, which would've made it my property too if I had accepted Sam's offer to marry him. I shivered. *Marriage* was a big word. Would I marry Henry? We were kind of an item now. But was marriage always the right answer when you loved someone?

"Hello?" Carper waved a hand in front of my face.

I blinked. "Did you say something?"

Carper grinned. "I asked how you knew that Jimmy was from Green Meadow, while you were day dreaming."

I put my hands to my hot face. "Uh, Jimmy told me before he died." I tripped over a shoe on my way to the closet door. "Where are we, anyway?"

"When Jimmy and I kidnapped you, this is where we took you. We didn't want you knowing, just in case you escaped. You'd passed out, so we didn't need to worry about that. A portal into the other world usually opens in this closet. Don't know what's special about this place. Maybe it's built out of magical wood or something."

"You said Mom would be in China. Are we in China?"

"No. The Oregon coast, the nearest portal from where you lived in Green Meadow."

"We're near Dad! I need to see him!"

"We can try." Carper pushed the door open.

Outside the closet was a large and well-furnished bedroom with a huge vanity where sat a middle-aged woman in a black-laced dress, aiming a curling iron toward us.

"Cherry?" Carper asked.

The woman's curling iron and voice dropped. "Calvin."

"Who's Cherry?"

Carper took a step back. "What are you doing here?"

The woman named Cherry stayed frozen. "I should be asking you the same thing. You're supposed to be dead."

"You say that as if you wish I was."

"What am I supposed to say?" Cherry's voice shook, then strengthened, like she wasn't sure if she held back a couple of tear drops or a torrent.

"You called me by my first name," Carper said.

Cherry's eyes narrowed. "I wasn't about to jump into your arms and call you *Daddy*."

Wait. Carper had a daughter? I took in the same dark eyes, round face, and skin tone. The woman had to be Carper's daughter, whether she wanted to be or not.

Carper's eyes sparked with what looked like pain for a moment before turning unreadable once again. "Your English has improved."

No wonder Cherry seemed to have issues with her father. He was terrible at small talk.

"Why'd you come back?" Cherry's chest heaved, her gaze like a laser trained on her target.

He remained standing, seemingly stung with every word she cast his way. Could words cripple a man?

Carper stepped forward. "I know you don't want to see me."

Cherry smirked.

"I don't blame you. I was a terrible father. I caused...you're in pain because of me. But I want you to know that things are different. You won't believe me yet, but I'll prove it to you."

"How?"

"The fact that you're in Rose's spare room, in a party dress, tells me that you're working for Rose and he's throwing another celebration to cover up his latest con."

Cherry's mouth gaped as if she'd just been caught stealing. Was this the same Rose who'd taken Mom, Henry, and Sam? The room seemed to shrink, like Moon City's walls, moving in, so tight, so confining. I needed to get out of here.

Carper kept his direction solely on his daughter. "Rose might've told me you were here, but I didn't believe it. I also happen to know that Rose's plan involves Pero here and that he won't be pulling me in this time. He knows I've changed, gone to the other side. However you want to say it. Rose took her family and is after her blood as a fulfillment to the prophecy, just as I used to be."

Cherry looked at me as if she'd only then noticed someone else in the room.

"Pero is one of the three chosen and the daughter of your old friend, Bahar."

"Bahar's alive?" Cherry clutched the edge of the vanity.

"As long as Rose doesn't hurt her. I'm making things right this time, and the first thing I need to do is get this fifteen-year-old girl to her mom."

Cherry's gaze lingered on my face, then scanned my clothes that were caked in dust from Moon City's crumbled walls.

"Hi." I waved. "I'm Pero, and I'm seventeen, not fifteen. Just so we're clear. You were friends with my mom?"

Cherry's lips curved into a slight smile. "You don't look anything like her. Maybe her nose."

Now was not the time to explain my adoption. I'd waited seventeen years to find out myself. Besides, Mom was still very much Mom, no matter the circumstance.

Carper clapped his hands. "Great. Since introductions have been made and we're all aware that Bahar and I are not dead, I will let you two get ready for the party." He bowed his head. "I trust Pero is in good hands." Carper turned and stepped up to a door leading out of the room.

What was he doing? He couldn't leave me there. Even as Carper's daughter, Cherry obviously wasn't on our side. Panic grew until I felt it might burst into a million pieces of tangible fear. What did fear look like, anyway? Sharding rocks? Splintering wood? This wasn't the time to play another one of Carper's games. This was my life he laid in his angry daughter's hands. "Where are you going?"

"Business." He winked at me.

My chest tightened. "I can come with you."

"Like I said, Pero." He narrowed his eyes as if I'd understand a message from one look. "Later."

"You can't leave the girl with me," Cherry called.

"How is Mr. Kilen?" Carper asked pointedly. "Don't tell me you left your husband for Rose."

Cherry folded her arms. "Are you threatening me?"

"Nope. Just reminding you that I know more about your history than you realize. And I can help you escape. You can't possibly prefer Rose's plans for you over Elohim's."

Cherry shook her head. "It's too late to change. What's done is done. Decisions were made."

Carper placed both hands on her arms and smiled.

Cherry leaned back but didn't pull away from his hold.

"New decisions can be made today," he said. "Trust me, *xīngān bǎobèi*. I promise this time I won't let you down."

Carper let go and left.

Appearing stunned, Cherry sighed and looked me over again. She walked to the bathroom, started the shower, and threw me a towel. "Get in."

I wasn't going to argue about taking a shower. After Cherry left and closed the bathroom door behind her, I undressed and stepped in, letting the hot water wash away all anxieties.

Cherry called from the room. "I have the perfect dress for you."

Maybe a party would give me and Carper a better chance of leaving without anyone noticing. Kind of like I'd left Moon City. Would I ever see Cathena again? Or Alexis? I never said goodbye. But I hadn't said goodbye to Dad either. I had to see him before finding Mom. Poor Dad. There had to be a hole in the floor where he'd been pacing.

Would Cherry come with us? It seemed like Carper wanted to repair broken relationships between father and daughter and Cherry and her husband who she'd possibly left behind. Perhaps I wasn't the only one to practice forgiveness. I squirted some body wash into my hand and lathered the suds. Wounds from the last month clung to my skin, begging to be scrubbed and washed down the drain.

Not every fall ends with pain.

ABOUT THE AUTHOR

Best-selling author **Amy Earls** writes fiction that explores intersections between life issues and faith. A professor of first-year college students, she holds a master's degree in education for adult learners, with an emphasis on writing. Amy lives in Oregon's Willamette Valley with her husband, daughters, and a never-dying goldfish.

Find out more about Amy at www.amyearls.com.